BACKSTAGE MURDER

BACKSTAGE MURDER

SHELLEY FREYDONT

Kensington Books
http://www.kensingtonbooks.com

KENSINGTON BOOKS are published by

Kensington Publishing Corp.
850 Third Avenue
New York, NY 10022

Library of Congress Card Catalogue Number: 99-071478
ISBN 1-57566-458-5

First Printing: October, 1999
10 9 8 7 6 5 4 3 2 1

Printed in the United States of America

One

Lindy Haggerty downshifted the Volvo up the slope of her driveway and reached toward the radio. The Rolling Stones replaced Offenbach's frenetic cancan music. The Rolling Stones. They must be fifty if they were a day. Hell, the whole world was getting older.

She stopped the car at the kitchen door and leaned across the front seat for her groceries. As she did, the waistband of her jeans cut into her stomach. Older, and fatter, she thought. I shouldn't have had that pizza for lunch. She pulled the bags out of the car and headed toward the kitchen.

As she stuck her key in the lock, balancing a grocery bag on each hip, the telephone rang. Bruno began to bark at the same time. The blue *New York Times* bag lay on the flagstone stoop. She opened the door and kicked the paper across the threshold in one smooth movement. With the grocery bags sliding down her thighs, she hurried across the mudroom and into the kitchen. Sixty pounds of Irish Setter leapt forward. "Down, Bruno." Both bags fell to the floor. A head of lettuce rolled out of a bag and under the table. Bruno buried his head in the bag, and Lindy lunged for the phone.

The message machine had clicked on. She stopped for a

second, hand resting on the receiver. Telemarketing? She picked up anyway.

"Lindy? Lindy, is that you?"

"Yes?" The voice sounded familiar. She sat down at the table, unbuttoned her jeans, and reached for the *Times*.

"It's Biddy." Lindy paused as she opened the paper. "Arabida McFee."

"Good Lord, Biddy. It's really you? I haven't talked to you in . . ."

"In ten years."

Had it been that long? They had been best friends. "That long? Well, you know when you take the Holland Tunnel to New Jersey you end up in Outer Mongolia. Where are you?"

"In New Jersey."

"You retired?" She couldn't believe it.

Biddy laughed. "Of course not. I'll still be on my feet when I'm eighty-five. I'm at the Endicott Playhouse. I'm rehearsal director for the Jeremy Ash Dance Company."

"Jeremy Ash? Didn't he retire?"

"Yes, but he's back. He's got a terrific group of dancers. We're on a Northeast tour and open in New York next month."

"That's great." Lindy was hit by a momentary pang of envy. Where had that come from? She hadn't thought about dancing in years. As good as it had been, she certainly wouldn't want that kind of stress back in her life.

"Anyway, I was really hoping that you'd come to the theater tonight. It's our opening night here, and it would be great to see you."

"Tonight?" She felt a flutter of panic. "Let me check my calendar." She scrolled her finger across the wall calendar above the phone. April 14. Biddy had an opening night at the

Endicott, and she had . . . an emergency meeting of the Jaycee family talent show committee.

"I'd like to, but . . ."

"Please." The word shot out of the phone, obliterating the last ten years and propelling Lindy into the past. She recognized the urgency in Biddy's voice, and in her mind, Lindy could see Biddy scrubbing her hair as she waited for her answer. She always did that when she was upset. The wildness of Biddy's hair was the weather vane of her feelings.

"Biddy, what's wrong?"

"Nothing."

"Biddy," she prompted.

"It's just—I'd just really, really like to see you."

Biddy's voice unleashed a tidal wave of reminiscence. The applause, the fame, the good times they had together hit her with an intoxicating rush. Even the bad times seemed not so bad when you had a friend to support you. Curiosity and loyalty tugged at her. It was obvious that something was wrong, and Biddy needed her, but did she really want to go back? Even for a minute, even as a visitor, even for a friend?

She glanced back at the calendar. Oh, what the hell, it was only one evening, for old times' sake. There'd always be another committee meeting. "Okay, I'll see you tonight."

"Thanks."

She pushed the off button and phoned the Jaycees.

A frump. When had she turned into a frump? Lindy looked down at her jeans and oversize fisherman's sweater. The jeans were designer; the sweater, imported. Casual chic on the outside, but the inside was strictly suburban frump.

"Frump, frump, frump," she yelled into the walk-in closet

in her bedroom. She hadn't seen Biddy in years, and she didn't have a thing to wear. A pile of rejects lay jumbled on the bed next to Bruno. He was whining in his sleep, a paw lying territorially over a navy-blue sequined jacket.

She pulled a teal-blue sheath from a hanger. She wore a lot of blue. It brought out the blue in her eyes. Well, a girl had to work with what she had, or in my case, thought Lindy, what I have left.

Rows of other clothes hung patiently waiting. Lindy pointed an accusing finger at them. "I know what you're thinking. I'm fat. The only thing that hasn't gotten fat is my hair. And it's too short to be fat."

She struggled into the dress, turned to the mirror, and gave her reflection an appraising look. Was this the figure of a once thin and lithesome dancer?

In her image of herself, she was still the eighteen-year-old who astounded the New York critics in her first professional season; as alluring as she had been throughout her full career; just as vital and in demand. Sure, that had been before marriage, children, and a decade in the suburbs, but still . . .

She frowned at the image in the mirror.

"Your gut is sticking out. Pull it in," she ordered. Bruno slunk off the bed and padded down the hall, his tail drooping.

"You're not in trouble, Bruno," she yelled after him. "I am."

She added the sheath to the pile and went back into the closet. She passed the size tens, then the size eights, caressing them distractedly with the tips of her fingers. In the remotest, darkest corner of the closet, shoved together like shimmering sardines, she found the sixes. Expensive, bought years ago on a dancer's salary off the clearance racks of exclusive boutiques. It had been a few years since she had been able to wear them. At the rate she was going, she would never see the inside of a six again. Well, someday she would go on a diet, tomorrow maybe.

She touched a full skirt of peach organza bought in Cannes, a white leather miniskirt from Milan, a gold knit sweater dress, so petite, from ... where? She couldn't remember. Even her brain had the frumps.

She pulled the miniskirt over her head. It wouldn't button. It wouldn't zip. It wouldn't even slip down her thighs to the floor. She pulled it back over her head, returned it to the hanger, and reached for her latest and largest old standby—the black silk pants suit. At least it fit, but why shouldn't it? It was a size ten and had elastic around the waist. She tossed it on the bed.

Six hours, a new dress, and twenty-five sit-ups later, she was speeding down the Garden State Parkway toward the Endicott Playhouse.

"You were meant for me-e-e ... ," she sang along with the radio. She felt good, if a little nervous. So she had retired. She had a successful life in the suburbs. So, maybe, she had gotten a little older, a little fatter. So had everyone else. Right? Biddy would still be glad to see her.

She could still remember the first day Biddy showed up at rehearsal, having aced an open audition over 150 other girls. Open auditions, known in the business as cattle calls, were notorious for never landing anyone a job. But Biddy with a formidable technique and an unparalleled joie de vivre had been the exception that proved the rule. The artistic director adored her; he would greet her each morning with *"Ca va? Poulet?"* and soon the rest of the company began calling the angel-faced Arabida, "Biddy."

They hadn't stayed in touch. When she and Glen had left the city in search of the perfect house, the perfect neighborhood, the perfect school system, Lindy had left her career and her friends behind.

And in the new adventure of life in the suburbs, she had forgotten them: the friends who celebrated when you got a good review, and commiserated with you when you didn't, the flowers backstage, the international tours, the applause as the final curtain lowered on a stellar performance. Hell, she had even forgotten the corner deli and how admiring construction workers whistled at her lean dancer's body as she raced to the subway.

Instead, she had transferred her professional zeal to amateur fund-raisers, tackled car pools like they were international tours, and gladly traded the flowers backstage for Rice Krispie treats at the neighborhood coffee klatches. While Glen rose to heights in the telecommunications industry, commuting daily to the city, and traveling to conferences across the country, she schlepped kids to school with all the enthusiasm of an opening night.

She had approached suburban life just like an extended run on Broadway and it hadn't disappointed her. There was no lack of angst on the playground, and plenty of drama in the PTA meetings. She had even witnessed a few diva attacks outside the principal's office and felt right at home, at first.

Okay, so there wasn't much applause, and the pay wasn't great, but her current audience could be just as fickle as any paying ticket holder. Maybe, the scenery *had* gotten a little dull over the years. Well, to be honest, so had the characters.

It was only seven o'clock when she pulled into the parking lot. Even though Biddy would be too busy to talk before the performance, Lindy had subconsciously arrived in time for hour call.

She hadn't been to the Endicott Playhouse since she had retired from dancing. Now that she was here, she had butterflies. She got out of the car and smoothed the skirt of her new outfit, a flamboyantly royal-blue dress with matching jacket, and picked her way across the graveled parking lot, wobbling dangerously on four-inch heels. They hurt like hell, but one had to make some concessions to art.

She climbed the stairs to the stage door holding tightly to the rusty handrail. Fighting off a serious attack of déjà vu, she stopped at the security booth. The guard buzzed her in. Biddy, as efficient as she was effervescent, had remembered to leave her name at the door.

Inside the theater was dark, like the inside of all theaters. Instinctively, she closed her eyes. It was an old theater trick to adjust the eyes quickly to the absence of light. She breathed in the musty air, years of accumulated dust and sweat assaulting her senses, and opened her eyes. Bright lights illuminated the stage, but the contrast only added to the darkness of the backstage area, reducing the figures there to amorphous shadows. She was jostled by someone carrying a pile of spandex and chiffon draped over one shoulder and holding an overflowing laundry basket with both hands.

She took a tentative step forward. She could see parts of the stage through the wings, the entrance areas to the stage separated by black curtains called legs. Metal pipes holding side lights were positioned at the back of each wing. Dancers, wearing layers of oversize practice clothes, were on stage, warming up to individual music that played from headsets.

A couple practiced a lift that was giving them trouble. The girl took a few preparatory steps toward her partner. He lowered in a deep *plié*, hands forward to catch her hipbones. He lifted her a few feet off the floor and gave up. The girl backed up, rolled her sweatpants down below her hipbones to give him a better grip, and tried again. She got a little higher on the second try.

He's holding her too high, Lindy thought automatically.

"Watch ya back." She jumped aside as a ladder carried by two stagehands careered around the corner. They maneuvered it through the second wing and onto the stage. Lindy followed them, stopping at the edge of the black curtain.

"Heads up!" All motion stopped, frozen midmovement. Every head turned upward as a long metal pipe, a batten, was lowered from the flies above them. It was burdened with lighting instruments. It stopped about six feet from the floor. Abruptly everyone returned to what they had been doing, avoiding the lowered batten and ladder.

One of the stagehands climbed up and began adjusting the lights. He was extremely thin; his sinewy arms stretched taut out of his sleeveless T-shirt as he handled the heavy equipment. He looked vaguely familiar, but Lindy couldn't place him. That wasn't unusual for her. She rarely forgot a face; she just couldn't always attach it to a name. All that visual training, she supposed. And anyway, she hadn't seen these people in years. Of course they had changed.

Biddy was standing at the front of the stage. She was easily recognizable; she hadn't changed at all. But I have, thought Lindy with a surge of panic. The stage lights silhouetted the cinnamon curls that wisped around Biddy's head like finely spun cotton candy. A sweater was tied around her still thin waist and fell straight past her narrow hips. She was leaning on a pair of crutches, surgery maybe? She was in her late thirties. It was probably time to start having everything replaced.

She caught sight of Lindy, waved energetically, and began hauling herself toward the wings. The toe of a plaster cast stuck out from beneath the left leg of her voluminous black stretch pants. She progressed in a syncopated rhythm; first crutches, then cast, crutches, cast, *lub dub*, *lub dub*, until she was standing next to Lindy at the side of the stage.

"Wow! I can't believe you're here." Biddy wrapped her crutches around Lindy and hugged. "You look great! It's just like you never left." She pulled back and looked at Lindy affectionately. "You're taller."

"Thanks, it's just the shoes. I'm still five-five and holding. But still taller than you."

"Heck, everybody's taller than me."

"But remember," Lindy started.

"Height is just a state of mind," Biddy finished.

"But a cast is not a state of mind. Biddy, what happened?"

"You know, graceful old me." She shrugged, lifting both crutches off the floor and bringing them down with a thud.

It was a standard joke: the most graceful dancer on stage could trip over a piece of paper anywhere else. But here, too, Biddy was the exception that proved the rule.

"An accident," she said. "Broken in two places."

"Ouch." Lindy moved aside as the ladder was taken offstage. She watched it pass. "Who is that? The skinny one with the black hair? He looks familiar."

"Lindy, that's Peter Dowd. You know him."

"That's Peter? God, I didn't even recognize him." Peter Dowd was a much sought-after production stage manager in the dance world, organized, intelligent, and patient. A PSM on the dance circuit was responsible for setting up and striking a show, dealing with the stagehands, laying the Marley floor, hanging lights, moving scenery, keeping everyone on schedule, as well as calling lighting and music cues during the performance. But this was not the Peter Dowd she remembered. Always svelte, he was now painfully thin. He was prevented from being truly handsome by acne scars that canyoned his cheeks. Those cheeks had become almost cavernous, and his face seemed etched in a permanent scowl.

"He's, uh . . ." Biddy's green eyes searched the air above her for the right word. "Changed a bit, I guess." She looked sympathetically into the darkness where Peter had disappeared. "But it's so-o-o good to see you."

While Biddy hauled herself from dressing room to dressing room, giving last-minute corrections and words of encouragement, Lindy stood out of the way, letting the ambiance take hold of her. It felt good to be back, even as an observer. The mania of preperformance was soothing.

She was drifting somewhere between the past and the present when Biddy shook her. "I'm done. Let's get out front."

She led Lindy to their seats at the back of the orchestra and sat on the aisle so that she could stick her cast past the row in front of them. Lindy reached across her to grab a program from a passing usherette.

Biddy opened her spiral notebook and turned to a fresh

page. "Remember these?" She pulled a ballpoint pen from her pocket and pressed a button on the side. A small beam of light illuminated the writing tip.

"Do I. Though I always preferred taking performance notes in the dark. It wasn't too bad as long as you didn't keep writing over the same line."

"And remember, you used to always keep a mystery to read during the intermission."

"I've got one in my purse."

Biddy laughed. "Just like old times."

Not exactly, thought Lindy. "So . . . what's on tonight?"

"A new commission. *Carmina Burana.*"

Lindy groaned. "Not another new *Carmina.*" *Carmina Burana* was composed by Carl Orff in 1937. For orchestra and voices, it was based on the secular texts of thirteenth-century Benedictine monks. Its combination of folk simplic-ity, ritual and infectious rhythm as it portrayed the joys of eating, drinking, and lovemaking was captivating, and it had been used or misused by scores of professional and student choreographers ever since. "Aren't there enough, already?"

"More than enough. But this was choreographed by David Matthews."

"No kidding. He's the hottest choreographer in town. It must have cost a fortune."

Biddy shrugged. "He wanted to do a *Carmina*, so we got him cheap. Anyway, he's a friend of Jeremy's."

"Lucky you."

"Yeah, you should see the audience perk up when they recognize the music from the car commercial. They feel really cultured. Anyway, it's pretty clever. A story line, which is more than I can say for most of the 'new' ones. It's a long first act, but we end the evening with a lighter piece. If the Orff music doesn't drive you crazy before it's over, I think you'll be impressed. The only thing is . . ."

The houselights began to dim. Before Lindy could open her program, they were sitting in total darkness, and the tape had begun to play.

"Still working with canned music, I see," she whispered to Biddy.

"For the tour and for the New York season. There's no room at the Joyce for an orchestra, much less a full chorus."

"I remember."

"But after that? Keep your fingers crossed."

The front curtain opened revealing a smoky stage. Whiffs of fog rolled out into the first few rows. Several people coughed. Lindy grimaced and slid down in her seat. A painted backdrop of black and gold slashes gradually came into view as the stage lit up with a soft amber wash. Stage right held a metal frame about fifteen feet high that looked like a jungle gym squeezed and twisted by a giant hand.

"I bet I can guess who the set designer is," whispered Lindy.

"None other. David always uses him. He has perfected mixing business with pleasure. If he ever gets a new boyfriend, maybe his work will get lighter, both figuratively and literally. Wait till you see the props."

A woman in the row in front of them turned in her seat and scowled. At least, Lindy guessed she was scowling. It was still too dark to see much more than the stage, itself, and the outline of the woman's perfect hairdo. Lindy pulled a face and settled into her seat, hoping she could sit through another *Carmina*.

Two male dancers, costumed in beige pants and tunics, entered from upstage left carrying a girl curled into a contraction above their heads. They laid her so that she draped over the lower bars of the tower. With long, open strides they circled the metal frame, climbed halfway up the back and hung there.

Lindy slid further down in her seat.

As the music crescendoed, another dancer appeared. She walked slowly across the stage, draped in a smoky-gray cloak that trailed several feet behind her. Her face was covered by a voluminous hood. Abruptly she turned to the audience, the cape swirling around her feet, and threw her arms open, revealing a sparkling gold lamé lining. At the same time, the hood fell back, and she was bathed in a blinding light.

Lindy jolted upright. "My God."

Several faces turned with disapproving looks.

"Biddy, it can't be. Tell me that is not Carlotta."

Biddy gave her a rueful smile. It was easy to see her expression reflected from the light that now radiated from the stage. "I'm afraid so."

"She's older than I am. What the hell is she doing out there?"

The sprayed-in-place perm turned around. "Sh-h-h."

"I'll tell you later," Biddy whispered.

Lindy opened her program and turned the pages until she got to the cast list. She held it up until she caught enough light to read. It was true. Carlotta Devine, ancient and ugly, not to mention mean. Carlotta had never been pretty even as a young woman, but she had always been mean. No, that wasn't fair. Life had made her mean.

With a knotting stomach, Lindy peered at the figure on

stage. Dark eyes, set too close together, eyebrows plucked to a thin, miserly arch that looked painted on, long face and chin that had to be expertly shaded with makeup to keep it from looking sinister even in her prime. Carlotta was no longer in her prime and hadn't been for a decade. And though makeup might do wonders for a less than perfect face, they hadn't invented a cover-up that could conceal Carlotta's vicious personality. She would wreak havoc in this company of young dancers. What had Jeremy Ash been thinking?

Carlotta flung herself about the stage. Lindy gripped the arms of her seat. Seeing the body draped over the railing, Carlotta ran to it and pulled the girl into her arms. The figure poised momentarily in Carlotta's grasp, then slowly moved her hands from her face. She stepped forward onto half point, arms falling gracefully to her sides. The light caught her features and held them for a breathless second. Then she crumpled to the ground, long blond hair cascading around her, blending with the gold of her costume.

Beauty and the Beast, thought Lindy with a shudder.

Carlotta walked forward and into a large circle. When she reached upstage center, two other dancers in robes removed her cloak and carried it offstage.

From downstage right, a male dancer stepped into a pool of amber light and reached longingly toward Carlotta. He was slender and sandy-haired and looked more like a schoolboy than the woman's enamored lover. Carlotta ran toward him, and he pressed her into an overhead lift that should have been beautiful. Carlotta, though thin, was not easy to lift. Her arms stretched out above her like unruly vines. Lindy could see the tendons in her neck straining with the effort of staying aloft. Her young cavalier seemed about to perish beneath his load, and Lindy's whole body tensed as she subconsciously tried to help him.

She could feel Biddy watching her and wondered what on earth could have made Biddy want her to see this. As if reading her thoughts, Biddy shifted her eyes back to the stage.

The *pas de deux* ended with one final lift, which carried Carlotta offstage. The boy barely got her to the edge of the stage, then dumped her unceremoniously into the wings. They were replaced by a quartet of male dancers. Lindy straightened up and breathed deeply as they bound over the floor in athletic jumps, falls, and turns.

By the end of the piece, she had begun to squirm in her seat and wondered what she would say to Biddy. Actually, the choreography wasn't bad, and the music didn't drive her crazy. But it would take a few changes to make this a success. First of all, recasting. Put the pretty girl, what was her name? Lindy looked in her program. Andrea. Put Andrea into Carlotta's part. Get rid of Carlotta completely. Paul (the schoolboy) would be a perfect lover for Andrea. Then . . .

Her attention was brought back to the stage by a sudden dimming of the lights. Two rows of robe-clad figures walked straight across the stage, each holding a three-pronged candelabra of flickering candles. The lights continued to dim until the stage was virtually black except for the twinkling of the artificial flames. Well, really, thought Lindy. David Matthews had turned a celebration of secular life into a morality play. But it was pretty effective.

Gradually light suffused the surface of the metal tower, now a funeral bower? The bodies of Carlotta and Paul lay draped over each other at the apex. At least, he's on top, thought Lindy irreverently. Blackout.

After a suspended interval, the audience began to applaud loudly. Biddy let out a long breath, snapped her notebook closed, and turned to Lindy.

"Thank heavens, they seem to like it. Now, intermission, an upbeat dance to end the evening, and they'll go home happy."

The curtain opened for the bows. The corps came forward, still in their robes, bowed in perfect unison, then backed away. Paul led Carlotta and Andrea forward and then backed them into line. Andrea stepped forward by herself. The applause swelled. A few whistles and cheers. Before she rose from her curtsy, Carlotta stepped forward, regarding the audience with a regal hauteur, and cutting Andrea's applause short. Andrea began to back into line.

The applause rose once again, then stopped suddenly as a gasp rolled through the house. Lindy jerked forward. From above Andrea's head, a batten from the flies plummeted toward the stage, slicing the air between the two women as they exchanged positions. Carlotta froze, arms held slightly outward from her body as the batten bounced on the floor at her feet, then rebounded into Andrea.

It hit her on the calves, and she pitched forward. Her hands shot out before her as she stumbled a few steps, then fell to her knees. The audience watched in suspended horror. Her hands grabbed the edge of the stage as she fought to keep herself from plunging into the seats below. Steel cables snapped in the air behind her.

The corps stood frozen, smiles hardened into a rote expression. The front curtain began lurching closed. Andrea pushed herself backward, struggled to her feet, and managed to limp upstage out of the way of the curtain. She tripped over the batten and fell headlong into Carlotta as the curtain closed, billowed out, and settled in a cloud of dust.

Biddy reached for her crutches. Lindy bolted out of her seat and started to climb over her. She stopped, surprised. What was she thinking? This was not her company; she was just a visitor.

"Come on," said Biddy. She swung her crutches into the aisle. Lindy followed her for a few frustrating steps, then ran ahead clearing the way.

The audience was vibrating with worried exclamations; a voice rose over the loudspeaker announcing the intermission. Lindy closed the stage door behind them.

The dancers stood in a nervous cluster around the prostrate body of the young ingenue. They talked in agitated whispers. Biddy and Lindy pushed through the crowd. Peter Dowd bent over the girl, smoothing her hair out of her face and talking quietly. Jeremy Ash stood just beyond them, staring at the scene. Biddy bent down next to Peter, her cast thrust awkwardly out to the side.

"Is she hurt?"

Peter glanced at her, eyes panicky. "I don't know, I don't think so."

Andrea lifted herself to her elbow. "I'm okay, really." Her stage makeup stood out starkly against her pale skin.

Peter turned back to her and began to lift her carefully to her feet. The company took a step backward. Supporting her with both arms, he led her toward the dressing rooms. Biddy followed.

"Clear the stage, now," ordered Peter over his shoulder.

Everyone moved slowly away from the batten and wandered into the wings. Carlotta took one step toward Jeremy, hesitated, then followed the others offstage.

Lindy and Jeremy were alone on the stage. It must be him, thought Lindy. His back was to her but she recognized his silhouette. He just stood there looking into the wings, where Peter had taken Andrea. Then slowly he walked toward the dressing rooms.

Lindy waited until he was gone, then looked up, careful not to stand under any of the battens or electrics. The one that lay on the floor was empty; no lighting instruments or scenery was attached to it. It wasn't in use for the performance. Why would it suddenly plummet downward?

The Endicott Playhouse was on a counterweight system. She remembered that from years before. The lock must have been triggered by mistake. She had seen that happen once before, years ago on Broadway. A dancer had been knocked out by a piece of flying scenery. She shivered; one batten could have taken out the entire line of dancers. It was too horrible to contemplate.

Peter walked back onto the stage and motioned to a stagehand who was standing by the rail on stage right. Lindy took the opportunity to disappear. This wasn't exactly a good time to renew old acquaintances. She watched from the wings as Peter reached down toward the batten and held it steady as the stagehand raised it into the flies and winched it off at the rail. He watched it stop above his head, then wiped his forehead with the palm of his hand; the stage lights tinged his skin with a yellow pallor. He would never have overlooked an unsecured pipe in the old days. What had happened to him?

He stood staring up into the flies, then smashed his fist into his other hand and walked toward the rail. Lindy's stomach lurched in sympathy for the stagehand who waited for him.

"What a nightmare," said Biddy, clunking up behind her. "She's not hurt, just a few bruises. She's scared out of her wits, but she's going on with the next piece. Jeremy's with her."

They watched Peter stride toward them. Biddy looked at him expectantly. "What happened?"

Peter stopped momentarily in front of them, then looked down at Biddy's cast. His eyebrows furrowed. Without speaking, he walked past them to the door to the dressing rooms. "Five minutes, everybody."

Lindy and Biddy exchanged looks.

They returned to their seats. Biddy sat down and dropped her crutches to the floor.

"The audience is jumpy as all get out," she said as she scanned the seats around them. "Let's just hope Jeremy's piece takes their mind off of falling debris." She opened her notebook. "It's a real gem. Edvard Grieg's *Holberg Suite.*" She sighed heavily. "God, what a night."

The audience didn't quiet down until the house was completely dark. The *Holberg Suite* music began abruptly; violins startled the audience into silence. The curtain opened. The stage erupted with a burst of nervous energy.

"Settle down," whispered Biddy.

"Settle down," echoed Lindy.

As the piece progressed, the dancers began to relax. The music seemed to carry them along as it embraced the audience and lulled it into tranquillity. Andrea entered, composed and in full command of the stage. Lindy could feel the audience respond to her as six men lifted her gently, then passed her from one to another like an elegant present. The movement at first enchanted, then wove a seductive web over the theater. The energy diminished so imperceptibly that Lindy jumped when the notes of the last movement began. The stage filled with the entire cast, moving expertly through intricate patterns.

When the curtain closed on the final pose, the audience burst into applause. They jumped to their feet with a roar when Andrea took her bow. They loved her, and the accident had given them a vested interest in her success. Lindy stood and joined in the applause.

The enchantment left with the darkness. Backstage was filled with pedestrian activity. The wardrobe mistress was collecting dirty socks and whatever needed mending. Stagehands hauled pieces of scenery back into the shop for storage until the following night. Dancers packed up practice clothes or lounged in their dressing rooms smoking cigarettes. Just like any other night in the theater. Just like nothing had happened, thought Lindy.

They met Jeremy Ash as he came out of the girls' dressing room. He was tall, solid but thin, and about as gorgeous as a man should be. Wavy blond hair curled over the collar of his black turtleneck. His camel-colored trousers still held an immaculate crease, not even a wrinkle at the hips. He must have been standing backstage during the performance. Lindy hadn't seen him in the house. Maybe he was too nervous to sit still; some directors were. Jeremy Ash didn't look nervous, just incredibly tired.

Biddy enclosed his arm in hers and led him forward. "Lindy, this is Jeremy."

"Hello." She held out her hand and pulled in her stomach. "It's a pleasure. The performance was impressive."

Jeremy's weary expression rearranged itself into one of politeness. "The pleasure is mine. I hope 'impressive' doesn't fall into the category of 'unbelievable' and 'you should have seen yourself up there.'"

Lindy felt a rush of embarrassment. "Of course not. I thought it was stunning."

Jeremy grimaced.

God, her conversational skills were as flabby as the rest of her. "I meant the dancing."

"Thank you." He smiled suddenly. It was dazzling. "You know, we've actually met. And of course, I've seen you on the stage."

"You have a good memory; that was quite awhile ago."

His smile disappeared. "Yes."

Behind him, the door to the first dressing room swung open and banged against the wall. Carlotta stormed out and descended on Jeremy, her Japanese robe flying out behind her, revealing more of her body than anyone cared to see. Black hair, dulled to a matte finish, brittle and broken from years of hair spray and dye, flew out stiffly from her scalp.

He turned around abruptly, then started back with obvious repugnance as she stopped in front of him. The entire backstage area was suddenly quiet, the dancers stopped in the process of leaving, eyes focused away from the outburst. They became a tableau behind Carlotta and Jeremy, exaggerating their every move.

"What is it, Carlotta?" he asked. For a man, known for

having a pet name for everyone, he seemed particularly formal. Lindy could guess why. She couldn't come up with a nickname for Carlotta that was anything but obscene.

"I know what you're trying to do. You think you can frighten me away." Carlotta turned in a dramatic slow-motion pirouette, mesmerizing her prey, forcing all eyes to look at her. She snapped her head back to Jeremy as if spotting a turn. "It won't work. Do you understand? Someone will pay, but it won't be me."

Jeremy looked at her blandly, except for one momentary bolt of hatred that shot from his eyes. Lindy saw it. He blinked, and it was gone. "What are you talking about, Carlotta? No one is trying to hurt you. It was an accident."

Carlotta raised a long finger to his chest. "If you think you can replace me with that little bitch, think again. I'll finish her, and don't think I won't."

Jeremy flinched. "That batten hit Andrea, not you."

Carlotta smiled, baring cigarette-stained teeth. She ran her finger slowly up his chest and under his chin. "Your aim never was that good." She flicked his chin with her fingernail, then turned spasmodically, her hair lashing across his face, and strode back into her dressing room.

The door slammed closed, and Jeremy turned to Lindy.

"A fitting exit for Medusa," he said. He seemed completely unaffected by her outburst. The dancers continued to stand where they were, faces strained, bodies tense.

Jeremy smiled slightly. "We should get so much drama on the stage."

Lindy smiled as graciously as she could, but she couldn't think of anything to say. No one would ever talk to a director the way Carlotta had. How could she get away with it? Even for Carlotta, her actions seemed extreme.

"Excuse me, Lindy, it's been delightful to see you again."

As soon as he left, the dancers crowded around Biddy.

"Why doesn't he do something?" asked Paul. "She's ruining everything, and he just takes it. I hate her." His lower lip trembled.

"Yeah," said a tall black dancer. "If he'd just cooperate, we could have the bitch out of here." He jabbed the air with an unlit cigarette.

"He's under a lot of pressure. Help him out, okay?" said Biddy.

"We've been trying, but he doesn't pick up on one damn cue. What's the matter with him? I'd kill the bitch if she talked to me that way."

"Look, Rebo, it's been a hectic night. Go back to the hotel and get some rest. Try to forget this. It was a great show; celebrate a little." Then she smiled. "But not too much."

Lindy remembered that smile. It had carried them through some rotten times, as well as some good. It looked like the Jeremy Ash dancers would be needing it now.

The dancers began moving toward the stage door. Only Andrea remained, braced against the wall.

Lindy walked over to her. "Rough night."

Andrea smiled feebly.

"Don't let her get to you. It's all show."

Andrea opened her mouth, and a convulsive sob escaped. Her eyes filled with tears, then she turned and ran down the hall after the others.

Lindy turned to see Biddy staring after Andrea's retreating form. She seemed pretty close to tears herself.

"Come on, old friend, I'll buy you a drink, or better still, why don't you spend the night at my house. That way, I won't have to not drink and drive, and you can see Glen." Lindy dropped her arm across Biddy's shoulders. "And then you can tell me what the hell is going on here."

Lindy could feel Biddy fighting with herself, torn between her need to stay with the dancers and a greater need to talk to Lindy. Just like the old days, when they had been so close that one could tell what the other was thinking just by walking into a room.

"Okay." It was quiet and calm, but Lindy knew Biddy as well as she knew anyone, and she suddenly understood why Biddy had asked her to come.

Two

They drove north on the parkway. Lindy's evening at the theater had piqued her curiosity and unearthed feelings that surprised her. She felt vitalized. First the batten and then that scene with Carlotta. It was awful. She had loved every minute.

"And remember those two Italian silk merchants in Tokyo?" asked Biddy.

Lindy slowed down at the token booth and threw in thirty-five cents. "The night of the earthquake? How could I forget? I thought it was the sushi that made the earth move."

"Well, it certainly wasn't the two Italians. And speaking of Italians ... ," Biddy paused. "I wonder what ever happened to Gianni?"

"My faithless *amoré?* Who cares? Probably still chasing after young American girls, only he's bound to be older and fatter and bald. At least, I still have hair."

Gianni BonGiovanni, purported count and definite rake, had wined and wooed Lindy from Milan to Venice to Portofino. He filled her dressing room with flowers, bought her presents, plied her with Chianti and champagne, and then promptly disappeared, leaving her to deal with the two unsavory gentlemen who wished to know his whereabouts.

"Maybe the Mafia got him." Lindy turned the car into the driveway and stopped at the front door.

"Wow, Lindy, this is gorgeous. I had no idea."

"Biddy, it's pitch black. How can you even tell what the house looks like?"

"There's the porch light and anyway . . ." Biddy inhaled deeply.

"If you sing, I'll break your other leg."

Biddy laughed. "Remember, we used to sing entire conversations."

"It's amazing what depths touring can plunge you to." Lindy opened the car door. "Take me back to Flagstaff," she sang. Biddy joined in and they warbled their way up to the front door, two girls again. Biddy, young and fiercely optimistic; Lindy, a little older and wiser, but immediately drawn to the insouciant charm of the younger woman.

It was Lindy who had convinced Biddy to take night courses in accounting at Pace University. And it was Biddy who had held Lindy's hand when Gianni had dumped her, bullying her into laughter and taking her shopping to forget her woes. It was great therapy, shopping. The habit had stuck with her.

"Don't mind Bruno, just don't let him knock you over," said Lindy as she opened the front door and led Biddy into the entrance hall.

There was no sign of Bruno. Lindy turned on the entry lights and ushered Biddy down the hall. "I'll get you settled in the guest room, and then we'll find Glen. If Bruno didn't greet us at the door, they're both asleep in front of the television."

They found Glen and Bruno in the family room, snoring in tandem. Glen sat in one corner of the couch, his feet propped on a leather ottoman. Bruno was stretched out beside him, his head resting in Glen's lap. The blaring sounds of a chase scene ricocheted around the room.

"Scratch that," yelled Lindy over screeching car wheels, police sirens, and gunshots. She closed the door, shutting out the noise. "Surround Sound," she explained in a quieter voice. "How about a glass of wine?"

Lindy poured out two glasses of white Bordeaux and returned the bottle to the pewter ice bucket. She sat down on the Sheraton sofa, slipped off her shoes, and tucked her feet underneath her. Biddy sat next to her with her cast resting on a pillow on the marble coffee table.

Biddy took a glass as her eyes scanned the room. She clinked Lindy's glass with hers. "It's so posh."

"Medium posh. You should see the other side of town."

"Is that a real Ming vase?" asked Biddy, indicating the object with her wineglass. "I'd have been a nervous wreck raising two kids and a dog with all this breakable stuff around."

"Oh, we lost a few pieces, but I broke most of them. Anyway, I've become an instant empty nester. No sooner did I get Cliff off to college, then Annie wins a music scholarship to spend her junior year abroad. Bern Conservatory. She's only sixteen, but . . ." Lindy shrugged. "I had to let her go. We're an independent lot, we Haggertys. Anyway, I left for New York the day after high school, and I've done okay."

"You've done great."

Biddy's superlatives were beginning to annoy her. She didn't want to talk about herself. She hadn't done much lately, she was just busy. "Glen made all the money. I just did the grunt work."

"I'd hardly call raising two children 'grunt work.' "

"You'd be surprised." Lindy stretched out her feet next to Biddy's on the coffee table and declaimed in a public-television voice: "I've perfected driving a station wagon into a fine art, taken grocery shopping into the next century, and created more amateur ballets in twelve years than all the choreographers in Soho put together. Two thumbs-up."

"Be serious."

"I am," said Lindy. "But in addition to the boring stuff, kids are pretty cool. And the suburbs is the best place to raise them. I mean, poor Cliff spent his first year of life on tour with me, sleeping in the bottom drawer of a hotel dresser. Now, he can communicate with the whole world, electronically, without ever leaving his bedroom."

"I think I'd rather tour."

"Hmm."

"Do you think you'll ever go back to work?"

The question hit her like an ice cube from the wine bucket. Lindy shrugged. "I don't know. I can't see spending the rest of my life doing amateur fund-raisers."

Biddy sipped her wine and looked at Lindy over the rim of the glass.

Lindy returned her look. Biddy's cheeks were mottled with pink. "Biddy, what's going on?"

"I wish I knew." She placed her wineglass on the coffee table and began to scrub her hair. "You saw what a mess things are. I'm so confused. I really wanted to work for

Jeremy. He's incredibly talented. I couldn't believe it when he actually hired me as rehearsal director, that he would trust *me* with overseeing his creations.

"And everything seemed fine until Carlotta showed up. It was about three months ago. No one had heard anything about her being hired. Jeremy just said she was in, and there was no use talking about it. Now, everything is falling apart."

"Odd."

"More than odd. Jeremy can barely look at her. He completely ignores her. You can imagine what kind of rehearsal environment that makes. Before she came, he was always around, shaping things, directing, hands on. Not like other choreographers who turn over their work the minute the last step is finished. He was really so powerful in rehearsals. But now, half the time he doesn't even show up when she's supposed to rehearse, and I have to take the rehearsals alone. And he's turned over everything in the theater to Peter; he's the only person in the company who attempts to control her. Then she insisted on Paul as her partner. They look ridiculous together. He's really talented, but he's so tied up in knots, he can barely move."

"He and Andrea would be the perfect casting for *Carmina*. Surely, David Matthews could have insisted that Jeremy use her."

"He did, but Jeremy refused. There was a big to-do, and we were afraid that David would pull *Carmina*, but for some reason he didn't. Everybody hates Carlotta. They avoid her like the plague and then play all sorts of practical jokes on her. It's a nightmare."

"Tonight was not a joke."

"No. It was just an accident."

Lindy pointed to Biddy's cast. "Like that?"

Biddy's eyes widened. "Yeah," she said slowly.

"How did it happen?"

Biddy picked up her wineglass and took a sip. "I was rehearsing Carlotta in that fast section in *Carmina*, and she kept moving too far downstage. I was standing in front of her trying to keep her in place. But the steps kept traveling forward, and I kept backing up, and pretty soon I was in the orchestra pit on my butt. Luckily, the pit was raised, or I might have broken my neck instead of my leg."

"You backed off the stage?" Lindy asked incredulously.

"It's hard to believe, I know, but Carlotta was so forceful. Everything is a power struggle to her."

"You think she did it on purpose?"

Biddy shrugged.

"What did Jeremy do?"

"Nothing." Biddy sighed. "Oh, he took really good care of me; paid for everything that insurance and workman's comp didn't cover. He's good that way."

"But he didn't put it to Carlotta?"

"Not while I was around, but Peter did. While we were waiting for the ambulance, he read her beads in no uncertain terms. I've never seen him so angry."

"He thought she did it on purpose?"

Biddy's hands shot into the air; the wine sloshed in her glass. "Nobody knows what Peter thinks. He was hired when Jeremy started up the new company, and he's been scowling ever since. He's efficient and uncomplaining, but stays completely to himself."

"And that's another thing. What's happened to him, Biddy? He looks eaten up. He would never have allowed a batten to remain unsecured in the past." Blood rushed to Lindy's stomach. "He's not . . . sick, is he?"

Biddy chewed on her lips. Lindy knew what she was thinking. Biddy had loved Claude faithfully for years with no reciprocation from him. He had finally "come out," and when he became ill, Biddy had nursed him and then buried him. His family didn't even come to his funeral. So many of their friends were dead. Please, not Peter.

"Biddy."

Biddy jumped, then shivered. "No, I don't think so. He's straight. Isn't he?"

"It's hard to tell in this business."

"No. I'm sure."

"Maybe, but, Biddy, this is not the Peter Dowd we all knew and loved."

"He's still wonderful with the dancers, cares about their comfort, and he always runs interference for them against Carlotta." Biddy's mouth worked spasmodically.

"Biddy, he's changed," said Lindy. "But, I guess, working around Carlotta could put a strain on the most benign personality. I just can't understand why Jeremy would keep her on. She should have retired years ago. She's awful and ugly, and—"

"And they love her in the suburbs."

"I can't believe it. Why?"

Biddy shrugged. "Why do they eat at McDonald's? She's been living off her reputation for years. If she weren't so awful, I'd feel sorry for her."

"Don't tell me Jeremy keeps her on because she sells in the burbs."

"Of course not; he's an artist. He cares more about the

work than satisfying the uneducated whims of suburbia."
Biddy clapped her hand to her mouth. "I didn't mean . . ."

"It's okay. We are pretty gauche out here in the hinter-
lands." Lindy leaned back against the couch. "So why doesn't
he fire her?"

"Not a clue. They may like her on the tour circuit, but
they'll crucify us in New York. He knows that."

"And why does he let her get away with talking to him
like she did tonight, and in front of everybody? I would have
fired her on the spot."

"So would I, but he just takes it, and doesn't even seem
upset about it. She's going to ruin us."

"It's not some kind of game, is it?"

Biddy looked blank.

"I mean, we've all seen some pretty sick relationships in
this business."

"Not Jeremy, he's not like that."

"Wasn't Carlotta a member of his first company?"

"I think so, but she should have retired even before that."

"People like Carlotta usually keep their jobs by sleeping
with the director."

Biddy made a lemon-sucking face. "Yuck."

Lindy raised an eyebrow.

"He would never. He hates her. You'd have to be dead
not to notice it."

Lindy raised the other eyebrow.

"Anyway, he's gay."

"Straight or gay, I can't see him diddling someone like
Carlotta," said Lindy. She tried to remember what she knew
about Jeremy. He had been the artistic director of a prominent New York dance company until about five years ago.

Then he abruptly quit and disappeared for several years. He had been talented, intelligent, and a savvy businessman, a perfect combination for success. Now, he was back. Why would someone with so much going for him let things get so out of hand?

Bruno padded into the living room as she was wrestling with the thought. He wagged his tail perilously close to the ice bucket.

Lindy reached over as it began to topple and righted it. "Bruno." He put his front paws on her lap and attempted to crawl up.

A head appeared around the corner of the archway to the hall. "Bruno, come." The voice was groggy with sleep.

"Glen, here's Biddy. Come say hello. I'll get you a glass." Lindy started to get up.

"Hi, Biddy," he said from the archway. "Good to see you. I'm beat," he said to the room in general. "Good night."

Lindy felt her cheeks tingle and sat down again. "He works long hours."

"Computers, right?"

"Telecommunications. Of the global variety." Couldn't he have at least made an effort at small talk with Biddy? He knew how close they'd once been and how excited she was seeing her again. Why did it suddenly strike her that Glen might be wiring the world, but had begun to tune her out?

"He's still cute."

"Yeah."

Biddy stared at the space where Glen had stood. "What am I going to do?"

The question hung in the air. Lindy poured the rest of the wine into the glasses.

"I need help." Biddy pulled her fingers through her hair, leaving wisps radiating from her face. "You and I were always a good team, weren't we?"

Lindy eyed her cautiously. "What are you getting at?"

"It's only a few weeks until the Joyce season."

"You want me to come to work?"

Biddy nodded her head in jerky, hopeful movements. "I'll arrange it with Jeremy."

"I'll be forty-four in November. I'm not in shape. I can't find my cheekbones much less my hipbones." Despite her protests, the idea of working with Biddy was growing like a bionic mustard seed in her brain.

"Just for a few days. I can't seem to manage this alone. I have to clunk around on these crutches, and I just feel overwhelmed." Biddy clutched her wineglass with both hands; her hair had maxxed out.

"I can't . . ."

"Please."

Lindy reached over and pushed away a strand of Biddy's hair. "Working for Jeremy is pretty important, huh?"

"Lindy, it's my life."

Well, how could she say no to that?

It was well after two o'clock when Lindy staggered upstairs to bed. Her head was reeling from wine, intrigue, and the possibility of actually having a job, even for a few days.

So much for a pleasant evening at the theater. The on-stage drama paled compared to what had happened back-stage afterward. Take one nasty diva, an impervious director, a brooding stage manager, and you had enough to tempt any mystery buff, or a desperate soap-opera writer. And then there was Biddy.

Glen and Bruno were snoring peacefully. Lindy tripped over a pair of shoes lying in the doorway.

"Ouch." Bruno lifted his head at the sound. "And get off my side of the bed, you mutt."

Bruno closed his eyes. Lindy groped her way through the darkness to the bathroom, feeling her allegiance drawn back into the past. She clicked on the light and began rummaging through the medicine cabinet for some aspirin. Just in case, she thought. She popped two into her mouth and stuck her mouth under the running water. It was a routine that she remembered well. Between aches, pains, strains, and the occasional hangover, Lindy had taken her share of aspirin over the years.

She threw her clothes in the hamper and pulled out a T-shirt from the top drawer of the bureau. When did we start wearing clothes to bed, she wondered as she pulled the shirt over her head. She looked at Glen, a little pudgier, a little pastier. He had been aggressive in his attentions to her, and after the nefarious Gianni, she was more than susceptible to his all-American, no-nonsense kind of charm.

He knew where he was going, what he wanted out of life. He wanted Lindy, and she had succumbed. And now he had just what he wanted and had gone where he wanted to go, but Lindy was afraid that he had left her behind somewhere along the way.

There was suddenly a hollow pit in her stomach. Probably the wine, she thought. She and Glen had made such grand plans, and they had achieved them. Or maybe, it was Glen who had achieved them. With Cliff and Annie away from home, it seemed like he hardly needed her at all. But Biddy needed her. She shivered. One phone call, one evening at the theater. Suddenly she didn't feel so sure of herself.

"This is not a good way to think," she said aloud and jumped at the sound of her voice.

"*Aarghgh,*" came the response from the bed.

Lindy sighed. She couldn't even tell if the sound had come from Glen or Bruno.

She climbed wearily into bed, grabbed Bruno by the collar, and pulled him onto the floor. He made one of those baleful doggy yawns.

Lindy growled back and tucked her feet under the comforter. Glen turned over, facing away from her. Bruno jumped back onto the bed and after walking over her for a few seconds found a comfy spot between them.

"Pick up my laundry tomorrow?" one of them mumbled.

"You will not cry," she said silently over and over like a mantra until she fell asleep.

Three

When Lindy came downstairs the next morning, Biddy was on the phone. She motioned Lindy over. "Jeremy" she mouthed. She handed Lindy the phone. Lindy shook her head. She wasn't ready to make any decisions. She hadn't even had coffee.

"Hello, Lindy. It's Jeremy." His voice was a smooth, unruffled baritone, and her doubts melted into the receiver. "Look, I'm sure this is an imposition, but if you're available, I would consider it a great favor if you could help Biddy out for a while."

She swallowed hard. "Jeremy, I'm really flattered, but I haven't done this kind of work in years. I'm not sure I can even touch my toes."

"Lindy, it's like riding a bike."

Well, she could ride a bike, probably. Her doubts flew out the window, down the street, and into the next county.

Biddy added Lindy's name to the roster at the stage door and led her down the hall. She swung the door open. "This is ours. I'll go find Jeremy." Biddy smiled, eyes twinkling. "Make yourself at home."

Lindy walked into the empty dressing room and tossed

her dance bag on the makeup table. She stood in the middle of the room watching dust motes dance in front of the dingy window. Bats were slamming around inside her stomach. Damn. She had stage fright, and it felt great. She took a deep breath, held it, then exhaled slowly through her mouth. With a last look around the dressing room, she wandered backstage.

A group of girls was warming up onstage. (All dancers were called "girls," "boys," or "kids" until they retired, usually around the age of forty.) The boys would show up at the last minute. Some things never changed.

Dressed in a wild assortment of sweatpants, cutout T-shirts, sweaters, and leg warmers, four girls stood at a ladder in the center of the stage. The Jeremy Ash Dance Company was a contemporary-dance company, but the dancers were classically trained. A ballet *barre* was as essential to their day as brushing their teeth. They had reached *grande battements*, the high kicks that ended that portion of the warm-up, before they moved into more strenuous movements in the center. Their feet curved as their legs kicked to the front, side, and back, high above their heads.

Two girls were stretching on the floor, legs spread out in a straddle. Deli coffees sat on the floor in front of them, and they sipped and talked as they curved their backs right and left and forward.

Laughter came from behind her. The boys. They could afford to take it easier than the girls. Competition between men wasn't as tough; there were fewer of them to choose from. She heard the rustle of paper bags being opened: the ubiquitous tour breakfast, coffee and a hard roll. It felt good to be back.

"Seems like everyone's making a comeback these days."

Lindy looked over her shoulder and into the brown eyes of Peter Dowd. "Hi, Peter. I didn't get a chance to say hello last night. It's good to see you." Lindy stretched out her arms to give Peter the customary theater hug and kiss on the cheek.

"It was a busy night." The tone of his voice stopped Lindy midgesture, and she dropped her arms to her side.

"Never a dull moment, especially with you-know-who around?"

Peter made no comment but looked past her to the stage. Lindy was acutely aware of his body next to hers. It exuded an unsettling mixture of standoffishness and invitation, and he seemed oblivious to it. She longed to ask him what was wrong.

"Yeah, he seems to have made a slip there," he said after a moment. "He's out front with Biddy."

Lindy watched him walk onto the stage. Peter Dowd had missed his calling. He should have been on the stage, not backstage. Tall, lean, with thick hair the color of obsidian, and cheekbones to die for. A little makeup over those scars, and he'd be perfect, not a leading man, but the mysterious, dark stranger.

Lindy crossed to the front of the stage. Biddy and Jeremy were sitting in the front row. Biddy looked up and motioned her over.

In the past Lindy would have jumped down and gone out to the seats. She quickly evaluated the possibility of landing on her feet and walked over to the stairs that led down to the house from the side of the proscenium. All this company needed was two rehearsal directors on crutches.

Jeremy rose when she approached them. "Good morning. We'll start with the *Holberg Suite*. It's pretty straightforward. The *Prelude*'s in good shape, except for the spacing of the girls' trio. They keep cutting off the boys' entrance, and you could get fuller movement from the *Sarabande*."

Did he want her to take rehearsal now? Lindy frantically ticked off corrections and organized the piece mentally as he talked. *Prelude*, whole company; *Sarabande*, a sextet for three girls and three boys; *Gavotte*, group again; *Air*, adagio for Andrea and six boys; *Rigaudon*, fast paced and short last section. Okay. She could wing her way through the piece easily; the movement flowed perfectly with the music. All she had to do was fine-tune. She'd worry about *Carmina* later.

"Then we'll take a break while they set up for *Carmina* and do a couple of hours on it. That way the crew won't have to set up the cage twice."

"Sounds good. What do you want me to do?" asked Lindy.

"We'll introduce you to everybody, and then you can take the rehearsal. You might as well jump in."

She took several slow, calming breaths. "Okay, but, Biddy, what are you going to do?"

"Biddy can help me with some paperwork. I've got two grant proposals due in May, and I'm tearing my hair over them. Lucky for me, Biddy is good at everything; keeps me from having to hire a bunch of specialists."

Biddy beamed.

Lindy swallowed. Just like that. She was back at work.

"Well, let's get to it, then." Jeremy led them to the stage and pulled himself up over the edge. Biddy and Lindy took the stairs.

Jeremy called the company together. Most had finished warming up, but a few sauntered out of the dressing rooms. She would have to give a lecture on warming up before rehearsal. She had a lot of work to do, but first she needed to win them over.

Jeremy introduced her, giving the particulars of her career. A few of the older dancers seemed to recognize her name. They might have been starting their careers when she had retired, but most of them had still been children.

I could be their mother, she thought as she looked at the faces in the assembled group. Sixteen pairs of eyes looked back at her. At least, Carlotta wouldn't be coming in until later. It would give her an hour to build a rapport.

"Let's get started, shall we?" She gave them her brightest smile. "And those of you who still need to warm up, do so on the sly, please, and try to be a little earlier next time."

She turned and walked to the middle of the stage, legs shaking. "Let's take the opening section with music just to get the juices flowing, and then we'll stop and work on a few things."

The girls took their places quickly. Paul did a few last jumps and trotted off to stage right. A couple of the boys slouched off to the wings muttering to each other. Grumbling she could deal with, but if there was going to be an attitude problem, it would come from the one they called Rebo. She had noticed his name in the program. No last name, just Rebo.

He was a tall, muscular black man, long legged with a well-developed torso. He wore a red bandanna around his head and had a gold loop in one ear. He cocked his head at her, then moved indolently to his starting position.

What crap, thought Lindy. She recalled how he had burst onto the stage, gobbling up the space and standing the hairs of her forearms on end. Power, strength, rhythm, and good looks. And such an attitude. Well, she'd get through to him. He had too much talent to waste his energy on self-indulgence.

She pushed the play button on the boom box at the front of the stage. It was cued to the beginning. Thank you, Peter. She had enough to think about without having to search for music cues.

She let them dance the *Prelude*, then turned off the tape player.

"Good. Now I want to work on the girls' entrance, the three of you there. What are your names?" Mieko, Laura, and Kate. "Please bear with me. I'm trying to learn people and steps at the same time, so give me a day or two, okay?"

The trio looked at her pleasantly but didn't respond. Lindy took them through their steps, adjusting the spacing and directions so that the group stayed cohesive. Then they tried it to music.

"That's much better," volunteered Kate, or was it Laura? Mieko she could remember: Oriental features, straight black hair, petite. And a name like Mieko Jones tended to stick in your mind. "I could never make it to my place for the next cue," said Kate. "Now I have plenty of time."

If all of life could be so simple, thought Lindy.

Next she worked on the lift that she had seen Andrea and Paul practicing the night before, using two boys as "spotters" to catch her if she started to fall. When they got to a series of turns that lowered until the dancers were lying on the floor, Lindy stopped them.

"Not bad, but you need to open up your feet and lower

your turns gradually until the end. Like this." She took a deep breath and demonstrated for them. The turns were easy. She ended stretched out on the floor looking up at them.

"Okay, I got down here by myself; who's going to get me up?"

Quiet laughter rippled through the group. Rebo waltzed up and made an exaggerated kowtow. "Madame," he said and pulled her up with one hand so easily that she sprang onto her feet.

"Thanks, getting up would not have been a pretty sight."

Rebo granted her a wide, toothy grin. "My pleasure," he said.

Gotcha, she thought.

She started on the *Air*, the section for Andrea and six men. Their movement was seamless. Lindy just fine-tuned, adjusted an occasional handhold, shifted a position slightly so that it would read better from the audience.

They had reached the final movement, the *Rigaudon*, when Carlotta appeared at the side of the stage. She was wearing a fur coat and sunglasses. Honestly, thought Lindy. The woman had no taste. It was the middle of April; she must be sweating in the ridiculous thing. But she had probably had to save all her life to buy it. Might as well get her money's worth. Carlotta stopped for a moment, gave Lindy a haughty, appraising look, and went into her dressing room.

"*Brr-r-r.*" Rebo hugged himself and flashed Lindy a challenging look.

"Carlotta may be older than me," she replied innocently, "but I can handle her."

She gave them a fifteen-minute break. That would be long enough for Carlotta to get ready and for Peter to have the stagehands set up the cage for *Carmina*. She wandered back into her dressing room for the bottled water she had brought. There was no sign of Biddy and Jeremy. "When you walk through a storm . . . ," she sang under her breath.

She came out into the hall just in time to see Carlotta come out of her own dressing room, her hand on the shoulder of the costume mistress. Lindy reminded herself to ask Biddy what the girl's name was.

"It wasn't Peter's fault."

Carlotta patted her shoulder. "I know, dear." The girl looked gratefully up at the aging dancer and scurried past Lindy down the hall.

Lindy walked toward Carlotta and stuck out her hand. "Carlotta, Lindy Graham." She had slipped back into using her stage name automatically.

Carlotta looked at Lindy's hand like it was some unrecognizable object. Then slowly she shook hands. Her limp fingers felt like bird bones in Lindy's firm grasp.

"Oh, yes, Lindy Graham. I thought you retired to have children." She looked Lindy up and down as if counting the extra pounds.

"I did; now, I'm back." Lindy flashed her a smile. "When you're ready." She didn't wait for an answer but went through the door to backstage, heart hammering.

Peter was standing at the edge of the stage. "Cage is up, dancers are ready."

"Thanks." Lindy walked briskly onstage.

"Okay," she said. "Let's take it from the top. Where is Carlotta?"

On cue, Carlotta appeared. After one disdainful look around the stage, she took her opening position. Lindy hit the play button. Andrea looked out of the wings and shrugged. Rebo and two corps boys hurried out of the first wing. "Sorry." They took their places quickly, and Lindy recued the music to the beginning. A minute later, Andrea and the boys were draped on the cage, and Carlotta had flung out her arms. But when she started to lift Andrea, she promptly stopped. Andrea dropped heavily onto the metal bars. The two boys winced.

"Really," drawled Carlotta. "This is impossible. The girl is a lug; perhaps *you* can do something with her." Her eyes pierced Lindy's, and Lindy noticed for the first time, they weren't dark at all, but a dull gray.

Lindy gritted her teeth, then said nonchalantly, "Andrea, when you feel Carlotta start to lift you, just pick yourself up, please."

Andrea picked herself up, raised herself on point, and fell.

"And she's too close to me after her fall. David always told her to fall forward." Carlotta turned to Andrea. "Forward, dear, that's downstage, that way, toward the pit."

Andrea crawled downstage and glanced up at Lindy.

Lindy willed her to stay in control.

"Well, that seems to be settled. Could we please try to get to some dancing?" Lindy turned her back on them and spoke at the boom box. "Let's cut to the second section." She fast-forwarded the tape.

They rehearsed, but there was no energy. Movements were cut short, steps forgotten, entrances made late. It was amazing to watch the degeneration. An hour ago, the stage was rocking with exuberance. Now it was peopled by clumsy amateurs.

They moved on to the *pas de deux* for Paul and Carlotta. The kid was visibly shaking. He missed the first two lifts, and Carlotta turned on him.

"You incompetent little . . . just like your father. Two untalented peas in a pod."

Paul glared at her.

"Take two minutes, everybody, but don't leave the stage," said Lindy. Paul was immediately led off by Andrea and Mieko.

Lindy faced Carlotta. "This is doing no good. Can we try to make this work, please."

"Dear"—the word dripped with sarcasm—"the poor thing couldn't dance his way out of a paper bag."

Lindy looked her straight in the eye. She had to tilt her head up to do it. Carlotta was a good four inches taller than she was. She needed to dye her hair; the lighter roots formed a line down her center part. Like a skunk, thought Lindy.

"He could if you would help." She raised an eyebrow. "We all need to keep our jobs, dear. Let's try to make this as painless as possible."

Carlotta's eyes widened, then narrowed, like a cat deciding whether the pounce is worth the effort.

Lindy turned back to the group. "We'll start the duet again. Be ready to make your next entrance." She recued the music.

Rehearsal limped along. Lindy was exhausted mentally and emotionally, as well as physically. As soon as Peter announced three o'clock, she cut them loose.

"Talk about time standing still," she said as Peter unplugged the boom box.

"It's really ten till, but you looked like you needed rescuing."

"You're a good man, Peter Dowd."

He wrapped the cord around the handle of the boom box and walked away. At the edge of the stage, he stopped as Carlotta appeared holding a crumpled piece of poster-size paper.

"Where's Jeremy?"

Peter shrugged.

Lindy walked up behind him. "Can I do something for you, Carlotta?"

"Look at this." She shoved the paper toward Lindy. As Lindy took it, she noticed the boys crowded into the door of their dressing room. She straightened out the paper; the crinkling sound seemed absurdly magnified.

Across the top were the words spelled out in block letters: NOW APPEARING, THE DIVINE SWINE. The head shot that Carlotta used for the program, and obviously taken when she was much younger, had been cut out and pasted to the body of a pig.

Lindy swallowed. Peter glanced at the paper, then walked away. The boys disappeared into their dressing room.

"Where's Jeremy?" Carlotta repeated.

"I'll deal with this," said Lindy. Her eyes met Carlotta's. An instant of wordless challenge passed between them.

"I doubt it." Carlotta snatched the poster out of her hand and headed toward Jeremy's office.

"Then I won't deal with it," said Lindy under her breath. Carlotta wouldn't accept sympathy, even if Lindy had found any to give. And she hadn't. All their old antipathies had resurfaced in that one brief look. She pushed the thought away. It was her job to remain neutral, and she needed some time to get her bearings before she started dealing with the company's intrigues. But a word of advice wouldn't hurt.

Lindy stopped by Paul's dressing room. The door was ajar. Paul sat at the dressing table arranging an already neat display of makeup. Rebo and two corps boys, Juan and Eric, were gathering their dance bags to leave for the dinner break.

"She acts like she was the queen of the Gypsies," said Eric.

"Bitch," whined Rebo. "Everyone knows I'm the queen of the Gypsies." He blew Eric a kiss and struck a pose, a broad-shouldered Venus de Milo with arms.

"Paul, do you have a minute?" asked Lindy.

"Sure, come in."

"Hey, catch you at the restaurant." Rebo led the others quickly out the door. Lindy heard their laughter as they walked away. "Too bad that batten missed her; we could be dining on pressed pork *au jus.*" Another eruption of laughter, and they were gone.

Paul began lining up makeup pencils in a row. "I didn't have anything to do with that," he said.

"That's not why I'm here." Lindy sat down on the edge of the table; it creaked under her weight. It was attached to the wall along one side with support legs at each end. The makeup lights surrounding the mirror were on, and Lindy felt their warmth through her shirt. "How about some advice from somebody who's been there?"

"You worked with Carlotta?"

"Hasn't everyone? But in those days she had more technique and less attitude."

Paul smiled slightly.

"Listen, there's someone like her in every company. They

only get away with it if everyone else lets them. You know what I mean?"

"I guess, but she doesn't ever let up." Paul fingered a container of pancake makeup, pushing it round and round in little circles.

"No, she doesn't. But my generation survived her. So will you."

"Why does she have to be so destructive?"

Lindy shrugged. "I guess it's the only weapon she has left. She invented her life. Spent all those years working as hard, harder, than everyone else, and they were still prettier, more talented, more lovable than she was. It's sad, really. She's at the end of her career. What will she have when it's over?" Lindy smiled at the boy. "She's finished, you're just beginning."

"You want me to feel sorry for her?"

"I just want you to take a step back from it."

"While I'm trying to lift her over my head?"

"You have a point."

"The really sick thing about Carlotta is that she treated my dad the same way."

Lindy blinked as she made the revelation. Allan Duke. Of course. "You're Allan's kid." She paused. "Sorry, that was the mother in me talking. You're not a kid, but a professional."

"Not much of one, considering the way I'm letting Carlotta get to me."

"Then stop it. If you don't buy into the power struggle, she won't have any power."

"It's not so easy. She's on her second generation of 'Duke bashing.' Dad used to have to partner her in Jeremy's old company. He'd come home mad as hell. He finally chucked it and retired."

"What's he doing now?"

"He and mom are in Cleveland. He's artistic director there."

A hint of an idea popped into Lindy's mind. "Paul, did he retire before Jeremy quit as artistic director?"

"About the same time, I think. I don't really remember. I could ask him when I talk to them." He blushed. "They like me to call them once a week, just to say hello and keep them up on the gossip."

"You might ask him if he remembers what was going on then."

Paul looked at her curiously.

"In the meantime, don't let Carlotta do this to you. You've got a great career ahead of you. Do what you have to do. Pretend she's somebody else." Paul blushed again. "Erase her, ignore her, and just dance your best."

"That's what Dad says. 'Dance around her, over her, or through her, just keep going.' "

"Smart dad."

"But I think she's doing it on purpose. She wanted me as her partner, like she wanted to keep punishing my dad. She's horrible. I hate her."

"Forget her." She pushed herself off the table. Another creak. "Paul, those guys didn't have anything to do with the batten falling, did they?" She looked at his face. "Of course not. Stupid thought. You'd better get something to eat."

Lindy sat in the audience, holding her breath. Her first day on the job and she already felt totally responsible for the outcome of the performance. The houselights dimmed. Biddy patted her knee. "Here goes."

"Easy for you to say."

"I'm sure you were a great success. They'll do fine."

The curtain opened. Smoke billowed out into the house as the stage lit up. Maybe there should be less smoke. Lindy opened her notebook and took her first theater note in twelve years.

It was easy after that. She wrote rapidly, keeping one eye on the stage. Carlotta reached to Andrea; the girl picked herself up. Lindy clutched her pen. Andrea rose on half pointe and fell forward—toward the pit. Thank you, Andrea, said Lindy silently. The *pas de deux* passed with only a few shaky lifts. The boys came on like gangbusters. Lindy began to relax. The final procession entered, their dark robes skimming the ground like phantoms. The last lift. Lindy crossed her fingers. Paul missed Carlotta but made a good save. No one in the audience would know that it had been a mistake. They climbed up the cage. The curtain closed, and Lindy snapped her notebook shut.

"Not so bad," she said to Biddy.

"They did great. Thanks."

"It ain't over till the fat lady sings."

Biddy opened her mouth.

"Don't you dare."

The curtain opened for the bows. The corps came forward, then the trio. Andrea stepped forward for her solo bow. Lindy held her breath. Carlotta replaced Andrea, reached both hands to the audience, and sank into a low curtsy, head barely lowering. The applause grew. Carlotta stepped back into line, and the curtain closed as the company took one final bow.

Lindy expelled her pent-up air. "Now, you can sing."

The *Holberg Suite* was danced impeccably. Jeremy was a master at his craft, blending the steps flawlessly with the music. When the audience left the theater, they were humming the last movement of the *Holberg Suite*.

Four

The next day, Lindy sat in the audience watching the dancers warm up. She hadn't slept well. Images of falling battens and outraged divas interrupted her sleep. Her body felt stiff. She should be taking a *barre*, too; give her muscles a chance to work properly, and take her mind off accidents and changed personalities. Or had she just gotten too soft to cope with the strains of tour?

All the dancers were onstage, even the boys. Maybe I'm doing something right, she thought. They seemed relaxed. Trained to be resilient, they had relegated the opening-night accident to the realm of interesting tour gossip, if it were an accident. I'm the only one still worried, thought Lindy. Just like a mother. She started rehearsal.

The company breezed through the corrections she had taken the night before. It was an intelligent and talented group. Jeremy really knew how to pick them. Except for Carlotta. Why would he hire her after putting together such a good company? Whatever talent she had in the past was gone. New Yorkers would go for her blood; he was asking for failure.

She gave the dancers a fifteen-minute break. She was watching Peter and the crew constructing the cage, when she saw the costume mistress watching her from the wings. It took her a minute to realize who the girl was; her manner was so self-effacing that she seemed to merge with her surroundings. When Lindy looked her way, she lifted her chin slightly. Lindy took the cue and walked over to the wings.

"We haven't met; I'm the wardrobe mistress, Alice Phelps." For someone who was responsible for so much beauty onstage, Alice was downright dowdy. Her brown hair, thin and straight, was pulled back from her face in a low bun. Strands had fallen from the clasp and hung limply over her ears. She was wearing a faded-blue smock that only accentuated her pear-shaped figure. Pins and threaded needles were thrust into the fabric of her pocket, and a pair of orange-handled scissors hung from a ribbon around her neck. The top of her head came to Lindy's chin.

"It's a pleasure to meet you, Alice. Did you need to speak with me?" Lindy asked softly, feeling an immediate compassion for the woman. Alice was one of the many anonymous workers who kept the dancers looking glamorous, and who never received any glory. Washing, mending, polishing shoes, and helping with quick changes made up the bulk of her life, and she looked it.

Alice made no reaction.

Honestly, thought Lindy, can we pick up the tempo a bit? But she smiled at Alice and thought about Walter Mitty. Perhaps Alice, too, had a secret life.

"Yes?" she prompted.

Alice began to speak as if she were unaware of the time that had elapsed since she had begun the conversation. "This probably isn't the time, but . . ." Her eyes were focused, not at Lindy, but on the stage. "I wondered if . . . I mean . . . well . . ."

"Well?"

"Someone is making a mess of Carlotta's costumes. Tying her shoes together, misplacing pieces. Like that. I'm sure it's just for fun. Like a joke. But with everything that's happened . . . Carlotta's not so bad . . . she just got off to a bad start."

Yeah, about fifty years ago, thought Lindy.

Alice's eyes were scanning the fly area above the stage. "I'm sure they aren't thinking about that, or they—But now, I practically have to dress Carlotta, you see what I mean. And maybe—it's not really your—you know—but I hate to bother Jeremy. Like that . . ." Her speech trailed off.

She glanced at Lindy for the first time since she had begun to talk.

Peter passed by them. "We're finished. Shall I call the dancers?"

"Please," said Lindy. She turned back to Alice, whose eyes were now following Peter into the backstage area. "I'll speak to the dancers when the time seems appropriate, okay?"

"Thank you." Alice's body turned and followed her eyes back to the dressing rooms.

Lindy turned back to the stage. Well, it took all kinds. Alice seemed to live in a fog. Not like the dresser they had when Lindy was still dancing. What was his name? Ari. She smiled at the memory. He was a wizard of poufs, coifs and flounces, mincing about with flying, efficient fingers. Ever present, always at your elbow when you needed him. "Dahlin', relax, let Ari take care of it." He was a far cry from this quiet creature who had drifted off backstage.

Peter called the dancers onstage. They reappeared quickly, but the rapport was gone. Before the break, they had been energetic, enthusiastic. Now, like Alice, they seemed to be looking anywhere but at Lindy.

This was so unfair. Lindy bent down to check the tape. When she looked up, everyone had taken their places for the beginning of *Carmina*. Only Carlotta stood at the side of the stage, weight thrust onto her right leg, hand resting on her hip. She looked her age this morning. Her skin was pasty. Two blotches of red sat on her cheekbones. She had eaten off most of the red lipstick that covered her lips, and her chin seemed longer than ever. Maybe she hadn't been sleeping that well, either.

"Places, please," Lindy said unnecessarily. Everyone was in place but Carlotta. She stared back at Lindy, grimaced, and walked lazily to the wing.

So that's how it's going to be, thought Lindy. Feets don't fail me now. She pushed the play button. Rebo and Eric brought in Andrea. Carlotta entered behind the music. She sauntered over to Andrea and yanked her off the cage. Andrea's head snapped back. Lindy tensed, but Andrea kept going. She fell forward away from Carlotta.

Carlotta began her solo. Lindy gritted her teeth. She was marking! The bitch. This was no time to relax. Paul entered for the duet. He missed the first lift. Carlotta shoved him away. He missed the second.

"Let's pull it together, you two. I don't want to have to stop the tape," yelled Lindy from where she stood. Carlotta hit him with such force on the third lift that the boy staggered backward.

"Okay, that's it." Lindy stopped the tape. "You're fighting

each other. Take a deep breath, and let's start the duet again."
She saw heads peeking out from the legs.

Carlotta turned and gave Lindy a withering look. "Maybe you should cut to the next section, dear. The boy seems incapable of dancing this morning."

"We'll take it from the beginning of the duet, please." They started again. The dancers had moved closer to the stage, watching. Paul missed the first lift and shot Lindy an anguished look. Carlotta hit him from behind.

"Stop this," Lindy demanded.

Carlotta turned on her. The music continued in the background. "This is ridiculous." Carlotta spat out the words. "I can't work like this." She lifted her chin like a spoiled child and stalked off the stage.

No one moved. They looked at Lindy. She looked at Carlotta as she left the stage, and made a decision.

"Neither can we. Ordinarily I wouldn't let this happen, but in this case—who's her understudy?" Andrea stepped forward, eyes on the ground. "And who's your understudy?"

"Mieko." Andrea's voice was barely audible.

"Okay, fellas, let's take it from the top. Haul Mieko up and bring her in."

"Yes, ma'am," boomed Rebo and hoisted Mieko effortlessly over his head.

It took a few minutes for the chill to wear off, but gradually the company began to recover. It was an incredible transformation; Andrea and Paul made every lift. Lindy yelled out corrections over the music. After several sections, she stopped them to fix a spacing problem. When she turned to the tape recorder, she saw Jeremy standing in the back of the theater.

He turned and walked away.

Lindy's stomach shriveled and sank with a thud. She shook it off. It felt great to be working again. Paul and Andrea were a perfect match. Even the spacing seemed to fix itself. Surely, Jeremy could see that.

After another hour, Lindy turned off the tape player. "That's enough for today. You did great, but you have to keep it at this level. No matter what. Your job is to make it work, under any conditions, and, believe me, it's going to get worse before it gets better." She gave them a theatrically meaningful look and walked off in search of Jeremy.

How long had he been standing in the back watching? He probably had seen her confrontation with Carlotta, but surely, after seeing how good the dancers looked without her, he would be forced to make a decision.

She knocked quietly on the door of the dressing room that had been commandeered as Jeremy's office. Without waiting for an answer, she poked her head inside.

Jeremy was sitting at the makeup table, staring into the mirror that ran crosswise along the wall. The makeup lights were turned off, and the light in the room was dull and gray.

"Am I fired?"

He glanced up at her and smiled. It was a weary effort. The corners of his mouth barely turned upward, and fatigue dulled the usual liveliness of his blue eyes. "No," he said, looking back into the mirror.

"Jeremy, I barely know you, and it certainly isn't my business to tell you how to run a company. But you must have seen how the whole group pulled together after Carlotta walked off."

"I saw."

"And?"

He didn't answer, just sighed deeply as if he were about to recite a speech he had said too many times.

"Lindy, you don't—" He broke off. "It was like witnessing a little bit of heaven. Only we're stuck in hell, and even a glimpse makes it pure torture."

"Then why don't you fire her?"

"Because Jack insists on keeping her. Jack badgered me into starting this company when I didn't care about anything in the world. He saved my life. He made this all happen. He works hard, though God knows why. He wants her. She stays."

He turned back to the mirror and stared vacantly past his own reflection.

Who was Jack? His lover, maybe? She walked to the back of his chair and put both hands on his shoulders. "Sometimes you have to be ruthless, Jeremy, even when it hurts someone you care for."

She felt his shoulders tighten, then relax. He reached up and covered her hands with his. "Believe me, Lindy, I know that."

Lindy groaned and collapsed onto one of the double beds in Biddy's hotel room. Biddy looked up from the pile of papers spread on the table in front of her. She was sitting at a round table positioned near the only window; her cast rested on another chair across from her.

Lindy groaned again.

"Heard you the first time," Biddy said over her shoulder.

"Biddy, what are you doing?" Lindy propped her aching body up on her elbow.

"Grant applications. Easier to do them here than trying to make Jeremy concentrate on what he's doing. He's good at paperwork, but he sure doesn't like it."

"*M-m-m.*"

"Hey, you'd better pop into the shower, or you'll be stiff as a board in the morning."

"I'm all ready stiff as a board."

"Some shape you're in. I thought you worked out at a gym."

"I do, but there I ride a bike that doesn't go anywhere, walk into the wall for twenty minutes, and climb stairs that end where you started. I don't stretch, kick, turn, and jump with a bunch of younger, thinner professionals looking on. Maybe I should be doing a ballet *barre.*"

"I'm sure you did just fine." Biddy began to arrange the pile of papers into stacks.

"Actually, I was a dismal failure. Carlotta stormed out of rehearsal, and I let her go. Jeremy saw the whole thing. I think you have just witnessed the shortest comeback in history."

Biddy turned to look at her, a mixture of horror and admiration playing on her features. "Wow."

"Biddy? Has it occurred to you that there is something more sinister here than just one nasty diva?"

Biddy looked perplexed. Of course not. She had lasted in the business for years only seeing the good parts and ignoring the bad. Lindy felt a pang of envy.

"What if that batten falling wasn't an accident?"

"I don't quite follow you."

"Maybe someone is trying to help Jeremy get rid of Carlotta."

"That's a horrible thing to say."

"Or, maybe someone besides Carlotta is sabotaging this company, and using her as the catalyst." Lindy shook her head. "It all comes back to the same thing. Carlotta. Why does Jeremy put up with her? He doesn't need her, he doesn't like her, and he said that it was hell working with her."

"He did?"

"Yeah. It doesn't make sense. Jeremy comes out of seclusion and starts a new company. He's got talented dancers, good ballets, and a New York season on the horizon. Carlotta shows up, and he hires her just because somebody tells him to. He told me that much when I talked to him after rehearsal."

"You talked to him about Carlotta?"

"I told him to fire her. Do I have nerve or what?"

Biddy whistled. "Well, Jeremy said to jump right in. So you did."

"Just like always. I could never stay out of trouble, and I'm such a nice person. But doesn't the whole thing strike you as a little too much? Why is he letting her destroy the company?"

Biddy chewed her lip and passed her hands through her hair. "I've been trying to figure that out for the last three months. It doesn't make sense."

"No, it doesn't, not yet, anyway. And I doubt if I'll be around long enough to figure it out. I think I'll take a hot bath."

After the bath and room service, Lindy felt a lot better. She and Biddy dressed and headed to the theater for hour call. Most of the dancers had arrived earlier and were applying makeup and chatting lightly. Reggae, the Gipsy Kings, and Bach poured out of the dressing rooms, joining in a cacophonous symphony in the hallway. The stage crew was making last-minute adjustments to the lights, and Lindy could hear hammering coming from the shop behind the stage.

She and Biddy were sitting in their dressing room, the door ajar, when Carlotta arrived. Her complaining voice echoed as she passed them. Lindy cringed and peeked outside.

Carlotta swept past the door. A slight, but paunchy man in a dark three-piece suit shuffled hurriedly behind her. A boutonniere of freesias stuck out of his lapel. Thin strands of hair were combed forward over his balding scalp, and even in the shadowy light, Lindy could see the sheen of perspiration on his face. And then she recognized him.

She closed the door. "That's Jack."

Biddy nodded. "Carlotta must have called him. He never comes on tour. What's she up to now?"

"No. I mean, that's Jack Sullivan."

"Yeah, he's the business manager."

"Oh, Christ, Biddy."

"What?"

"He was Jeremy's business manager years ago. He was fired—for stealing money from the company. Surely, you knew that; I even heard about it in New Jersey."

"But—" Biddy's hands shot to her hair. "That was just a rumor."

Lindy shook her head slowly. "Oh, my kind and trusting friend. Jeremy, Jack, and Carlotta back together again? Biddy, I think this company is in deep shit."

* * *

That night's performance went well, in spite of Carlotta's aggressive dancing. The rest of the company seemed to have benefited from a day of rehearsing without her, and Lindy began to hope that they might be able to sustain it.

But she encountered a group of despondent dancers when she and Biddy returned backstage after the performance. They were standing in a tight group that virtually hummed with unhappiness.

"Now what?" sighed Biddy as she and Lindy approached them.

"Guess what?" exclaimed Rebo. "Still no paychecks, and Jeremy says we have to go straight to Connecticut instead of back to the city for our days off."

"Yeah, it stinks." Juan was standing safely behind Rebo's lean body, using it as a psychological shield.

Biddy faced the group. "You know, guys, Jeremy made this clear from the beginning. This is a tour, and we need to keep focused. We can't have people running back and forth to the city all the time."

"But, Biddy, we have things to take care of. I mean, we do have lives," pointed out one of the girls.

"Of course you do, but right now your lives belong to the company. *Capisce?*"

Rebo appealed to Lindy.

"Look," she said, "you know Biddy's right. So get something to eat. Watch TV. Bitch and moan, but be on the bus tomorrow."

"Are you going to be on the bus?"

"I've got my car, but quite frankly, I'm not sure I still have a job. Now get back to the hotel." They started to move away. "And be on that bus."

She turned to Biddy. "No paychecks?"

"Just the last week or two."

Lindy threw up her hands. "Unbelievable." She cast her eyes heavenward. Maybe it was just as well she was about to be fired. "I guess I'd better go face Jeremy. I'm sure Carlotta has put the screws to me by now."

"Do you want me to come with you?"

Lindy shook her head. "I'd rather be humiliated in private, if you don't mind."

The sound of voices came through the closed door of Jeremy's office. Carlotta's rasping screech was unmistakable.

"Do you really expect me to take corrections from that hausfrau?"

"That hausfrau happens to be . . ." Jeremy's voice was low. Lindy leaned into the door but she couldn't make out the rest of the sentence.

"Well, I won't. You can try to sabotage me all you want, but I'm not budging."

Jack's voice rose in a thin plea. "Carlotta, be reasonable. No one is trying to hurt you. They're just kids playing games."

"They tried to kill me; I'm not even safe on the stage."

"Too bad they missed." It was Jeremy. Lindy jerked back from the door, horrified.

"Jeremy, really." Jack's voice.

Carlotta's laugh swelled derisively. "Jeremy, darling, you're pathetic."

"I'll buy out your contract."

"She needs this job, Jeremy." Jack. Imploring.

"I *want* this job. And I'll have it."

The sound of a fist slamming onto the makeup table, then Jeremy's carefully controlled voice. "How long are you going to keep punishing me?"

A silence. Lindy held her breath; her ear was resting against the door.

"I want her out. Get rid of her. Try acting like a man— for once." Footsteps across the concrete floor. Carlotta was making her grand exit.

Lindy managed to jump into the shadows as the door flung open, and Carlotta swept toward the stage door. Jack followed on her heels, leaving the door open behind him.

Lindy steeled herself and walked inside.

Five

She had a job. For some reason that was not at all clear, Jeremy had asked her to stay on. And for reasons just as unclear, she had said yes. Now, she just had to pack. And tell Glen. He could certainly survive a few days without her. He could probably survive without her completely, but that wasn't an option she was willing to pursue.

She attacked her wardrobe, choosing clothes for their look rather than their fit. She was sure she'd be dropping a few pounds with the schedule she'd be keeping. She gathered jeans, practice sweats, evening wear, and an assortment of shoes that ranged from her new four-inch heels to her oldest treadless Nikes and crammed them into her suitcase. Not the matching Samsonite luggage that she and Glen used for vacations, but the old green tour bag that she had whimsically saved and stored in the attic.

She spent the rest of the day canceling appointments and finding her replacement for the talent show.

At six o'clock she started dinner. She pounded veal until it was paper thin, floured it, and stuck it back in the fridge. A quick sauté and it would be ready. She cut tips off asparagus, washed lettuce and field greens. She pulled the wooden salad bowl from the top shelf of the pantry, wiped off the dust, and seasoned it with garlic.

At seven o'clock the dining table was set, complete with candles and her best wineglasses; the wine had breathed, but Lindy was holding her breath. She puttered around the table, straightening forks and refolding napkins. When Glen hadn't shown up by seven-fifteen, she went out into the garden and picked a few early daffodils and hyacinths and arranged them in a vase, sticking the stems down between crystal marbles to keep them in place.

At seven-twenty-five, Glen's BMW pulled into the driveway. A minute later, he emerged from the garage and walked toward the house. He was carrying a bouquet of flowers wrapped in the pastel paper of the local florist.

"Hi." He handed Lindy the flowers and gave her a peck on the cheek.

"Thanks, sweetie. What's the occasion?"

"Just because I love you, and," he added sheepishly, "because I wasn't very friendly to Biddy the other night. I was tired. I've worked ten days straight." He slipped his arms around her and gave her a more meaningful kiss.

Better get this over with, she thought. She led him into the house and poured out two glasses of Medoc, put the flowers in water, and took the veal out of the fridge.

"Speaking of occasions, this is pretty elaborate."

Lindy concentrated on the veal.

They were having after-dinner coffee when Lindy's nerves forced her to bring up the subject of her new job. Glen had loosened his tie and thrown his jacket over one of the extra chairs. He looked pretty good. She smiled at him.

"Jeremy asked me to come to work."

Glen puffed out his cheeks. It made him look like Dizzy Gillespie. "Who's Jeremy?"

"The director of the company Biddy works for."

"What makes him think you would want to go to work? Doing what?"

"Biddy's on crutches, for crying out loud. Do you know how hard it is to carry on a rehearsal when you can't jump up and demonstrate how to do things?"

"No."

"No, what?" Lindy held her breath.

"No, I don't know how hard it is. What did you tell him?"

"I said . . ." She exhaled slowly. "That I'd have to discuss it with you."

Glen smiled. "Sure you did. And how long is this little jaunt going to take? Surely, you don't really want to go back to work, especially now that the kids are out of your hair. You could start having some fun."

"Just for a few weeks until the New York season."

"Weeks? I don't get it. Is this some kind of midlife crisis or something?" His eyebrows quirked together above his nose. She could see the corners of his mouth beginning to tighten. Eyebrows and mouth together. His "I don't get it" expression.

"Sweetie, you're gone all day, and you're tired at night." She refrained from mentioning that he'd have the TV to keep him company. "I'm kind of bored. I thought it would be fun; you know, like a busman's holiday."

Glen leaned back in the chair. "Hell, why not? I'm hardly at home, anyway. Go and get it out of your system. Just don't stay too long, okay?"

And that was that. Monday morning she posted her itinerary on the fridge, threw her suitcase into the Volvo, and headed toward the Tappan Zee bridge.

Spring had come to the Northeast. It was one of those sunny, blustery days, the air crisp and vitalizing. Trees lined the highway like spectators at a parade, leaning in the April breeze as if trying to get a better view. Spires of evergreens punctuated the hillsides of lighter green, and their branches swayed contrapuntally to the quiver of budding maple, dogwood, and locust trees.

She sped along the Cross Westchester Expressway, humming along with a Mozart piano concerto that played from the radio. If it weren't for the number of cars on the road, you'd never believe that New York City was just a few miles away, thought Lindy. That's why the suburbs are bearable. You could be surrounded by trees and flowers, and just when it started driving you stark raving mad, you could escape. Civilization was only thirty minutes away.

Two hours later, she passed through the center of the quaint, but upscale, Connecticut town where the company would spend the next six days teaching master classes and performing at the University Theater on campus. Six days anywhere was a luxury. To fill out every week of a tour, companies sometimes had to book frightening excuses for theaters: old movie houses that had been converted into stages, dressing rooms that were no more than old storage rooms, one-night stands when time was so limited that there was only enough time for a quick spacing rehearsal, while the crew hung the lights. As soon as the performance was over, the crew would strike the sets, roll up the floor, and truck it all over to the next theater and set up for the next performance. The costume mistress would gather all the costumes, dry out the worst of the sweat with a hair dryer before packing them into the costume trunks, only to have to unpack them the following morning.

But Jeremy still commanded a good deal of clout on the dance circuit. He had managed, or Jack had, to book longer runs in the best theaters in the area. The company should be strong and prepared when they finally arrived in New York, and Lindy would be a part of it. She felt energized; she would even make Carlotta come around. It would be glorious.

She almost missed the turnoff to the Sheraton. A woman with a mission, she had passed right through the town without noticing it.

The Sheraton University Parkline appeared unexpectedly before her, its six stories rising like a squat monolith above acres of pastureland. In the distance, the grasses gave way to a line of trees. It was the only building in sight, but that was an illusion. The sprawling campus lay only five minutes over the horizon, and where there was a big campus and a convention-size hotel, there was bound to be a brand-new mega-mall, a tenplex movie theater, and other modern harbingers of rural death close by.

She walked into the lobby. It was spacious, with high ceilings. Modern upholstered chairs were grouped comfortably together in several places throughout the room. A restaurant showed through open doors across the hall from a bank of two elevators, and a bar with a separate entrance stood beyond. She walked across the terra-cotta tiles toward the registration desk; her steps sent up little echoes around her. She signed the registration card and took her key from the congenial desk attendant, a young man with thick glasses and a calculus textbook, which he had slipped quickly under-neath the desk. An equally young and studious-looking bell-hop took her luggage and followed her into the elevator.

Biddy was sitting at the table immersed in grant applica-tions. "Hey, it's like I never left," announced Lindy as she handed the bellhop two dollars and dismissed him at the door.

"How was the drive?"

"Typical." Lindy threw her bag on the empty luggage rack. "Traffic at the bridge, and I daydreamed the rest of the way. Lucky for me, I'm not crossing the Canadian border by now. Anything scheduled for today?"

"Not unless you want to see the theater; the crew's load-ing in."

"Normal-size stage, number of wings, enough dressing rooms?"

"Old, but yes."

"I think I'll pass, though I thought we might take a drive over to the campus. My friend Angie Levinson teaches here. I want to say hello."

"Sounds good to me; I could use a break from these applications. They get more convoluted each year, thanks to the ever-changing status of National Endowments."

A few minutes later they were driving into the campus commons. They stopped at a little bakery in the row of brownstone shops at the base of the college.

"A pound of rugalach," Lindy said to the girl behind the counter. "Angie's downfall," she explained to Biddy. "We used to ply her with them in hopes of making her gain weight. While the rest of us filled up on rice cakes, Angie stuffed herself with sugar and carbos and never gained an ounce. Maybe she's gotten fat."

The dance department was located in an impressive new Movement Education complex: concrete, steel, and lots of glass. Angie was just dismissing a class as they arrived at the second-floor studios. She was as thin as ever.

"Some people have all the luck," whispered Lindy as Angie recognized her and came running over.

"My God, Lindy Graham, what brings you here?"

"I'm back on the road . . . for a minute. Angie, this is Biddy McFee, and this is for you." She held up the bakery box.

"Still up to your old tricks, I see. Hi, Biddy. It's nice to meet you. You guys have perfect timing; I've got a fifteen-minute break before my next class. I'll make some tea, and we can pig out."

As they followed Angie out of the studio, Lindy noticed the slightest, almost imperceptible, layer of fat silhouetted by her shiny jazz pants.

Yes, she thought. Yes, yes.

Angie poured tea into mugs and handed them round. Each mug had a picture of a famous ballet dancer glazed on its side. She shoved a stack of theme books to one side of her desk and put her feet up.

"So how do you like my little enclave?" Angie shook her shoulder-length hair back from her face and dug into the box of rugalach.

"Impressive," said Lindy. "Do you have a big staff?"

"Three full-time, two part-time, and a bevy of teaching assistants. Dance is booming in the boonies, and I'm as pleased as punch about it. The politics, of course, are lethal, but I've developed a thick skin, a complacent attitude, and, all in all, I adore this cushy life." She reached for another rugalach and blew a strand of hair away as she leaned back in her chair.

"So what about you? Did you marry that charming Glen what's-his-name?"

"Haggerty. Yeah, we live in New Jersey."

"So what are you doing here?"

"Doing a brief stint with Jeremy Ash, giving Biddy and her broken leg a little assistance."

"It must be a bitch hauling that thing around a theater," Angie said.

Biddy smiled in agreement.

"And taking a break from fund-raisers, church bazaars, and movement therapy at the local nursing home," Lindy continued.

"Hey, you do that, too? I go over to Hollingwood Gardens twice a week myself, Tuesday and Thursday mornings. Keeps me sane, working with geriatrics and trauma victims. The least I can do."

"I know what you mean," Lindy agreed. "It's pretty satisfying stuff."

"It really is. Plus I visit Sandra DiCorso while I'm there, not that she's even aware of it." She shook her head thoughtfully. The brown strands swayed back and forth against her cheek, the kind of hair Lindy coveted. "Still, you know how easily you're forgotten once you leave the business, and what happened to her was such a tragedy."

"Sandra DiCorso?"

"Sure." She looked at Biddy. "If you're working for Jeremy, surely you remember her."

Biddy shook her head. "I don't think . . ."

"Sandra was the young dancer who had that accident a few years back. It was right before Jeremy dropped out of sight. A big to-do at the time, but now she's completely forgotten. A real shame. The only visitors she gets are me and Peter."

"Peter?" Lindy and Biddy exchanged looks.

"Where have you been? Peter Dowd. She's his sister."

"Sandra DiCorso is Peter Dowd's sister?" Lindy didn't even know Peter had a sister.

"Sure. DiCorso was just a stage name. A name like 'Dowd' doesn't exactly sparkle with glamour, now does it?"

Lindy turned to Biddy. To judge by the look of dismay on her face, this was news to her, too.

"Doesn't Peter work for Jeremy now?"

Biddy nodded. "But he's never said anything. Not that he would; he keeps pretty much to himself. But you'd think somebody would have said something. I mean, that's pretty insensitive of us."

Angie shrugged. "Well, he probably doesn't want anyone to know. He was really broken up after the accident. The two of them were *mucho* close. I was shocked to hear that he was working for Jeremy."

"Why?" Biddy's question came out in a squeak.

"Everyone blamed Jeremy for the accident. And then Jeremy left the dance scene but good. Nobody could find him. Everyone figured it was guilt."

Lindy heard Biddy choke back a cry.

"Oh," said Angie, looking at Lindy and nodding her head slightly at Biddy. "That's only what I heard on the grapevine."

She shook her head energetically. "Probably none of it is true."

"And where is the—what was the name of the nursing home?" asked Lindy.

"Hollingwood Gardens. It's about a twenty-minute drive from here, down Fox Hollow Road, right before you get to the mall." She put her cup on the desk. "Listen, it was a long time ago, and I've probably got my facts all mixed up. I wouldn't worry about it, Biddy." She stood up. "I've got to go teach; Beginning Jazz Dance, my fave, but it jacks up the enrollment numbers. I'll see you around campus."

Angie left them at the elevator and hurried down the corridor to her class.

Biddy was staring at the down button. "God, it must be awful to be forgotten like that. It's the worst kind of nightmare. And poor Peter. He never said anything. How can people who are supposed to be such sensitive artists be so cruel?"

"Because they get caught up in their own little worlds at the expense of everything else," said Lindy. "No one has ever called me to see how I've been. I could be dead for all they know. But in all fairness, I haven't given them much thought, either."

"But to be left like that."

Lindy touched Biddy's arm. It was a gesture of empathy. She felt compassion for Sandra Dowd, but what frightened her was the tiny crack that had appeared in Biddy's unquestioning loyalty to Jeremy. And how did Sandra Dowd fit into the current puzzle? Just another accident? It was too coincidental not to mean something. But what? Should she pursue it? Maybe it would be better for Carlotta to destroy the company, than for Lindy to destroy Biddy's faith in Jeremy. What had she started? And should she finish it?

"Do you think we should visit her?" asked Biddy.

"I think Peter would be furious if we did."

"Poor Peter."

"Wait here for a second." Lindy ran back down the hall to Angie's office, where she scribbled a quick note and taped it to the back of Angie's chair: I'd like to join you at the nursing home tomorrow if it's convenient. Call me at the University Parkline. Room 324.

Six

"Okay, I give up."

Lindy looked up from where she was clutching the bathroom doorknob. Biddy's head was hanging over the end of her bed; the morning sun set her sleep-disheveled hair into a blazing aureole. "What on earth are you doing?"

"A *barre.*"

"Like in ballet? And I suppose that's a *grande plié?*"

"Doesn't it look like one?" asked Lindy, sitting on her haunches, both knees turned out to the side.

"You look more like a frog waiting to snare the wallpaper. See any flies in that floral print?"

"Cruel, cruel," said Lindy, using the doorknob to pull herself back to a standing position.

"Try it again, and this time keep your back straight and don't sit on your heels." Biddy shifted around on her side like a break dancer until her cast hit the floor, and she came to a sitting position.

Lindy straightened her back and began the descent, keeping her knees out by her ears and stopping when her butt was a few inches from her feet. She straightened up with a creak.

"It's only eight-thirty," said Biddy. "Why don't you wait

until you're at the theater and can use something more substantial to hold onto?"

"And take the chance of anybody seeing me? When Swan Lake freezes over. Anyway, I have to meet Angie at Hollingwood Gardens at ten o'clock."

Biddy watched silently. Lindy moved on to *tendus*. They were a lot easier than *pliés*. Stretch out and close, four to the front, side, back and side, *en croix*, the shape of a cross.

"You still have the best feet I've ever seen," said Biddy.

"And you still have the greenest eyes that ever lied," returned Lindy beginning to sweat. "Why don't you order some coffee?"

Biddy scooted around the edge of the bed and reached for the phone; Lindy moved on to *rond de jambes*. It *was* just like riding a bike, she thought. After all these years, her muscles were still programmed to dance. She was feeling quite pleased with herself until she heard Biddy singing "Aloha-ee."

"Are you saying that my *derriere* is wiggling?" A trickle of sweat dripped off the end of her nose. She wiped it away with the back of her hand.

"Nice *port de bras*. And yes, it looks like you're doing the *pas de hula*," said Biddy. Lindy squeezed her butt and concentrated on the circular motion of her leg. "But you're doing better than me. I can't even get into fifth position. My cast is too big."

"Well, I can't get into fifth position because my thighs are too fat."

"You are a mess. Try *developé.*"

Lindy raised her foot to her knee, stopping briefly in *passé* position to rest before extending her leg out to the side. Then slowly she lifted her foot, aiming it shoulder level. She had almost straightened her leg when it began shaking and fell with a thud.

"Oh, God, is there any reason you can think of why a middle-aged, suburban housewife should be able to touch her knee to her ear?" asked Lindy, rubbing her thigh.

"Well, if I had a husband like Glen ..." Biddy raised her eyebrows until they disappeared under the puffs of her uncombed hair.

"Arabida McFee, I'm shocked and horrified. That's a deliciously perverse idea." Lindy began kicking to the front.

"And an inspiration to go on with *'grahn bahttemahn.'* " Biddy drawled out the French pronunciation.

"God, you sound just like Madame Koussekovsky."

"Euw, yahz," replied Biddy, crumpling her torso into a Transylvanian pose. *"Yand a one."* Lindy kicked. *"Yand a tehoo."* Lindy kicked again. *"Yand a thre-e-e-e."*

Lindy kicked and collapsed with a giggle. "God, she was frightmare theater, and that was the dirtiest studio I've ever been in. You couldn't even stretch your feet for the cracks in the Marley. What were we thinking of when we left Maggie to take class with her?"

"It only lasted a week, and, thank God, Maggie was understanding enough to take us back."

"Yeah," said Lindy. "She was the best. She kept me on my feet when I was too tired to even feel my feet."

"Yep, there will never be another ... ," Biddy began to sing.

Lindy finished the second side of her *battements*, and the coffee arrived.

* * *

Angie was waiting for her at the nursing-home entrance when Lindy got slowly out of the Volvo. Her legs were still twitching from her first *barre* in twelve years, and she nearly fell over when she reached back across the front seat to get the bouquet of flowers she had bought in the hotel lobby.

"How did you manage to get the morning off?" asked Angie. She was wearing the pinkest warm-up suit Lindy had ever seen. "Jeremy is the taskmaster of all taskmasters. Who are the flowers for?"

"Everyone is teaching master classes this morning, as you well know, and I thought I might drop these off for Sandra, get my volunteer fix in, and be back at the theater for twelve o'clock rehearsal."

"Indefatigable as ever, I see."

"Nature and me and the state of vacuums," Lindy said. "Of course, the only vacuums around me these days are of the cleaning variety."

Angie's laugh was a clear, soprano trill.

"Nice color," said Lindy, indicating Angie's warm-up suit.

"Bright colors are very cheering. Come and meet my old folks."

They entered through the double doors of the brick building into a comfortable lobby. A burgundy Queen Anne couch and wing-back chair stood at one side. Potted ficus graced each side of the couch, and an enormous chandelier hung from the ceiling.

Angie signed them in at the desk and led Lindy into a bright sun-room off to the left. It was cheerful, warm, and conspicuously free from the usual nursing-home odors. A row of wheelchairs were lined up across the room. Some of the patients slumped, asleep in the chairs, strapped in so they wouldn't inadvertently tumble out. Others waved feebly. A few actually seemed eager to begin.

Angie slipped a tape into a boom box that had been set up on one of the institutional tables that ran along one wall. She had chosen songs from the 1930s and 1940s, songs they might recognize. One lady, fragile and brittle as antique china, began singing along to "Slow Boat to China" before Lindy even recognized the tune. She was joined by the reedy voice of a corpulent gentleman a few wheelchairs away. The woman next to him started howling.

An attendant appeared at her side and took her hand. "Minnie. It's time for your exercising. It's all right, dear." She turned to Lindy. "Unexpected noises frighten her. She should settle down soon. If she doesn't, I'll take her away."

Angie was already in the middle of the room facing her audience. "Okay, everybody, hands in the air. And point your fingers up and down, wiggle them all ar-o-u-nd," she intoned in a singsong voice.

Lindy joined her, flexing her fingers along with the rest of them. Next they moved the wheelchairs into a circle, and the participants batted a balloon around to the strains of "I'm Looking Over a Four-Leaf Clover." It took some effort for Angie and Lindy to keep the balloon aloft. Some of the folks had surprising strength, but most only made feeble swipes at the balloon as it came near them. A few made no effort to play at all, and the balloon would settle into their laps or roll onto the floor. Angie would pick it up and bat it to the next person. The session ended with a fairly rousing rendition of "If You're Happy and You Know It" accompanied by hand clapping, feet clattering, and head nodding.

Before they left, Angie and Lindy stopped at each wheel-chair to say goodbye. Minnie started to cry, Lindy patted her hand, and the attendant whisked her away. Some seemed sprightlier after the exercise, but a few had not even awak-ened from their aged dozing.

"Whew," said Angie as she collected her tapes and waved a cheery goodbye to the room in general. "See you on Thurs-day, everybody."

Lindy picked up her flowers and followed her out. Several corridors and turns later, when Lindy was thoroughly lost, Angie stopped at a nurses' station. The nurse on duty smiled in recognition. "And you've brought a friend, how nice," she said as if continuing a conversation they had just been engaged in. "She's quite popular this week. I'm so glad, though I doubt if she even realizes it, poor thing. Daneeta will show you down."

Daneeta turned from the file cabinet with a stack of manila envelopes in her hand. She was a tall black woman in her early twenties. Without a word, she plunked her folders down on the counter and turned left down the hall. About fifty feet later, she entered a door on her right and crossed to the figure sitting in a wheelchair that was turned toward the window.

"Miss Dowd, you have visitors," she said in a melodious croon. She turned the chair around toward the center of the room.

There was not a hint of movement from the blank, but beautiful, features that faced them. Sandra DiCorso didn't move. Her head didn't lift. Her hands didn't catch the edges of the chair. Wherever her thoughts were, they were not in this room and not for her visitors.

Daneeta continued crooning as if she were having a conversation instead of a monologue. "It's Ms. Angie, your friend, and she's brought someone with her."

Lindy gazed at the seated girl. Black hair offset the stark whiteness of her face. Her features were fine, the cheekbones high, the mouth sculpted. Lindy knelt down beside the chair. "Hello, Sandra, I'm Lindy Graham. I work with your brother." Not a flicker from the dark lashes. "These are for you. Shall I put them in some water?" she asked quietly. Daneeta's tone was catching.

Daneeta took the flowers from Lindy and pulled off the paper covering. "Well, would you look at this?" Sandra didn't look, but Lindy and Angie did. "They're lovely daisies and pink pompoms. Won't they be fine on your dresser?" She turned to Lindy. "I'll just get a vase; be right back."

Angie had taken over the monologue. She was explaining about Jeremy's company being at the university, adding bits of related information as if she expected an answer. She didn't get one.

Lindy swallowed away the sudden tightening in her throat. God, what a waste. She looked desperately around the room, focusing on the contents in an attempt to quell the tears that had suddenly sprung to her eyes. The walls were covered in bright posters: Degas dancers, a New York City Ballet advertisement in primary colors, a kitten in a pink tutu bounding into the air while his companion chewed at the ribbon of a point shoe. A ceramic ballerina in a brittle tulle tutu balanced on one leg on the dresser. A stuffed bear with a red plastic heart was propped up next to the ballerina. An enormous bowl of white and yellow flowers was set on the bedside table.

Someone had taken pains to make this room special and intimate. Peter, of course. Efficient, no-nonsense, loving Peter. Lindy imagined his cut and scraped fingers unwrapping the delicate figurine, finding just the right place to display it, trying to reach the vacancy in his sister's face, and it broke her heart.

Daneeta returned with the vase of flowers, and Lindy pulled herself together. "Here we are. Aren't they pretty? Where shall I put them?" Daneeta looked directly at the girl who didn't look back. "How about on the dresser, next to Teddy?" She pushed the bear aside and placed the arrangement next to him. "I do think this is a perfect place, don't you?" Lindy wondered who she was talking to, but managed to mumble yes.

They said their goodbyes and followed Daneeta back to the nurses' station, where she picked up her files, smiled at them, and walked away.

"God, that was depressing," said Lindy.

"Which part? The seniors or Sandra?"

"Sandra, mostly. I mean, at least the older ones have had lives; now they just want to go home. Home to the past, or home to their Maker. But when you see someone cut off in their prime—"

"I know, you start thinking 'There but for the grace' . . . etc."

"Exactly. What's wrong with her? Will she get any better? I vaguely remember hearing about it, but I was in Jersey by then, and it didn't really touch my life, you know?"

"I know. She fell in a rehearsal. Only, for some reason she was rehearsing alone at night, and no one saw it happen.

Luckily, she was found by the custodian who came in to clean later that night."

"Yikes." Lindy shuddered. It was every dancer's nightmare. One misstep and your career was over. In this case, that misstep had taken more than a talented girl's career.

"Well, there's nothing you or I can do about it. Nor, apparently, the doctors, and we have some of the best trauma specialists in the country at the U. Hospital. I just come and talk to her. Maybe someday she'll get better. Maybe she even knows what's going on around her. You have to act like she does, just in case."

Lindy breathed away the lump in her throat. "Why do you think everyone blamed Jeremy for what happened? If she was rehearsing alone, how could he be responsible?"

Angie shrugged. "It was awhile ago. All I know is there was a big scandal. Questions about whether it really was an accident and about Jeremy's involvement; then *lots* of talk. Right after that, Jeremy dropped off the face of the earth. Then later, the business manager was fired. Even with a new staff, the company couldn't recover and was disbanded about a year later."

"Was Peter working there at the time?"

"I don't think so. Wasn't he at City Ballet then? Everyone moves around in this business so much, it's hard to keep track. Well, I'd better get back to campus and check on the master classes. You headed to the theater?"

Lindy nodded.

"It's a great old theater. One of the original buildings. A bit outdated, but lots of class. I'll hate it when they build the new one."

"They're going to tear it down?"

"The trustees want to; it isn't big enough for the current campus and too expensive to renovate. But there's a move to keep it intact as a part of the new complex and use it for student productions. I'd hate to see it go."

Lindy drove back to campus in a quandary. Jeremy, Jack, Carlotta, Peter. Why would people with such enmity toward each other work together? She couldn't begin to untangle their motivations. For all the mysteries she read, she had never learned to pick out clues unless the writer tap-danced around them, and those she recognized usually turned out to be red herrings. There was definitely a mystery here; she just hoped it wouldn't have the usual outcome. Most of the deaths in the theater world either occurred onstage, where the deceased rose from the dead in time to take his bow; or from AIDS, which was the ultimate and final curtain.

She was so lost in thought that she arrived at the theater without realizing it. It took a few minutes to comprehend the parking code: blue for handicapped, green for faculty, orange for students.

She parked in a black-lined visitors' space, unloaded her dance bag, and stopped for a minute to appreciate the ambiance of the old theater building. Even in the midday sunshine, its brownstone facade evoked images of a gaslit New England street. It was a massive box, not elegant, but inviting. The entrance was set off by Ionic columns, free standing in front and mantled into the brownstone around the doors. Rail balconies fronted two upstairs windows, and the whole of the structure was topped by a black slate Georgian roof.

Lindy walked around to the back. Jeremy was just going into the stage door.

"It's a grand old building, isn't it?" she said.

"Yes, very substantial." He looked down at a stage weight that held the door open. "Let's just hope the equipment isn't as ancient as the edifice. And let's just hope we can fill it for five nights."

"How are ticket sales?"

"Good for tonight, *ish* for tomorrow and Thursday, better for the weekend. The usual. If we get a good review, things will pick up. A lot of people will wait to see if the critics like it before they'll commit to leaving their televisions for an evening of live theater."

Lindy smiled. "Is that a hint of cynicism I hear?"

"Moi? Never. I'm as eager and optimistic as ever." He opened the door and followed her inside.

Why is it, wondered Lindy as they entered backstage, I can never figure out whether he is being serious, ironic, or just plain obtuse?

They were early. Only the stage crew was moving around in various states of lethargy. The trouble with using resident crews was that they rarely showed a sense of immediacy. With rehearsal only thirty minutes away, they were just beginning to roll out the Marley floor. If they didn't speed up, they would still be taping it down when the rehearsal began. Dance companies always traveled with their own Marley to insure consistency of the dance surface. It was heavy, took up lots of room in the trucks, and added a small fortune to freight costs when it had to be flown, but it paid off in the long run.

Lindy noted the unevenness of the old wooden floor of the stage. It was dry and splintery and would be disastrous for dancers who spent much of their time rolling, falling, and sliding as did the dancers of the Jeremy Ash Dance Company. The warped planks were broken up in several places by shorter squares of wood that fit unevenly into the floor like one of those children's sort games—squares in square holes, circles in circle holes; old-fashioned trapdoors used for entering ghosts and deus ex machina.

Peter almost knocked them over as he sped onto the stage. "Half hour, guys. Ralph, put another man on the Marley, and let's start focusing the sides."

Ralph grunted and rose from squatting at the first roll of Marley. Lindy looked away from the flabby skin that showed between his T-shirt and jeans. She had seen enough beer-enhanced stagehand flesh to last her until her next retirement.

"Thank God for Peter," said Jeremy.

"Yes, how did you get him?"

Jeremy shrugged. "When we started up, he came looking for a job. Beats me. He had a good job, but who can turn down more work, less pay, and a constant headache when you get the chance?"

"Maybe he missed touring."

Jeremy looked at her in disbelief.

"Some people do, you know. Or, maybe it was your winning personality." Peter seemed, if not exactly happy, at least content with his job. Did he blame Jeremy for his sister's accident? She certainly didn't see any signs of hostility, which, if he did, should be hovering pretty close to the surface.

"Definitely, my winning personality. And Alice came along right after that. What a team."

A team? Lindy had never even seen them speaking together. But they spent a lot of time in the theater. Familiarity could make for a smooth-running machine.

There was a rustle of activity behind them. The company

was wandering in, loaded down with dance bags and paper bags of food.

"Half hour," Peter called over his shoulder without taking his hands or eyes off the side light he was adjusting. "Dressing rooms are through that door or up the stairs."

Jeremy turned to Lindy. "Hurry the kids along, will you? I've got to check the box office."

A half hour later, the floor was laid, and the dancers were in place for spacing the *Holberg Suite*. It went so well that Lindy decided to move on to *Carmina*, hoping to have some time at the end to run the understudies through a few sections.

The cage was assembled and so were the dancers when they realized that Carlotta hadn't arrived.

"We'll space without her and use the understudies until she gets here," announced Lindy. They finished the spacing; Carlotta still wasn't there.

Peter was setting cues at the light board backstage left. It was a mammoth, archaic contraption that required two men to run the cues. And it was positioned so that anyone entering from the first wing had to detour around it. "I'll call the hotel." He disappeared into the darkness of backstage.

"Well, while we're waiting, let's try the procession. Andrea, stand in for Carlotta, will you?"

Andrea took her place center stage next to Paul. The other dancers exited stage left, picked up candelabras from the prop table, and formed a double line for their entrance.

"It's really important to keep exact unison on your turns," said Lindy. "Even the smallest discrepancy is exaggerated because of the lights. Let's try it with counts."

They entered slowly as Lindy clapped the rhythm. Each

foot hit the ground at the same time; strides were matched so that the whole line moved as one organism across the stage. They were beginning the slow, descending turns behind Andrea and Paul when the first hitch occurred.

"Okay, hold it. These candelabras should move around exactly at the same speed. If you get off, it looks terrible." She took one of the candelabras to demonstrate. Her arm dropped about six inches. "Heavy little monkeys, aren't they?"

"Yeah, your arm's dead meat by the end of the piece," complained Eric.

"This is what they mean when they say you must suffer for your art." Lindy smiled at him and handed back the candelabra. "Better you than me. Try to keep them even. And Eric, why does your group keep moving upstage here? It should be a completely straight line."

"Because Carlotta keeps moving in on us when she leaves Paul for the lift. Christ, it's scarier than the first act of *Giselle* back here."

"Yeah, she gives us the Wilis," added Juan, who punctuated the sentence with ghostly howling.

Rebo clutched his stomach and fell to the floor, writhing. "Bad joke," he groaned. "I'm having a bad-joke attack."

Mieko grabbed him by his shirt and pulled him up. "The Wilis are in the second act, bonehead."

"She loves me." Rebo tried to embrace the girl, but she ducked gracefully out of the way.

Lindy shook her head, smiling. They were actually having fun. And then she saw Carlotta standing next to Peter by the light board. Her smile disappeared.

"You weren't supposed to start *Carmina* until two." She faced Lindy with a stance of studied intimidation.

"The call was for twelve o'clock. If you want a dispensation, talk to the Pope."

Carlotta turned to Peter, who shrugged and turned back to the light board.

"Can you please hurry? You're keeping everyone waiting." Well, that wasn't exactly true. They hadn't even missed her. "We'll continue on until the end and fix this when Carlotta is ready." Lindy turned to the house to see if Jeremy was there. The house was empty. She really had to be more disciplined. She had worked with real divas before and had never lost her cool. She wouldn't let Carlotta be her downfall.

Carlotta returned faster than Lindy had expected, and it occurred to her that she had been in the theater all along but was waiting to make an effective entrance. They started with the procession. As Carlotta turned from Paul to take the final lift, the center of the procession moved upstage out of her way, destroying the unity of the turning lights.

Lindy stopped the tape. "Right here, guys, you're moving upstage. Carlotta, stay closer to Paul when you circle behind him. You're getting too close to the corps. It's throwing off the line."

Carlotta took a deep breath like she was being lowered into boiling oil. She began again, avoiding the line of candelabras by making grotesque contortions. It looked ludicrous.

"Thank you. That's so much better."

They broke at four o'clock. Most of the dancers returned to the hotel on the bus; a few opted for eating in the university shopping area and napping in their dressing rooms.

"Hey, Lindy." Paul's voice came through the open door

of the boys' dressing room. She poked her head inside. "I talked to my dad."

"How is he?"

"Fine, but he gave me the dish on Jeremy's old company."

Right. Lindy had almost forgotten their previous conversation. She came all the way in and closed the door. They were alone except for Rebo stretched out on the floor; a towel lay across his shoulders as a makeshift blanket.

Paul lowered his eyes. "Rough night, I guess."

"As long as he keeps his days together." Lindy gave Rebo a sidelong look. "He's talented, but he's on the road to burn out. I'm sure you guys will put it to him, right?"

Paul nodded.

"So what's the story from your dad?"

"He left a few months before the company disbanded. He said it had been a total disaster. Some girl fell at a rehearsal, and the police were questioning Jeremy about his whereabouts or something. They finally decided it was an accident, but then Jeremy left, and nobody knew where he went to. But, Lindy, Dad's sure it wasn't Jeremy's fault, and he said to only tell you and nobody else. That it shouldn't color how I feel about Jeremy, because he's a good guy, and he'll do right by us."

"Anything else?"

"Well, here's the funny part." Paul lowered his voice to a whisper. "Jack was the business manager. A few months after Jeremy left, Jack quit. Only the rumor was that he was fired because he was embezzling money from the company. Lindy, do you think he's taking our money, too? Is that why we haven't been paid? Why would Jeremy let him do that?"

And why had she gotten this kid involved? She wanted

to kick herself several times. She sat down in the chair next to him. He looked miserable.

"You know, Paul. Dance companies are like soap operas. Too much angsting without knowing the truth. By the time stories get passed around, the most innocent bystander can look like Charles Manson."

"But—"

"I'm going to look into things. I'm sure there's a rational explanation to our current money problem, and you are not to worry about it. Understand?"

Paul nodded, but he looked like a jurist who had just been told to ignore that last outburst by the witness. It was impossible.

"But I do think you should keep this to yourself. It won't help upsetting everybody."

Paul blushed.

"Who did you tell?"

"Nobody, but at the end of the conversation, Eric came into the room; he's my roommate. And he kinda overheard the part about Jack. He started pumping me, and it just sort of came out. Not the part about Jeremy, but the last part about Jack embezzling the money."

Lindy closed her eyes. Her neck muscles were gnarled and her shoulders hurt. Rebo snorted and turned facing the wall. He had probably heard the whole conversation. What had happened to her brain? All she needed was the entire company panicking.

"Rebo, are you listening?" Lindy asked sotto voce. "Open your eyes and come straight."

He rolled over to face them. "Not straight, anything but that." His grin was seductive. Huddled on the concrete floor, dance bag for a pillow, he looked like a desert sheik. He propped his arms behind his head and waited.

"Okay, I'm a total ditz for letting Paul talk while you were here."

Rebo sighed. "It's a good thing you're not a brain surgeon. The patient would be dead by now."

"I should just stick to fixing steps and spacing, huh?"

"And getting us a paycheck." He sat up and groaned. "You should definitely stick to steps and spacing, my dear."

"You're right, you're right." He reached for a pack of cigarettes on the makeup table. "I'll go—not straight—but clean. Will that do?"

"It's a deal. You curtail your social life, and I'll get you a paycheck. And don't say anything about this conversation. Any of it. Got it?"

He tossed the pack back onto the table. "Got it. But, man, it's weird. These guys are a bunch of whacked-out masochists. They make me look like Julie Andrews."

"I'll talk to Jack, but erase the last ten minutes from your memory banks, I mean it."

She left them staring at each other in total silence. They wouldn't stay quiet for long. You couldn't keep secrets in a group that worked, lived, ate, and slept together. Her head ached, and her shoulders felt like they were growing out of her ears.

She found Jack in the lobby of the hotel. He was collecting phone messages from the front-desk clerk when she walked up beside him. He was wearing the same three-piece suit he was wearing the first time she had seen him. It was shiny in places and seemed too snug to button comfortably.

"Got a minute?" she asked.

He looked surprised. "Sure. Shall we step into my office?" He led her into the bar and to a booth off to one side. He ordered a scotch; Lindy ordered a seltzer. After the waitress had left the drinks, Lindy got down to business.

"Jack, I might be way out of line, but we need to pay these people. I'm surprised they haven't walked out already. What kind of trouble are we in?" She looked him straight in the face and tried to look businesslike. It wasn't easy. Her throat was dry in spite of the seltzer, and she kept expecting Jeremy to pop in at any moment. That would finish it. Ms. Buttinsky at it again.

But Jeremy didn't appear. Jack took a prim sip of his scotch and flicked the air with his fingers. The hem of his sleeve was frayed with age. "There's no real problem, just a sluggish cash flow. We've had some big expenditures lately. That *Carmina* contraption and the candelabras came in way over the estimates. A few late payments from sponsors; everybody is suffering from cash-flow problems, thanks to our illustrious, art-bashing congress. But it will all be sorted out soon. In fact, a big check just cleared today, and I'll have paychecks for everyone tonight."

He gave her a condescending smile, which wasn't at all convincing. "So," he continued with a shrug. "Nothing to worry about. Anything else on your mind?"

There was plenty on her mind, but she had accomplished the one thing she needed from Jack. She was sure he had

had no intention of paying anybody until she had confronted him. What she needed now was a long talk with Biddy.

"No," she said lightly. "See you tonight." She left him with the check and walked briskly out of the bar. She didn't see him slug back the rest of his drink.

Seven

Biddy was not in their room. The beds were neatly made; the grant proposals were stacked in two even piles on the table. Not even an empty soda can disturbed the cleanliness of the room. Biddy had obviously not returned since they had left this morning. Lindy spent a few minutes pacing from the window to the beds in frustration. When she finally heard the door click, she advanced on Biddy with unreasonable impatience.

"Where have you been?"

Biddy looked startled and a little hurt. "Teaching a Rehearsal Techniques Seminar to graduate students. Did you need me?"

Lindy smiled contritely. "I always need you. I'm bursting with gossip and haven't been able to share it. If you had come in much later, you would have found me exploded into little pieces."

"Nasty rehearsal?" Biddy dropped her bag and collapsed on the bed, hoisting her cast up with one smooth tug. The mattress bounced under its weight.

"Not too bad, though Carlotta was late. The usual stuff. But I went with Angie to the nursing home this morning. I saw Sandra Dowd. It was pretty awful. To end up like that." Lindy described the visit and what Angie had said about everyone blaming Jeremy for the accident.

"That's ridiculous. It wasn't Jeremy's fault."

Lindy ignored her reaction. "And the next part is, Paul talked to his father, and Allan said that there was actually an investigation before it was declared an accident. Jeremy was under suspicion."

"No, I don't believe it." Biddy's hands shot to her hair. "Jeremy is the most wonderful person, and he would never hurt anybody. You just don't know him well enough."

"Biddy, I don't think Jeremy would hurt anybody, not intentionally anyway. I'm just saying—I don't know what I'm saying. Let's try to think this out. I'm beginning to think that whatever happened then may in some way be responsible for what's happening now."

"You mean that Jack and Carlotta have some hold over Jeremy because of Sandra, and this has all been some sordid game?"

"Not a game, Biddy, but sordid and destructive." Lindy sat down on the bed and faced her. "What exactly do we know? One, Jeremy is in seclusion, maybe because of the accident or for some other reason we're not aware of. Two, Jack, after stealing from him, somehow convinces him to start a new company with Jack as the business manager. Jack would have to have a pretty persuasive argument, wouldn't he?"

"Maybe he really cares about Jeremy, or maybe he was desperate for work. I don't think anybody would hire him after what happened, do you? Maybe Jeremy felt sorry for him, or knew he was innocent?"

"And get saddled with Carlotta in the bargain? That would be a harsh sacrifice even for the most loyal of friends."

"But Carlotta didn't come until a few months ago." Biddy tugged at her hair.

"I realize that; I can't figure it out at all. I've read hundreds of mysteries, and I've never figured out who dunnit until the last page."

"And you think if we could figure this out, we could make everything right again?"

"Or destroy it."

"Lindy, you're scaring me. Maybe we don't want to find out."

"How long do you think the company can go on like this?"

"Oh, God," moaned Biddy and dropped her arms across her face.

"And I talked to Jack. He said he'd have paychecks tonight."

Biddy sat up. "I'm beginning to get a nasty feeling about this. I want to take a look at the books. I don't know how, but we'll have to figure out a way."

"My exact thought."

They spent a half hour piecing together what they knew about the convoluted relationships in the company: Jeremy and Jack, Jack and Carlotta, Peter and Jeremy, ending up more confused than when they started. They made plans for raiding Jack's briefcase, some practical and some hopelessly outlandish.

After a quick bite to eat, they drove to the theater. Lindy prepared herself to look at everyone in a new and unbiased light, but her resolution shattered when they entered the stage door.

Alice was sitting on a folding chair next to the prop table. Tears were dropping off her cheeks onto her smock. She must have been at it for a while; her face was swollen and blotched. The effect did not enhance her features. Peter stood next to her, his arm loosely draped over her shoulder.

"Carlotta's costumes are missing from her dressing room," Peter said. "Really, Lindy, this is going a bit far. A few pranks against Carlotta are okay, but it's hardly fair to do this to Alice."

"You're right. Call the company onstage, will you, Peter?"

A few minutes later, sixteen dancers stood before her. She had a good idea who was behind the practical jokes, but she didn't want to alienate any of them. "Look," she said, careful not to gaze at any one person too long. "Carlotta's costumes have been taken out of her dressing room. Alice is very upset. I know this is not what was intended, but when a little fun begins to hurt the wrong people, it has to stop. The four of us are going into the shop now. We'll be there for fifteen minutes."

The costumes were hanging in Carlotta's dressing room when Lindy came out of the shop. "Good show, everybody, for tonight and for this." She and Biddy went out to the audience early. Better to leave things on a positive note.

They were taking their seats when Biddy stopped her. "Don't look now, but there's Carlton Quick. The *Times* must have sent him. Wow."

"Oops, too late." Lindy pasted on a smile and walked down the aisle to where Quick was sitting. "Carlton, what an unexpected pleasure."

"Lindy, darling, it is you. You look divine. And Arabida McFee. Well, well, we've come full circle."

"Only we'll be sitting through the performance tonight," said Lindy. "And you, Carlton? Still sleeping through the boring parts?"

"Of course, darling." He gave her a fleshy, gold-speckled smile. "How else would I catch up on my beauty rest?"

"Well, I think we'll manage to keep you awake tonight. Have you taken a look at your program?"

"Just got here. Are wonderful surprises in store?"

Lindy flashed him an impudent smile. "Stay awake and see for yourself. See you later."

As they sat down a few rows behind him, Quick turned to face them. His mouth performed a series of Silly Putty expressions before it relaxed, and he turned back to the stage.

"He must have seen the program," said Biddy.

There were no major problems that night. Carlotta even managed to stay away from the candelabras, and the processional proceeded without mishap. Jeremy's piece was danced with joyful abandon; when a famous critic is in the audience, news spreads fast.

Quick managed to snag them before they could escape backstage after the final curtain. "Darling, I nearly had a coronary; you should put a disclaimer in the program in case anyone is frightened to death by the old bag." He put the tips of his fingers to his forehead. "Jeremy must have gone round the bend."

"So you did stay awake."

"I had to. Afraid of nightmares." He shuddered, jowls

vibrating. "But in all seriousness, darling, the company is fresh and talented. Dump the dreadful diva, and you'll be a hit."

"If it were only that simple," sighed Biddy as she clunked after Lindy.

Jack was handing out paychecks when they arrived backstage. "But only one?" Rebo said. "You owe us two."

"All in good time, boy." Jack turned and walked into Carlotta's dressing room.

"Did that asshole just call me 'boy'? I'll kill the motherfucker."

Eight

Lindy blinked her eyes open. Morning. A hotel room. Tour. It felt comfortable, familiar. She smiled and got out of bed, feeling only minimally sore from her first ballet *barre* in years. She climbed into her sweats and headed for the doorknob.

She was finishing *battements* when breakfast arrived. Munching on English muffins and squeezing the last drops from their grapefruit halves, she and Biddy reviewed the corrections from the previous night and decided what areas needed the most work.

Rehearsal began each day at noon. This gave the dancers the mornings for sleeping in, relaxing, and considering the general notes Lindy had given them the night before. The day started with Jeremy's *Holberg Suite* and was followed by *Carmina*. The break in between allowed time for the setup of the cage. It was a quick procedure considering the size and bulk of the metal tower. There were three major sections: base, middle, and top, which fit together and were stabilized by inserting cross bars into els; the crossbars also served as climbing rungs.

The rehearsals were beginning to take on a rhythm of their own. It was a satisfying feeling. If they could just maintain their work habits until the New York season, they would be assured of favorable reviews, in spite of Carlotta.

Carlton Quick's review was being circulated around the dressing rooms when Lindy arrived at the theater. Quick was one of the last critics who still made the midnight deadline for the next edition. Sometimes it took several days for a review to appear in the paper; not much help in boosting ticket sales for a short run.

Lindy walked into Paul's dressing room. A huddle of six heads bent over the paper. Eric looked up. "Review's out. They don't call him Quick for nothing, and it's good, mostly."

Andrea sat scrunched in a chair, arms folded over her head. She looked out from under them.

"Expecting a cave-in?" asked Lindy.

"She's going to kill me."

"Let me see." Paul handed Lindy the paper. She skimmed the complimentary paragraphs about *Holberg* and found the item she was looking for: a glowing accolade for the "golden-haired beauty that danced David Matthews's arresting chore-ography with grace and intuitive understanding." The only allusion to Carlotta was the very pointed statement that "unfortunately, all casting choices were not as successful as the choice of Andrea Martin in the supporting role. The critic hopes to see more use made of this talented dancer in the future."

"Well," said Lindy as she plopped the paper onto the makeup table. "Fasten your seat belts, guys . . ."

"Yeah, it's going to be a bumpy ride, but, Andy, look what happened to Bette in the end." Rebo writhed in top diva imitation, bulging his eyes and rolling them until only the whites showed.

"Right now I'd rather face Bette Davis than Carlotta. Oh, God." Andrea slumped down in her chair.

"We'll protect you from the 'Demon Diva,'" said Paul gallantly.

"Thanks, Paul." Andrea smiled at him.

"I'll beat her with my do-rag."

"Thanks, Rebo."

"Just like in *The Wiz*. The Scarecrow." He pointed Vanna White-style to Eric. "The Tin Man." He put his arms around Paul and gave him a sloppy kiss. "I guess that makes Jeremy the Cowardly Lion, 'cause I be Toto. Gonna bite de old witch on de ankle and steal her shoes."

Paul pushed Rebo away. "You're so full of crap, Rebo."

"Dat's why dey luv me."

"What would your middle-class, Midwestern mama say if she heard you talk like that?" asked Lindy.

"Madam, I never talk 'like that' when conversing with the grande dame, I assure you," quipped Rebo, and he pinched her on the butt.

"You're incorrigible."

"Like I said, that's why they love me."

"Let's get to work," said Lindy. "What time is it?"

"Don't know. Peter, that keeper of the timepiece, hasn't shown up yet."

"Well, get onstage and start warming up, please."

Lindy fetched the boom box from the prop room and plugged it into the floor plug at the front of the stage. Peter wasn't around, though he must be somewhere in the theater. He was always there before the others. Or maybe he had gone to visit his sister. They could get by without him for a while. She began the *Holberg* rehearsal.

It was during the *Air*, that Lindy first became aware of Peter standing in the wings. He was gazing at the movement onstage, a faint smile on his lips. Standing behind him, loaded down with dresses that needed to be steamed free of wrinkles, was Alice, also watching.

He must have felt Lindy observing him. He caught her eye momentarily, frowned, and turned away, bumping into Alice. The pile of dresses slipped to the floor. He didn't stop to help her; he seemed unaware of what he had done. Alice bent down, quickly gathered up the fallen dresses, and followed him backstage.

During the break Lindy watched the crew construct the cage. They lugged the middle portion onto the base and hammered retaining pieces into numbered slots. Peter was putting up the crossbars, slamming them vehemently into the fittings.

She wandered over to him. "How's it going?"

"Fine." He didn't look up, just banged another bar into place. His tone of voice and the sound of metal hitting metal had the same teeth-jarring grind.

"Five minutes more."

"Peter, is something wrong?"

"No."

"Peter."

He stood up so abruptly that she took an involuntary step backward. His long fingers wrapped around her upper arm and drew her toward him. "Why did you go there? Leave us alone. It's none of your business. Just leave me alone."

His face showed no emotion, but his voice was barely controlled. Rage. Lindy recognized the emotion immediately. He was containing it, but barely. Why hadn't she realized it before? His demeanor had always been calm, efficient, even caring, but she should have guessed from his physical appearance. His thinness could have been caused from stress, bad diet, even illness. But Peter wasn't ill, just sick at heart. Lindy's stomach flipped over and dropped. She had violated his defenses by visiting Sandra. How could she have been so unthinking? She hadn't even considered how he would feel. In fact, she hadn't thought about him at all.

Now, she could feel the years of pent-up frustration rumbling just beneath his veneer of icy acceptance. His anger was escaping now like air through the pinhole in a balloon. Aimed at her. Enough force and it would explode. She stood frozen, indecisive. She didn't know how to comfort him or diffuse his anger. With a jolt, she realized that she was afraid of him.

He had grabbed her arm so forcefully that her right side was crumpling from the pain. He glared at her with harsh, penetrating eyes.

"Peter."

Her voice must have sounded pained; he loosened his grip and stared at her arm in dismay. "Sorry." He released her. "Why shouldn't you be curious? God knows, I should welcome any show of concern. No one has even bothered to visit her in five years. Five years. Like she never existed. Jeremy has never been to see her. Not once. That cold-blooded bastard. I'll never forgive him."

She reached to touch him, to make some human contact, but he jerked away. "I'm sorry. I didn't know."

"Why should you? Just forget it, please." He picked up the last crossbar and banged it into position. "Ready."

Lindy turned away, ashamed at her insensitivity. Carlotta was standing in the wings, watching and smirking.

Damn the woman. The whole world might be a stage to Shakespeare, but this stage was becoming their whole damn world. Nothing was private; everything was magnified. Lindy felt sick. She'd like nothing more than to smother the old bag with her insufferable fur coat and walk away from the whole convoluted mess.

"Call the dancers, please."

Peter walked off toward the dressing rooms pointedly ignoring Carlotta as he passed her.

They started in the middle of *Carmina*. Lindy wanted to do as much work on the piece as she could before rehearsing any part that would bring Carlotta in close contact with Andrea. There was going to be a scene. Scenes were what Carlotta did best, and after the review praising the ingenue, she knew that Carlotta was just waiting to come in for the kill. For once, she wished Jeremy would appear at the rehearsal, but he had come in and gone directly into his office with Jack, closing the door behind him. He must be aware that things were going to be tough today, and Lindy was a little miffed that he left the situation entirely in her hands.

She couldn't keep the two women separated for long. There was too much interchange between the characters they were portraying, though what their theatrical relationship was supposed to be was a little vague. The younger woman representing the other's past exploits? The symbolism of dreams lost? It would make more sense for Andrea to carry the story line using Mieko as her alter ego. That's what Lindy would have done, but she didn't know what David Matthews had intended. He was supposed to come to the

Thursday performance. She would try to pin him down on certain dramatic situations that were still eluding her.

Her mind had been wandering for just a few seconds, but it was long enough for the rehearsal to slip from her control. Carlotta had gone into action. Lindy snapped to attention as the older woman gave Andrea a shove. Peter appeared from offstage. His presence was so immediate that Lindy looked unconsciously at the floor where the trapdoor lay hidden beneath the Marley. It was the perfect deus-ex-machina entrance: the god suddenly appearing to set things right in Greek dramas.

The cast looked on openmouthed as Peter grabbed Carlotta by both arms and lifted her off the floor. "Get this straight and get it now. There will be no disruptions like this on my stage. This is a professional company, and you will act accordingly. Understand?"

Carlotta's face was colorless as parchment, but whether from surprise, fear, or anger was impossible to tell. Peter shook her like a locked door. Her feet sputtered against the surface of the floor.

"Do you understand?" The words seemed to strangle him.

"Keep your hands off me, you miserable worm," she hissed. "Jack won't stand for this. You're finished."

"No, Carlotta, you're finished." The voice was low, calm, and melodious in spite of its directness. Jeremy stood at the edge of the stage. He didn't even have to raise his voice to be heard. Talk about your Greek gods. Lindy silently thanked the deities for his fortuitous appearance and for his total control of the situation.

Peter released his hold, and Carlotta stumbled backward.

"There will be no more outbursts, Carlotta. Just do your

steps and leave everyone alone." He glanced at Lindy and then turned to Peter. "What happened?"

"She pushed Andrea." Peter jerked toward Carlotta. "You could have hurt her. What if she had—" He stopped, then recoiled from her as if she were a venomous snake.

"Get back to rehearsal. And no—more—of—this." Jeremy turned, jumped over the edge of the stage, and sat down in the first row, dead center. "Carry on, Lindy."

Lindy reached for the play button with shaking hands. She hadn't reacted fast enough. Now Jeremy was sticking around to make sure everything ran smoothly. She glanced at him through lowered lids.

He returned her look with an encouraging smile. He settled back in his seat and draped his right leg over the armrest, the picture of studied calm.

Rehearsal plodded on. The troops were massing. Jeremy had given them an unspoken order to stand their ground. They kept their spacing, even when Carlotta moved too close. They danced past her if she moved too slowly. They effectively erased her from the stage. These tactics wouldn't work in the long run, but for the first time since Lindy had joined the company, she felt them embrace their own power.

Lindy's respect for Jeremy jumped way up the scale. He had gotten himself into an untenable position, but he was taking control. She felt a surge of optimism.

She fine-tuned the girls' trio, encouraged the boys to higher energy levels, demanded more drama in some sections, more subtlety in others. Carlotta caused no more trouble. She would later, no doubt of that, but for the moment, life seemed wonderful.

When she turned to stop the tape, she saw that Biddy

had joined Jeremy in the audience. Biddy smiled and made a surreptitious thumbs-up sign. They looked like a kooky, two-headed beast, sitting there together, Jeremy's right leg over his seat arm, Biddy's cast stuck out to the left.

Lindy turned back to the stage, wiping the smile off her face. "Let's cut to the end. I want to try something. Paul and Carlotta, that final climb seems a bit crowded to me. Hang back just a bit, Paul. Let her get a few steps ahead of you and then speed up a bit at the last minute. Not too melodramatic, okay? Just a bit of space." Paul nodded, Carlotta made no objection, and Lindy cued the tape.

Carlotta was on the fourth rung of the climb, when it suddenly gave way. One leg tangled in the metal as the rest of her hit the floor. There was a communal gasp from the dancers, but no one moved to help her. Finally Paul stepped cautiously toward her. Carlotta lay sprawled on the floor, trying to disengage her leg from the cage.

Then everyone seemed to move at once. Lindy rushed forward; Jeremy was, somehow, right behind her. Carlotta began shrieking and yelling obscenities at Paul, who was trying ineffectually to help her up. Lindy was vaguely aware of Peter running across the stage. Alice shuffled behind him, carrying an ice pack. Lindy could see Jack hurrying through the wings.

Carlotta had managed to untangle herself and was half standing, groping at the structure for support. She stood on one leg; the other leg hung limply from the knee. She knocked Paul out of the way and turned on Peter. "You did this. You and—" Her head spun to look at Lindy. "And her. You planned this. Jack! Jack!" Her voice was shrill and hysterical. "They planned this, just like the last time. Look at the bar. They've cut it so I would fall. She made me go up first."

Every head turned to look at the cage. The fourth rung dangled from one end. Peter stooped down and picked up the loose end. "The welding has broken through." He turned to Jeremy, confused. "I didn't do this. Look. The welding hasn't been cut, it's broken. It's hard to believe this could happen. Atlantic always does impeccable work."

"It's not hard to believe." Carlotta lunged at Peter. Alice, who had been trying to apply an ice pack to Carlotta's foot, tumbled backward onto her butt. Before Peter could react, a bloody trail from Carlotta's nails streamed down his face. Jeremy and Jack pulled her away.

"Carlotta, you're not acting rationally," said Jack. "Let's get you off your feet and assess the damage."

"Assess the damage, you fool!" She whirled around and grabbed him by the lapels. Freesia petals dropped to the floor, and the rest of Jack's boutonniere followed as Carlotta twisted the fabric in her fists. "I'm not some bloody piece of merchandise. You'll be doing the assessing soon, you little charlatan."

"Jack, maybe you should take her to the emergency room. Alice, give him a hand, will you?" Jeremy turned to Lindy.

"Right," she said. "Let's get back to work. Understudies. And stay away from the cage."

Peter came to stand beside her. His face was smeared with blood where he had tried to wipe it away with the sleeve of his T-shirt. "I'll check out the structure thoroughly. I've never had any problem with Atlantic's work before."

"Fine." Lindy touched his shoulder. "But first, get yourself a Band-Aid."

Carlotta was still screeching at Jack offstage. The sound shot through the wings and onto the stage. Lindy turned up the music, hoping to drown her out and return to some kind of normalcy. She had to force herself to concentrate on the dancing. She wanted to send everyone back to the hotel and check out the broken cage herself. If the structure had been weakened, wouldn't Peter or one of the stagehands have noticed? They set it up and dismantled it each day, storing it in the shop. Could someone have sabotaged it? But why?

Stop it, she demanded silently. Keep your mind on your work.

A few minutes later, she saw Jack and Alice helping Carlotta out of her dressing room. Jeremy watched them leave and then came over to Lindy.

"They're taking her to the emergency room. I don't think it's broken, but she'll be out for tonight." He paused for a minute, surveying the stage. "Get the understudies in shape. And Lindy, you're doing good work."

Lindy breathed a sigh of relief.

The cast was nervous at first. They were prepared for their parts physically, but to be abruptly pushed into performing without the psychological preparation would take its toll if Lindy didn't settle them down. So she started at the beginning and just let them dance their nerves away. They would find their stride; she was sure of it.

Biddy and Jeremy watched the last few minutes of the rehearsal from the wings. When they broke for dinner, Jeremy made a short speech, telling the dancers they had all worked hard, and he had total confidence in them. Lindy had stood through hundreds of similar speeches from many directors, but none had been as simple and eloquent and believable as

Jeremy's. She marveled at his ability to always turn a situation to the better, with such naturalness and ease.

While he stood talking to individual dancers, Biddy motioned Lindy into the wings. She had been looking at Lindy throughout Jeremy's speech with barely disguised excitement. Her hair was standing on end, an experiment in static electricity.

"I thought he'd never stop," she said breathlessly. "We've got to hurry."

"What?"

"The books. In the excitement, Jack left his briefcase. Maybe there's something in it. You know . . ." She prompted Lindy with an urgent look.

"Biddy, we can't rifle Jack's briefcase. What if he comes back to get it?"

"That's why we have to hurry. You said we needed to look at the books."

"I thought you said that."

"Well, you agreed."

"Okay, I did agree," admitted Lindy. "And I guess we have to do it. But we'll have to wait until the theater clears out and risk Jack's coming back. Let's just hope the local emergency room is really busy today."

"Excuse me, Lindy." Lindy and Biddy jumped guiltily.

"Yes, Andrea?"

"What about my costume?"

"What about it? You do have one, don't you?"

"No, they ran over budget, so they didn't have the extra one made up. There's fabric, but it isn't made. Mieko can fit into mine, and Kate can fit into Mieko's. But I guess Alice will have to alter Carlotta's for me, and Alice has gone with them to take care of Carlotta—"

"Don't worry," Biddy broke in. "I'm sure Alice will be back in plenty of time to take a few tucks. You'll be all right. Now get back to the hotel and rest." Andrea nodded and left them.

"Just hurry up, and take everybody with you," said Lindy under her breath.

They watched from the office window until the bus pulled out of the parking lot. Then they turned to the briefcase. It was open, surrounded by financial sheets. A blue ledger sat on top of the papers.

"This is the first time I've ever been glad of Carlotta's nasty temper," said Biddy. "Jack must have been too rattled to lock it before he left."

"Or there's nothing incriminating in it. I can't understand any of this," said Lindy, poring over the ledger pages.

"But I can. Thanks to some friend who badgered me into taking night courses in accounting."

"Thanks, but I didn't mean for you to use your math skills for breaking and entering."

"So it's a good thing the briefcase just happened to be sitting open on the table." Biddy handed her a stack of papers. "Bills, probably. See if you can find anything that looks suspicious." She had already opened the ledger, and her fingers were flying over the portable calculator on the table before her.

After a few minutes, Biddy looked up. She sounded disappointed. "All the numbers add up. Of course they would.

Maybe he keeps two sets of records. Isn't that what embez-
zlers do?"

"I guess, but I don't have a clue as to how it works."

"Me neither. They don't have a course in Doctoring the
Books in night school."

"But maybe there's something here." Lindy pulled an
invoice from the stack of bills she was holding.

They didn't hear him approach. He was suddenly there
in the doorway, blocking their escape.

"Oh, God," whimpered Biddy.

"What the hell are you up to?" He stepped inside, closing
the door behind him.

"Oh, Jesus, Peter. We must be in heaven 'cause you just
scared the hell out of us."

"Funny."

"How are those scratches?"

"Forget the damned scratches. What are you doing?"

Biddy looked at Lindy; Lindy looked at Peter. "Well,"
she began. Her mind was blank. They should have thought
up a believable reason to be here in case they were caught,
but they hadn't. Could Peter be trusted? He already thought
she was an insensitive busybody. How would he react to
her snooping into company business? Especially in view of
what she had just discovered. Or worse, could Peter be
siphoning the funds, and not Jack at all? He might just hate
Jeremy enough to weasel his way into a job and then destroy
the company. She tried to see him as the villain, but it just
wouldn't work. Maybe she was too damned naive, but she
thought of Peter as one of the good guys.

"Have you taken enough time to come up with a good
story? I'm not going to believe anything but the truth, but

you can try." He leaned against the edge of the table and crossed his arms. Keep your mind focused, she pleaded with herself.

"Okay." She expelled a long sigh. "You caught us red-handed."

"Lindy." Biddy looked at her imploringly.

"It's okay, Biddy, I hope. We're looking through the books. Come on, Peter, something is wrong here. We all know that sponsors pay before the performance. Nobody lets fees trickle in after the fact, or we'd all be bankrupt."

"Right." He encouraged her to go on, but Lindy could see from his face that he was already several steps ahead of her explanation.

"The payments have been entered," said Biddy. "Every theater on the last tour has paid."

"So where's the money? Is that what you're looking for?"

"Yes," said Lindy. "Peter, I have to ask you this before we go on. Do you know where the money is going?"

His response was more of a bark than a laugh, but it took away one more doubt from Lindy's mind. It had the harshness of someone who wasn't used to laughing, but it was genuine.

"You're not very subtle, Lindy." Peter shook his head. "I don't know. Jack doesn't pay me, either."

"Then why do you stay?" Lindy cringed at her own stupidity.

Peter frowned. She could almost hear the gates locking around him.

"Sorry, I'm off the subject. Didn't you say something about Atlantic making the cage?"

"I always use them. They do excellent work, until now anyway, and are very reasonable for a union shop."

"Do you deal directly with them?"

"Yeah, I send over the specs. They call or fax if they have any questions. But we were on the road with the last tour when most of the construction was done. Jack stayed in New York, and he'd fax me the communications from the office. There weren't many; I went over it pretty thoroughly with Atlantic before I left. Why?"

"Because there is no invoice from Atlantic here."

Peter stuck out his bottom lip. He had very full lips. "Maybe it's in another stack."

"But there is an invoice from Barton Scenery for the construction of a metal frame: seventeen thousand dollars and change."

"What? Let me see that." Peter grabbed the invoice out of her hand. "That son of a bitch. I've never even heard of this company. The Atlantic estimate was eight thou with a twenty percent margin."

"You're sure the bid was supposed to go to Atlantic?"

"There was no bid as far as I know. Jeremy asked me who to use. I said Atlantic; he and Matthews agreed. Hell, I talked to the shop several times before I left."

"Could Jack have pulled it and given the job to this Barton company?"

"And get a little kickback for his effort? I guess. I only check the bills when there's a discrepancy. The paperwork I get is just a glorified packing list."

They nearly missed the sound of the car driving into the parking lot and coming to a halt just outside the stage door.

"Oh, no," cried Biddy. She began shuffling papers together and threw the ledger into the briefcase. She tore the paper out of the calculator and pushed it into Lindy's hand. Lindy crammed it into the waistband of her sweatpants.

"Is the stage door locked?" she asked Peter.

"No, damn it, I don't take the pig iron out until everybody's gone. Horrible for security, but it's better than running back and forth to open the door all the time."

They had barely returned all the papers to their approximate places when Jack came in. He gave them a startled look and glanced uncomfortably at the open briefcase.

"Oh, Jack, good," said Lindy. "We were just standing here wondering if you'd be back for your briefcase, or whether we should take it to the hotel for you."

"Uh, thanks. I'll take it." Jack slammed the top down and grabbed the handles. "I have to run."

"How's Carlotta?"

"Oh—she's okay. Just a bruise, the doctor said. She'll probably be fine for tomorrow." He turned and hurried out of the room.

No one spoke until they heard the car leave the parking lot. "That was close," said Biddy, turning from the window. They breathed a collective sigh of relief.

"Let's get out of here. We can figure out what to do later," said Lindy. "Want a ride to the hotel?"

"No, thanks," said Peter. "I think I'll stay around and check over the cage one more time. If this was done by some fly-by-night company, there's no telling what else might be wrong with it."

"We'll bring you a sandwich."

"Thanks." He smiled at Lindy for the first time since she had arrived.

Nine

The performance couldn't have been better. There were a few near misses and shaky balances, but the company danced with expression and dexterity. The absence of Carlotta was an instant panacea; the Jeremy Ash Dance Company had been released from an evil spell and had come back to life.

It had been touch and go until the curtain rose. Backstage before the show had been tense and jittery. Lindy went from dressing room to dressing room with bits of encouragement and words of advice. She had to be careful not to give too many last-minute corrections and overload their racing minds and nerves. She repeated the same words again and again. "Breathe, get into your legs, focus on what you're doing. Pay attention, you'll be fine, just do one thing at a time."

She had dropped into the costume room mainly because she had nothing to do. Alice was completing the alterations to the dress for Andrea while the girl squirmed and shook herself, trying to dispel a nasty attack of stage fright.

"Hold still, I'm working as fast as I can," said Alice through lips holding a row of straight pins. She deftly pulled the fabric between her fingers and secured it with the pins.

After a few minutes, she struggled up off her knees.

"There, you're done." She pulled the dress carefully down the length of Andrea's slender body, manipulating the fabric so that the pins didn't stick her as the dress fell.

It was forty-five minutes to curtain before Alice completed the alterations. Lindy was sitting in the girls' dressing room chatting with Kate and Mieko. Andrea was staring into a small makeup mirror, applying false eyelashes with trembling fingers. She looked up into the large mirror to compare her eyes and snatched off one of the lashes.

"I can't get it even," she moaned and started applying more glue to the strip of lashes.

"Clean off the old glue first, then reapply it. And let it dry a little before you put it on," said Lindy. "Relax. You've got plenty of time. How many times have you put on lashes? A thousand or so?"

"You're right. I'm being a nervous Nellie. I just wish Alice would finish with that dress. Paul and I haven't even tried the lifts with it yet."

"Alice will be done any minute. You worked the lifts with the corps dress, and they're pretty similar."

"She's even making me nervous," said Mieko to Lindy's reflection in the mirror.

"Ladies, you have heard a first." Kate raised her arms like a ringmaster. "The inscrutable, unflappable, 'don't let them see you sweat,' Mieko Jones has butterflies."

Mieko stuck out her tongue to Kate's reflection.

The distraction worked. Andrea's second eyelash was in place, and she moved on to applying lip liner. Her face had the perfect bone structure for the theater, prominent and finely chiseled. She didn't need to use the brown contour powder to accentuate the curve of her cheekbones. Her lips were full and expressive. Her face projected freshness and vitality even when covered by the heavy layer of stage makeup: pancake, mascara, blush, and heavily lined lipstick.

Alice slipped in through the door. The room was narrow, and the door banged back, hitting the wall opposite the makeup table. She squeezed past Lindy and hung the dress with the other costumes on the metal rack attached to the wall. The rack was rusty and had been covered with one of those plastic shower rods that opened along one side and then snapped back into place.

The whole theater was pretty shabby, Lindy mused, as Alice bustled around the costumes, fluffing some, smoothing out others. It was appalling how beautiful, old theaters were left to a slow death. Faded paint, rusted pipes, splintered stage, not even a sentry at the stage door. It was sad.

"I could have finished much earlier," Alice said, "but Carlotta wouldn't let me leave the hotel. If she wasn't so upset, she would realize that I had a lot of work to do."

"Alice, even when you're trying to be mean, you're nice," said Mieko.

Alice looked flustered.

"The old hag knew you had lots to do. She was putting the screws to you. Even in pain, she's busy orchestrating revenge."

"She's such a bitch. I thought people like her only worked for the opera," said Kate. "Here, Andrea, try this color." She tossed a tube of lipstick toward Andrea. She missed it, and the tube rolled toward the edge of the table.

Lindy caught it as it dropped and handed it back to her. "Okay, girls, no more diva dishing. Get those little muscles in working order."

Andrea quickly brushed the new lipstick onto her lips. The three girls rose from their chairs as one person and walked out the door, grabbing headsets, extra shoes, and leg warmers. Alice followed them.

Alone in the dressing room, Lindy looked into the mirror. Computer operators had nothing over the theater. You heard about people in the same room, talking to each other on screen instead of bothering to turn around to face each other. But the four of them had just carried on a conversation to each other's reflections in the mirror. Lindy pursed her lips and remembered just in time that it was bad luck to whistle in a dressing room. She bit her bottom lip instead. This was not the real world, or was it?

She stood in the back of the house during the show. Biddy had opted for sitting. It was hard to pace convincingly while lugging a heavy cast back and forth. She picked up one crutch and tapped Lindy on the butt.

"Merde," she said and made her way down the aisle. There were two empty seats beside her. Lindy wanted to be on her feet in case there was another disaster. And Jeremy was unable to hold still. She had seen him pacing in his office, pacing in the lobby, and now he was pacing in the small standing-room area in the back of the house.

He was immersed in his own thoughts. Lindy watched him at a distance, too nervous herself to wonder how Jeremy had ever gotten himself mixed up with two such destructive people as Jack and Carlotta. She could only worry about tonight and what Jeremy would think if she wasn't able to pull it off.

Stop being so self-centered, she admonished herself.

You're only one little piece of this. But egocentrism was the staple of their trade and a necessity if not taken too far. It was the quality that turned talented proficients into artists or failures.

Jeremy jolted to a stop when the houselights dimmed. He came to stand beside Lindy, the side of his arm touching her shoulder. It was a subtle appeal for comfort, and she didn't move her arm away.

It was the longest fifty-five minutes she could remember standing through. She did every step, every lift, every entrance and exit of every dancer on the stage. She was sweating, but smiling, when the curtain finally was drawn on the bodies of Andrea and Paul draped on the still intact and standing cage.

Relief replaced tension. Biddy turned in her seat, smiling radiantly. Lindy nodded back, but she was afraid to turn to Jeremy. She had tried to sneak a peek at his face on several occasions during the dance, but he stared straight ahead, his features immobile, and she couldn't read his feelings from his profile. They continued to stand side by side until Biddy joined them.

"Wow." Biddy bounced the ends of her crutches off the floor like a drumroll. She beamed at Lindy and beamed at Jeremy. "Well? Are you guys going to stand there in a daze, or what?"

Lindy shrugged her shoulders slightly and glanced sideways at Jeremy.

He opened his mouth and then closed it, took a deep breath and winced as if the act of breathing had hurt.

Lindy wanted to shake him until his thoughts tumbled out.

For once, Biddy looked like she wanted to shake him, too.

"Jeremy," she prompted.

He looked from one to the other of the expectant women in front of him. The audience was moving past them in a rush to the bar or outside for a cigarette. Normally, Lindy would have followed them, picking up comments in order to get a pulse on the audience's reaction. But right now, she only cared about Jeremy's reaction, and it was slow in coming.

"I'm such an asshole," was what he said when he finally chose to speak.

It was an odd response. Lindy expected ecstatic congratulations and a rush backstage. She could have coped with disappointment if he hadn't liked what he had seen. But "I'm an asshole" didn't leave much for her to work with.

She swallowed. "Would you care to elaborate?"

"Huh?" He shook his head slowly back and forth. "They've been ... I've let them ... I could have lost this." He looked back and forth at the two women.

It was Biddy whose patience finally broke. "Jeremy, what did you think of the performance?"

Jeremy's eyebrows lifted in mild astonishment, and then he grinned. "Wow." He draped his arms around both of them and started walking them toward the hall that led backstage. They had only gone a few feet, when he stopped.

"I know what I have to do. I shouldn't have let this go on so long. I owe Jack a lot, but ..." He paused; his face clouded over.

Biddy and Lindy waited expectantly, but he said no more.

Except for the sounds of the cage being dismantled, backstage was completely silent. Lindy's heart constricted. She knew that feeling. They were waiting. Waiting for Jeremy's reaction. Every dressing room's door was ajar, but the light banter that usually followed a good performance was completely absent.

Jeremy walked to the door of the boys' dressing room. He didn't enter but braced himself with his hands on both sides of the door frame. He stuck his head in. "Great *Carmina*, kids. Pauly, very nice."

He spoke in a normal voice, but it carried to every door. The backstage exhaled in a big sigh of relief, like a woman being released from a too tight corset. He stopped at each door, giving praise, showing his pleasure. He was the perfect director: part demanding boss, part doting parent.

When he gave Andrea a hug, murmuring "Andy, good girl" into the top of her head, Lindy's eyes welled up with tears. Embarrassed, she turned away, only to see Biddy blubbering happily behind her.

"God, I love the theater. No stiff upper lip for me. Give me good old sloppy emotion any day." She ruffled Biddy's hair. "Let's get out front before we embarrass ourselves."

Lindy waited for Jeremy at the standing-room wall. When he appeared, his euphoria was gone. His shoulders were rigid beneath his silk jacket. The muscles at each side of his mouth tightened and relaxed, broadcasting his warring emotions like a blinking neon sign. He gave Lindy a cursory look before turning to the stage and leaning on his elbows on the half wall.

Lindy turned to the stage, too. The houselights blinked, and she watched the audience members hurry to their seats.

As the houselights began to dim, Jeremy spoke into the air before him. "It's my company. I have to do what is best for it, and that means Carlotta has to go. David will be here tomorrow. As choreographer, he has to be consulted, though I'm pretty sure what his reaction will be. He almost pulled *Carmina* when we insisted he use Carlotta. I don't think she'll go without a fight. I shouldn't have waited so long." He snapped his head toward Lindy. His feverish blue eyes held hers for an instant before their image faded as the lights lowered to black. "Lindy." She peered at his silhouette in the darkness. "Don't say anything. I want to talk to Jack first. I do owe him that." He jumped as the *Holberg Suite* began and turned back to the stage. "This is not going to be pretty."

The entire company gathered in the hotel bar after the performance. It was an impromptu celebration. Jeremy bought the first round of drinks and made an eloquent toast. The company had taken over the bar, standing or sitting at tables in animated groups. They congratulated each other, laughed at the near misses they had overcome. No one mentioned Carlotta, and Jack was conspicuously missing.

Toward the end, Peter entered the bar with Alice in tow. His hand rested fraternally on her shoulder as he guided her to the bar and deposited her between Andrea and Kate. He glanced toward Lindy and took his beer to the other side of the room.

By the time Lindy and Biddy retired to their room, they were both a little drunk. Biddy lumbered crablike down the hall.

"Can't find my key," she said, both hands stuck into the pockets of her dance bag.

"I've got mine." It took several attempts before Lindy managed to get the key into the lock and open the door. Her hand groped for the panel of light switches inside the door. She slapped at the panel, turning on several lamps and the entrance light. She stared, understanding coming slowly to her intoxicated brain. Biddy bumped into her and giggled.

"Someone has been in our room."

"Whad'ja mean?" asked Biddy, nudging her way around Lindy. She stopped. "I don' see anythin'."

The room hadn't been disarranged, much. Drawers weren't emptied onto the floor. Papers hadn't been thrown around the room; the beds were only a little rumpled. But it was clear that someone had been searching for something.

"Oh, m' God, have we been robbed?" Biddy fell toward the dresser and opened the top drawer. "No, my money's still here. I know you're not supposed to leave money in your hotel room, but you gotta trust people sometime."

"Whoever it was, wasn't looking for cash. Look at your grant proposals. You'd never leave them that messy. And everything else is just a little off." Lindy's brain was beginning to clear.

"Should we call the manager?"

"No—No, let me think."

"What if they're still here?" Biddy looked around in horror.

"Oh, shit." Lindy jumped away from the bed and looked underneath it.

"Don't, Lindy. What would you do if you found somebody under there?"

Lindy looked under the other bed. "Check the bathroom."

"I'm not going in there alone."

They both went to the door of the bathroom. Lindy stuck her hand around the edge of the door and turned on the light. "Nobody here, thank God."

"Whew. I wish I hadn't drunk so much downstairs; I could use a drink."

"Forget it. Who would be searching our room, and for what?"

"Jack." The name came immediately to Biddy's lips. "He wasn't at the theater tonight or at the party. He could have searched our room then, but what would he be looking for? We didn't take anything, did we?"

Lindy shook her head. "Only the calculator tape, and he didn't know about that." It dawned on her in a point of blinding clarity. "Did Peter return the Barton Scenery invoice?"

Biddy grabbed at her hair, balancing her crutches under her arms. "I don't know. Everything happened so fast. We were all throwing things back into the briefcase. But if he didn't put it back, that means Jack thinks we have it. But we don't. Or maybe—" She turned to Lindy slowly, a look of incredulity spreading across her face. "Oh, Lindy. You don't think Peter could be involved, do you? He didn't come to the bar until later. Maybe it was him after all, and he thinks we know something more than we do."

"Sounds like you've been reading too many mysteries. Maybe the maid dropped the papers and wasn't neat about putting them back. Maybe there's a perfectly reasonable explanation for this." Lindy didn't believe it, but she knew her brain was still too fuzzy to think clearly. She didn't want to think that Peter might be the embezzler, and she didn't want to worry Biddy. What she needed most were two aspirins and sleep; they could figure it out in the morning.

"You're right. It's probably just our imaginations. Too much excitement." Biddy babbled on unconvincingly.

"Let's get to bed. I'm beat."

Ten

The telephone was ringing. Lindy rolled over and groped for the phone. The receiver bounced off the bedside table and hung from its cord. She managed to get it to her ear.

"Hello," she croaked. The sun shone through the partially opened curtains, casting a rectangle of light across the ends of the beds; the rest of the room was dark.

"It's Jeremy."

Lindy sat upright, willing the rest of her body and mind to consciousness. "What's up?"

"My blood pressure. Jack left a message. He's gone to New York. He won't be back until tomorrow."

"Shit. Does that mean tonight won't be 'Dump the Diva' night?"

"I don't know. David is coming in this afternoon. Carlotta's already been on the phone to me twice. There's no way she's going to miss tonight's performance. How a woman with a brain that small has made it this far is astounding."

"She's managed to use what gifts she has pretty effectively."

There was silence at the other end of the line. Lindy cringed. "Well, never mind," she said lightly. "We'll let David take a look tonight and wait until Jack gets back if we have to."

"I know you think I'm being a wuss on this, Lindy. You're probably right, but I owe Jack a lot."

"I think you're wonderful. What's one more day in the scheme of things? We'll see you at rehearsal." She hung up the phone. One more day. It would be hell, but they had made it this far. What was one more day?

Carlotta was back in form. She showed up to rehearse early, limping slightly. No one suggested she take another day off. She lurched through her steps, mowing over Paul, pushing dancers off their spacing, getting in the way. Lindy didn't stop to correct her. No one complained. There was an unspoken conspiracy to let Carlotta burn herself out. When the procession entered carrying the candelabras, she moved uncomfortably close to them. They held their straight line, and she narrowly missed knocking them over.

Not a moth to the flame, thought Lindy. A behemoth, and she held her tongue.

Most of the dancers stayed around the theater after rehearsal. Biddy sent out for food. They ate quietly in their dressing rooms; no one turned on music. A few dancers sat on the stoop outside the stage door smoking cigarettes; their hushed voices carried back into the theater through the crack left open by the pig iron.

By seven o'clock the tension was unbearable. Lindy went through the motions of giving last-minute notes. She reminded them that the choreographer would be in the audience that night—as if they could forget.

Carlotta was the only person who seemed unaffected by

the change in mood. She called for Alice every few minutes. Everyone else dressed themselves, helping each other with zippers, snaps, and hooks and eyes.

Jeremy came in with David Matthews around seven thirty. Matthews was short, wiry, and energetic. They made the rounds, saying hello, and wishing everyone a good performance. The dancers' responses were demure.

At seven forty-five, Lindy could stand it no longer. She found Biddy and herded her to their seats in the audience.

Jeremy and David Matthews were sitting several rows in front of them. Matthews was studying his program. Jeremy made an occasional comment. Lindy was pretty sure they weren't discussing business; Jeremy had decided to let the action speak for itself.

"I just hope they dance half as well as they did last night," whispered Biddy, and Lindy realized that she had been so preoccupied over the break-in and Jeremy's call, she had forgotten to tell Biddy what he had planned and how Jack's departure had postponed it. Biddy had managed to sleep through the entire conversation.

The houselights went out. The music began, and the curtain opened onto the foggy stage. Rebo and Juan carried Andrea to the cage. Carlotta entered and picked her up. The girl collapsed onto the floor, straight down, not forward where Carlotta had demanded she fall. Carlotta walked forward, kicking the girl's feet out of her way as she did.

Lindy flinched. "Hold on, Andrea, hold on," she said under her breath. Biddy patted her knee without taking her eyes off the stage.

The boys entered. They were electrifying. Matthews's head turned toward Jeremy. The girls' trio followed. Their timing and spacing were flawless, and Lindy began to relax. By the end of the trio for Mieko, Andrea, and Rebo, she had almost forgotten that Carlotta was back.

She shouldn't have. Carlotta entered for her solo. She looked ancient compared to the girls. Was this what the choreographer intended? Lindy didn't think so. The corps entered behind Carlotta, moving to the right. Carlotta should have moved with them, leading the group, but she stayed dead center like some idiot opera singer rooted to the spot. What did the bitch think she was doing? She only made herself look bad. Surely, she couldn't be that stupid, or was she just so arrogant that she didn't care?

The corps danced right past her. They were doing what they were supposed to do. They wouldn't be to blame if things went wrong. If they just stayed determined and didn't start embellishing, Carlotta would finish herself off.

By the time the final procession entered, Lindy was exhausted from holding her breath. Biddy sat bolt upright; her hands clenched the armrests. And then it happened. The procession started its turns; Carlotta moved away from Paul and ran right into Eric's arm. The force of the impact knocked the candelabra out of his hand, but he kept turning. Rebo's foot caught the edge of the candlestick, and it skidded across the stage. Carlotta tripped over it, and the flickering light mercifully went out.

Lindy covered her face with both hands and peeked through open fingers. Pick it up, somebody, she pleaded silently. Mieko kicked the candelabra into the wings.

Carlotta managed to regain her footing but hit Paul with such force that he staggered backward. He fought to press her above his head, but he couldn't manage it, and Carlotta dropped heavily onto his shoulder.

"Shit," said Biddy.

The people in front of them turned around and stared. Lindy even lowered her fingers in amazement.

"Sorry," said Biddy.

Lindy didn't even see how Carlotta and Paul managed to get to the top of the cage for the ending. The curtain was closing before she knew what had happened. Matthews rocketed out of his seat as the curtain rose for the bows. Jeremy followed him, eyes straight ahead.

Lindy jumped out of her seat and climbed over Biddy's legs. "You're on your own." She raced after the two men, squeezing past the early risers making their way to the lobby for intermission.

Jeremy and David Matthews were standing in the hall near the door to backstage. The hall was empty; the audience exited up the aisles and through the back doors.

Lindy stopped short as she rounded the corner. Pressing against the wall, she peeked out at the two men. Matthews had turned back to face Jeremy. His face was contorted with anger. Lindy could see his right eyebrow twitch rhythmically even from where she was standing, and not for the first time, she marveled at how insignificant details could leap out to capture one's attention.

"I want her out. What's wrong with you, Jeremy? You've always been smart, intuitive. Have you lost your grip?"

No answer. Another string of emotional accusations. Jeremy didn't attempt to interrupt him.

"I don't know what hold that bitch has over you, but I'm pulling *Carmina* if you don't get rid of her. Now. Understand?

Fire her, bribe her, break her goddamned leg if you have to, but she doesn't go on that stage again. I mean it."

He turned toward the stage door, then spun around and strode back up the hall toward Lindy. Lindy ducked back around the corner. He marched past her without seeing her, jostled a few people in the lobby, and hurried out the front doors.

Jeremy waited for his exit before he looked up.

"Well . . ." He waited for Lindy to emerge from her hiding place.

Lindy peered around the corner. "I guess he'll get a cab back to the hotel."

Jeremy seemed to be unscathed by the barrage of insults he had just sustained. He merely quirked one side of his mouth, casually slipped his arm around her shoulders and walked her to the door.

And then she realized that he had orchestrated the events completely. Of course. He had made David give him the ultimatum. David was the bad guy. Jeremy had no choice, and Jack would have no recourse but to accept the decision. She wanted to throw her arms around him and tell him how brilliant he was, but she just walked beside him grinning like an idiot.

Jeremy opened the door, and Lindy stopped smiling. There was pandemonium backstage. Carlotta held one of the candelabras, swinging it inches from Eric's head. He had been right. It looked like a modern version of the mad scene from *Giselle*. It would have been funny if Lindy hadn't known how heavy those candelabras were. Jeremy moved with feline speed, but Peter was there before him. He grabbed the candelabra from Carlotta and slapped her hard across the face.

She reeled from the force of it. Andrea grabbed Peter, wrapping both arms around him and trapping his arms in hers.

"Don't, she's not worth it," she sobbed.

Peter dropped the candelabra. It landed with a thud at his feet.

"It's all right," he said, freeing his arms and enclosing them around the trembling girl. "It's all right. She's gone."

Carlotta *was* gone. The door of her dressing room was shut. No one had even noticed her exit.

Jeremy picked up the candelabra and put it back on the prop table. He turned to Eric, ruffled his hair, and slapped his butt. "Well, bold one, had enough excitement? I think I see a gray hair or two."

Eric started to cry. Jeremy enclosed him in a bear hug. "I'm sure Lindy has notes. Get onstage." No one moved. "Now, and if you hurry, I'll buy the drinks." He led Eric away toward the office.

"Last one onstage buys the next round," yelled Rebo, who bounded off through the wing. Everyone else followed.

"Let the kid compose herself," said Peter, still embracing Andrea. "I'll send her out in a minute."

Lindy nodded. God, she loved these people. Self-indulgent, pampered, competitive, they sure knew how to pull together when they had to. She followed the others onto the stage.

She hadn't taken any notes. There was no time to give any, even if she had. There was another piece to do, and intermission was almost over.

"Look, guys—" she began.

"Some serious shit just went down," interrupted Rebo, "but we be cool. Right?"

"That's all I ask. Some serious shit has gone down, as

you say, but it's going to be okay. Just don't let this screw up the next piece. Got it?"

They nodded.

"Then change costumes and get back out here."

She didn't return to her seat for the *Holberg Suite* but stood in the back. She saw Biddy hobble back down the aisle and sit down. She must have been out front listening to the audience's comments. Well, she'd get the whole story when they got back to the hotel. Lindy was too agitated to explain things now.

Carlotta's dressing-room door was still closed when Lindy returned backstage after the show. With any luck, she had gone back to the hotel already. Maybe Jeremy had fired her after all. No, he would wait for Jack to return—as long as he returned before tomorrow's performance.

The dancers were still onstage. No one seemed eager to leave the comfort of the proscenium.

She walked into the cluster of bodies. "That was pretty good. You really pulled together. *Carmina*, however, was a bust, and I have a few notes. These things happen. Sometimes the poltergeists get onstage with you, and there's nothing you can do but keep muddling through." She spent the next few minutes giving notes that didn't really need to be given. She just wanted to spend time with them.

"Boys, you got too far downstage in the quartet. Andrea . . ." But Andrea wasn't onstage. "Never mind, I'll give her corrections tomorrow." Maybe she's seeking comfort from Peter, Lindy thought; they would make a nice couple. "All right, that's enough. Get dressed and on the bus. I'll find Jeremy. He owes us drinks."

"But what did David Matthews think?" asked Mieko.

The air was rent with a loud wailing.

"That bad?" said a voice from the back.

"Oh, shit," said Lindy. "Now what have you guys done?"

"That's not Carlotta," said Rebo. He rushed off the stage followed by Juan and Eric.

Carlotta's dressing-room door was open. Rebo stopped suddenly, causing a domino effect as dancers piled up behind him. Lindy slipped under his arm and froze.

Carlotta lay on the cement floor, still in her *Carmina* dress. One leg was bent under her, the knee sticking out in a grotesque parody of a ballet step. One arm was flung dramatically out to her side. It was the last theatrical gesture Carlotta Devine would ever make.

Kneeling by her feet, Andrea rocked back and forth, keening in a heart-wrenching soprano.

"Get back, all of you," shouted Lindy. There was movement to her right, and she started. Alice moved jerkily from behind the open door.

"I—I came in to get Carlotta's costume, and she was there—leaning over her." Alice began to whimper.

"Oh, Christ. Rebo, get them out of here."

Peter skidded through the door as the others backed away. "I was—what happened? Oh, shit."

"You'd better call nine-one-one. No, first, do you know how to find a pulse? Should we touch her?"

Peter stood mesmerized by the sight. Blood oozed out around Carlotta's head in a black Rorschach pattern.

"Peter."

He jerked convulsively, knelt down, and placed his fingers

under Carlotta's jaw. "Nothing," he said without looking up. "I'll call." He rushed out.

Lindy backed out the door and into Biddy and Jeremy. She turned to them, her lip trembling. But they were both staring at the figure on the floor.

Eleven

Jeremy was the first to recover. "Is she . . . ?"

Lindy nodded.

"What happened?"

She shrugged. Her voice seemed to be buried under piles of rubble.

Jeremy turned to Biddy. "Call the company together. Quick."

Biddy turned away, then turned back and looked at Jeremy as if seeing him for the first time.

"Move." She hurried away.

"Someone's called the police?"

"Peter." Lindy mouthed the word. She noticed the sheen of perspiration on Jeremy's forehead. It had sprung out suddenly, the only evidence that he was upset. She wondered for a second if he was going to be sick. She certainly felt sick, and she couldn't gather her thoughts. They were floating around the top of her head, but she couldn't catch them.

He didn't say anything else, nor did he move toward the body. He took Lindy by the elbow, pulled her out of the dressing room, and shut the door.

"Don't fall apart on me now." She saw his mouth moving, but the words sounded far away. His hand enclosed her jaw in a viselike grip, and he turned her face toward his. "Lindy, for Christ's sake."

She snapped out of her shock. "Right." She followed him to the huddle of dancers waiting near the prop table. They were all there. Some were crying; some had their arms around each other. Peter was standing like a sentinel between Alice and Andrea, who were sitting on two folding chairs.

Jeremy spoke. His voice pierced through the charged atmosphere. "Listen, and get this right. The police will be here soon. They'll probably ask all of us a lot of questions. If you know something, tell them. Do not embellish, do not guess, do not try to impress them and, above all"—he looked directly at Rebo—"do not give them attitude."

His eyes roved the faces that looked out from the shadows. His voice softened. "We all like to tell a good story. That's what makes us artists. But do not try to be entertaining. Just answer their questions, don't add anything.

"Now go to your dressing rooms. Don't talk. Don't try to guess what happened. Keep your minds blank." The sound of sirens rose in pitch as the police cars pulled into the parking lot, then warbled down to silence, punctuated by the slamming of car doors.

Jeremy walked over to Andrea, who was rising slowly out of her chair, and knelt beside her. "They will want to talk to you and Alice. Try to be clear and only tell the facts."

"I know, Peter already told me."

Jeremy shot Peter a questioning look.

Peter turned away.

Three uniformed policemen came through the stage door followed by EMTs rolling a stretcher.

"In there." Jeremy pointed into the hall toward the closed door of Carlotta's dressing room.

The older of the policemen nodded and motioned to one of the EMTs, who followed him toward the door of Carlotta's dressing room. The officer's squat frame progressed like a bulldozer. His flesh bulged over the collar of his police jacket.

The two accompanying officers stood aside as they passed. They were both young and seemed nervous.

One pulled out a notebook and crossed to Jeremy. "You're?"

"Jeremy Ash, the director of the company." The young man nodded solemnly. "If you could just tell everyone to stay put, our chief is on the way. He was off duty," he added by way of explanation.

Jeremy nodded.

The chief of police arrived minutes later. He was dressed in jeans and a plaid woolen jacket; the smell of cigar smoke wafted around him. He was accompanied by a taller man, also in jeans, who surveyed the area and moved casually off to the side.

"Chief O'Dell," said the young cop who had spoken to Jeremy. "Williams is in there with the rescue squad."

O'Dell nodded and walked toward the dressing room. His companion stayed behind.

"Hey, Bill, is that you?" asked the younger cop, suddenly aware of the other man's presence.

"Hi, Rory. Yeah, it's me. What do you have here?"

"Don't know yet." He shrugged. "We haven't talked to anybody. We were waiting for Chief O'Dell. What are you doing back on home turf?"

"Playing poker with my brother-in-law until a few minutes ago. I wanted to get away from urban crime for a few days. I hope this isn't going to be a busman's holiday."

Lindy's dulled senses snapped to attention at the words. She had been standing out of the way, watching the activity of the police with a detached calm. Now she looked at the man who was talking. He was big: big-boned and angular. He towered over the curly-headed Rory. His voice was low but resonated across the air so that his words were clearly audible to Lindy where she stood in the shadows several yards away. His seeming nonchalance was a stark contrast to the bustling activity around him, but it didn't have a calming effect. Lindy's teeth started chattering. He emitted an air of urbanity in spite of the jeans and worn leather hunting jacket he was wearing. There was something in his manner that unnerved Lindy. She took several deep breaths and yanked her gaze back to the other officer.

O'Dell stuck his head out of the door. "Bill, do you mind coming in here for a minute?"

Bill shoved his hands into his pockets and moved laconically toward the dressing-room door. He was interrupted by the entrance of a cadre of campus policemen, who crowded through the door and looked expectantly into the room.

"Oh, Christ." O'Dell nodded to Rory, who moved to stop the newly arrived group. "I need a goddamned circus."

He lowered his voice as Bill reached him. "Hartford is sending us a Scene of Crime Unit, but it'll be a while. Would you mind taking a look?"

Crime? thought Lindy. Of course. Carlotta could hardly have bashed in her own head. She hadn't seen a wound, but the amount of blood around Carlotta's head couldn't have come from a fall.

O'Dell called over to the other officer, who seemed to be trying to melt into the shadows as Lindy had been doing. "Joe, you and Rory start some interviews. And make sure no one leaves." He looked around. "Hey, you, there."

Lindy jumped.

"Who are you?"

"Lindy Graham, uh, Haggerty." Lindy was suddenly aware that she was the only person who had not fled to a dressing room. There was no sign of Biddy or Jeremy. She was completely alone. "I'm the rehearsal director."

O'Dell looked at Bill.

"Like a unit leader."

"Oh." He looked back at Lindy. "Well, Ms. Haggerty. How many people are still on the premises?"

"Sixteen dancers," she began, "if you don't count Carlotta." She motioned to the door behind him. "And the crew and—about thirty people, maybe more in the front."

"Oh, shit." O'Dell rolled his eyes heavenward.

Bill laughed. It changed into a cough when O'Dell shot him a glaring look.

"Williams, get out here. It's going to be one hell of a long night."

O'Dell and Bill replaced Williams and the EMTs in Carlotta's dressing room and closed the door. Several more uniformed men had arrived and were talking to Rory. They dispersed, and Rory knocked on the door to Jeremy's office.

"Sir, would you ask everyone to come out here?"

Jeremy began tapping lightly on each door. Two of the new policemen went to the prop room and herded out the crew, Peter and Alice among them.

Williams faced the group that was now crowded into

the backstage area. He unbuttoned his jacket. "Maybe you should all sit out in the auditorium. We'll need to talk to everyone present. It may take awhile; there are so many of you."

Lindy followed the others through the side door and out to the house seats. Williams came out onto the stage and explained briefly about the procedure of getting statements from everyone. He looked self-conscious, like an understudy who hadn't had time to memorize his lines.

The houselights were on. The light was harsh. Most of the dancers had not had time to remove their makeup, and their faces stood out in garish, Fellini-like masks.

There is nothing less glamorous than a fully lit theater, thought Lindy. And then it hit her. Carlotta was dead. The rescue squad hadn't even tried to resuscitate her or rush her to the hospital. Could we have brought her back to life, if we had tried? Were we guilty of not trying? She jerked out of her seat when she heard her name called, and a uniformed man beckoned to her to follow him.

She was led through the backstage to a room near the prop room. It was a large dressing room used for the chorus of large-scale productions. The company hadn't needed it, since they were a small group, and it had been locked since their arrival.

Now, Detective Williams sat at a wobbly card table in the middle of the room. His jacket lay on one of the benches that ran the length of the makeup tables. Standing next to him was a tall, spindly policewoman. Her uniform seemed pinned to her shoulders and dropped straight to the floor without a curve. Lindy inanely recited "Jack sprat could eat no fat" as she tried to calm the bats in her stomach.

Williams motioned her to the chair that faced him across the table. "Ms. Haggerty?"

"Graham." She sat down. "I use Graham for the stage," she added. It was a stupid thing to say. Williams raised his eyebrows. They were very bushy, but short, barely extending to the ends of his eyes. "My married name is Haggerty, but I go by Graham here. It's my professional name." She should cram a fist into her mouth before she made herself sound more ridiculous.

Williams nodded his head gravely and said, "Yes, I see." He asked her about the position she held with the company, some background information, and about the events of that night.

She told him about the scream, finding the body, calling the police. She willed herself not to elaborate. She gave the bare facts as she knew them. She recited them dully, as unemotionally as she could. Surely, they didn't think anyone had deliberately hurt Carlotta. It must have been an accident.

He was asking about doors. She dragged her attention back to what he was saying. "Excuse me?"

Yes, the stage door had been propped open. Yes, anyone could have come in. But that didn't usually happen. Security? Alice always collected everyone's valuables and locked them in a theater case in the costume room. The door to the hallway? Yes, it was unlocked so the directors could come and go. Sometimes, friends or fans came backstage. Did she see anyone come back that night? No, she hadn't noticed. Peter usually kept the area free of unnecessary visitors.

"Did anything unusual occur backstage tonight?" The

question jarred her from her rote responses. Clammy fingers seemed to creep around her neck.

"No, I didn't see anyone that shouldn't have been there. Why?"

Williams shifted in his seat. The policewoman shifted her weight to her other foot. Her limp uniform shifted to her other side.

"Among the company members."

"Oh."

"Was there?"

What should she say? How could she make this man understand that what had happened at intermission was not that unusual.

"When?" she stalled.

Williams leaned forward in his seat. "Was there not an altercation between Ms.—" He glanced down at his notes. "Ms. Devine and some of the company members?"

"Oh, that. It was just Carlotta having one of her attacks. She does that sometimes."

"Attacks?" He raised his eyes to hers, his pencil poised above his writing pad.

"Diva attacks. She likes—" Lindy took a strangled breath. Carlotta was dead. "Or rather, liked to throw her weight around. Just emotional outbursts. She did it all the time." She knew she was beginning to babble. She bit the inside of her cheek to stop herself. She concentrated on the sweet taste of her own blood. It helped her to concentrate. She told him about Carlotta stabbing at Eric with the candelabra.

"It's a prop in one of the dances, but Peter took it away from her." Carlotta had gone back to her dressing room.

They had gotten ready for the next piece. No, she didn't notice Carlotta leave. The door of her dressing room was closed. She hadn't seen her again until they heard the scream and found her on the floor of her dressing room.

She felt herself trembling. Delayed shock, said part of her brain. Carlotta dead. Lying on the cold, hard cement, stretched out in that ridiculous pose.

The policewoman handed her a tissue. Lindy put it to her face and bit harder into her cheek. Don't fall apart on me now.

"Do you know of anyone who would want to harm Ms. Devine?"

He looked directly at her face, trying to read the answer. Well, she didn't have one.

She steeled herself and returned his look. "She wasn't nice. No one liked her. But she was a common type in the theater; we were used to her."

Williams stood up. "Thank you, Ms. Graham."

"Am I free to go?" She sounded just like some suspect on one of Glen's cop shows. She wished now that she had paid more attention.

"Yes, but we'll need you to come down to the station tomorrow and sign your statement."

Lindy nodded and walked on wobbling knees to the door. She reached for the knob and turned it. "It was an accident, wasn't it? I mean, you don't think that . . ." She didn't finish the question. The two police officers were bent over the papers on the table. They didn't look up, and she closed the door behind her.

Joe was waiting outside the door to accompany her back to the auditorium. Several more uniformed men and women had arrived and were now moving methodically about the hallway. A yellow tape cordoned off Carlotta's dressing room and the surrounding area. They skirted the edge of the tape and returned backstage.

The man whom she had seen entering with Chief O'Dell was leaning against the light board, apparently comfortable to wait and watch. One leg was crossed over the other, and his arms were folded across his chest. He looked like a mummy from the set of *Aida*.

Lindy walked slowly forward. He watched her openly, a slight smile on his lips. "Kurt Weill comes to Connecticut," he said softly as she passed him. She didn't look at him; his words had chilled her very soul.

Lindy spent the next hour shuttling dancers back to the hotel. Jeremy stayed on until everyone had finished being interviewed and returned on the bus. When she finally staggered out of the elevator to the third floor, she found Biddy leaning over her dance bag, her cast balanced out to the side as she rummaged inside the bag. Papers and unidentifiable pieces of clothing were dumped haphazardly about the floor.

"Biddy, what are you doing?"

Biddy looked up from her bag. Her face was red from leaning over. "I still can't find the darn key. I always put it in the side pocket, but with all the distractions, I just can't find it."

"I bet someone returned it to the front desk." Lindy raised her eyebrows and handed Biddy her own key.

"Jack." Biddy pushed a wild mop of curls out of her face,

took the key, and turned the lock. Lindy gathered up the mess, tossing everything indiscriminately back into Biddy's bag and took it inside.

Biddy stood hunched over her crutches, staring into the minibar. "What's the strongest liquor in here, do you think?"

Lindy sank into one of the chairs at the table and dropped her bag to the floor. "Beats me. Brandy, I suppose, for shock. They're always giving ladies a nip of brandy in Victorian novels. Even though alcohol is a depressant not a stimulant. I had forgotten how much we drink on tour. It will make me fat."

"How can you think about your weight when Carlotta has been murdered?" snapped Biddy. "Oh, I'm sorry. I didn't mean to yell at you. I'm just so, it's just so, oh, dear."

"We don't know she was murdered."

"Juan saw them putting one of the candelabras in a box when he was going for his interview."

"What?"

"Juan saw the police . . ."

"I heard you. Maybe he was mistaken. Everyone's nerves are pretty strung out."

Biddy shook her head slowly. "They think Carlotta was murdered. That one of us did it."

"That's ridiculous," said Lindy, pushing her own conclusions aside. "People don't get killed with stage props. The candelabras are heavy; they might give someone a concussion, but you couldn't bash somebody's head in with one of them."

Biddy's face turned a sickly shade of gray.

"How about that brandy?" Lindy asked.

There was a light tap at the door. "Now what?" Lindy rose wearily from her seat and opened the door. Rebo, Eric, Juan and two corps boys named Richard and John were crowded around the opening. "We be bad," said Rebo, with his head lowered penitently.

"Is this your idea of comedy relief?"

"Shit, no, we're in deep shit." His eyes flashed at her.

"Then you had better come in." Lindy opened the door wider, and the men filed inside forming a perfect semicircle in front of her.

"For crying out loud, sit down and tell me what this is about." She paused, a sickening feeling rising in her stomach. "You didn't kill her, did you?"

"Lindy," gasped Biddy. John and Richard dropped onto the bed. Juan, Eric, and Rebo began a chorus of denials.

"Okay, just one of you talk." Lindy's own nerves were painfully near overload. She slowed her breathing, willed her heart rate to lower, closed her eyes, then opened them.

Rebo began talking. "We played the tricks on Carlotta." He looked around at his comrades. There was no hint of his jive accent when he spoke again. "It was my idea. You know, a bit of humor to take the edge off the bitch. But we didn't hurt her."

"The candelabra?"

"I stuck it outside her door. So when she opened it, she'd see it."

Lindy shrugged, not understanding.

"There was a note." Rebo wiped his face, his strong fingers spreading across his features. "It said . . ." He seemed genuinely embarrassed. "It said, 'If you can't stick it to us, use it on yourself.' " His voice cracked on the last word.

"That's disgusting," blurted out Biddy.

"*She* was disgusting. We tried to get it back before the police came, but Jeremy had shut the door, and it wasn't outside. The note wasn't there, either. Then Juan saw them bring it out of her room. Someone must have used it to kill her, and my fingerprints are going to be all over it."

"Our prints will be all over that room. We were always doing stuff in there," said Juan. He was visibly shaking.

"Did you tell this to the police?"

They shook their heads in perfect unison.

"Well, I think we had better. The police are smart, I think. They'll understand."

"Are you sure?" The question came from John. He looked so young and innocent, Lindy wanted to pat his head.

"Pretty sure. But regardless, you have to tell them before they ask you. It will save them a lot of trouble, and I'm sure they'll appreciate it in the long run."

"They're gonna crucify my ass," said Rebo.

"Why?"

Rebo looked at her incredulously. "Black and gay? The note? I'm dead."

"The cops are not all thick-necked racists, Rebo. They are concerned with finding the truth."

"Shit, Lindy, what movies have you been watching?" He had a point. She only knew about policemen from books, television, and the occasional precinct scandal reported in the newspaper. But wasn't there always at least one good guy on the force who fought for truth and justice? If there was, she would find him and badger him into doing the right thing.

"Guys, there is nothing we can do tonight. Just go to bed.

I don't know what's going to happen tomorrow, but the first thing we're going to do is tell all. Jeremy, Biddy, and I will go with you." They stood up and clustered around her. She found herself in the middle of a group hug, silent, slightly swaying, comforting one another.

The telephone rang. The group broke up. "Okay, guys, outta here." Lindy walked around the bed to answer the phone. "Pour those brandies will you, Biddy?"

"It's Jeremy, are you asleep?"

"Hardly. Are you back at the hotel? What happened after I left? What did they say?"

Lindy heard him release a heavy sigh. "I'm at the hotel. I hope they finish looking for whatever they're looking for before tomorrow's performance. If not, we'll have to open one of the chorus rooms and camp out until the week is over. I'll try to get rehearsal space at the campus for tomorrow. It's probably best to keep the kids busy. They asked a lot of questions and were still working when I came home on the bus. Oh, God, Lindy, she would have been out of here tomorrow. I shouldn't have waited."

"Did you call Jack?"

"I just tried. His machine was on. I left a message for him to call me. Oh, Christ." There was a long silence. "You and Biddy had better get some sleep. We'll need to meet pretty early tomorrow and get organized."

"There's just one more thing, Jeremy." She told him about the visit from Rebo and the boys, and what they had confessed.

"Damn, damn. I should have stopped them. I knew who was doing it, but quite frankly, I was enjoying it."

"Give yourself a break, Jeremy. You're responsible for running a company, not being mother, father, and nasty nanny to your employees. They're adults, every one of them." She took the glass of brandy that Biddy was holding out to her. "We'll see this through. You get some sleep, too."

Twelve

A chorus of uniform-clad policemen moved across the stage and climbed up the cage, carrying candelabras. The stage lights changed colors at an alarming rate: blues, reds, ambers succeeding each other with dizzying speed. The uniforms turned as a group and marched forward. Keep your lines, you're out of line, she yelled, but they kept coming, replicating themselves as the music crescendoed. It was deafening. Lindy clasped her hands over her ears and woke up.

She lay in the dark, heart pounding, breath labored, stuck in the abyss of interrupted sleep. The numbers of the clock on the bedside table glowed 3:22 A.M. She sat up, drawing her knees to her chest. Carlotta was dead. That was it. It came back to her with horrible clarity—the body, the questions, the boys' confession.

She pulled her body out of bed and crossed to the window. The parking lot below was quiet. Evenly spaced lampposts cast dim cones of light onto the parked cars that formed a perfect line around the perimeter of asphalt. When the sun rose, people would get into those cars and drive away, going on about their lives, carrying their own set of tragedies and disappointments with them.

A black car pulled slowly out of the lot. He was getting

an early start. Probably anxious to get on with his vacation or back to his wife and children. Lindy envied him; she wished she were on her way home. Or did she? Glen would be working. Cliff and Annie wouldn't be there. They didn't even know she had gone back to work. In her excitement, she had forgotten to call them.

Lindy pressed her forehead against the window and watched the blinking turn signal of the car as it turned into the street. Cliff and Annie had their own lives now. Even the weekly phone calls had gotten further apart. If this was the empty-nest syndrome, she thought, why am I the one who feels left out on a limb?

No, it was better that she was here and working, even with a murder, than rambling around an empty house waiting for the next adventure. This *was* the next adventure. She'd call the kids tomorrow. She wouldn't mention the murder. The car disappeared around the corner of the hotel, and Lindy turned from the window.

She had to get some sleep. Keeping order would be up to her tomorrow. Don't fall apart on me now, she whispered. She crawled back into bed and pulled the covers over her head. The next thing she was aware of was daylight.

The bedspread had fallen to the floor. Biddy was tiptoeing around the room, and the smell of coffee wafted from a trolley, which stood in the middle of the room.

"Breakfast," said Biddy, her voice barely above a whisper.

Lindy blinked at her. Whoever said that things always looked brighter in the morning was right about the first thirty seconds. It took about that long for Lindy to remember what had happened the night before. She didn't feel better at all.

She threw her feet onto the floor and took the cup of

coffee Biddy handed her. Neither of them spoke. It was an awkward silence, but neither of them was ready to face what had to be faced.

Biddy walked back to the trolley, added sugar to her coffee, took a sip, and put the cup down. She turned to face Lindy. "Who did it?" Her voice held an accusing note.

"Well, I didn't."

"Don't be ridiculous. I know you didn't, but who do you think could have? Was it one of us? Maybe somebody sneaked in."

"I think that's probably what happened." Lindy didn't believe that, but she wasn't ready to contemplate the alternatives. She also felt uncomfortable talking to Biddy. She had a comfy suburban safety net to run home to. She had Glen. She would have lots of activities to keep her mind off what had happened. Biddy only had this life, these people. If one of them turned out to be a murderer, Biddy's life would never be the same. There was a good chance the company would fold, even if Jeremy or Jack weren't involved. The publicity alone could finish them. Lesser scandals had destroyed companies before.

"Biddy, I won't desert you." She blurted it out.

"No matter what?"

Lindy looked at her cautiously. "No matter what."

"Do you think it's too early to call Jeremy?"

Lindy shook her head. Biddy dialed his extension. The conversation lasted only a few seconds.

"He's coming over. The police want to talk to us again."

"All of us?"

"Just the three of us, and Peter, and Jack when he gets back, for now anyway. What are we going to tell them?"

"Whatever they want to know. First, about the boys and their tricks. And then . . ." Lindy shrugged.

"Not about what we found in Jack's briefcase," Biddy pleaded. "Don't even tell Jeremy. It might not have anything to do with Carlotta, but they would think the worst. Please, Lindy."

"They'll probably find out in the course of their investigation."

"Please."

"Okay, we'll wait for a while. Maybe Jack will have an explanation, though it seems pretty incriminating."

"It couldn't have been Jack. He wasn't even here. And not Jeremy, or Peter, or you, or me."

"Well, at least not you or me. Even if you had tried to brain her with your cast, I doubt if you could have kicked that high." Lindy sighed. "I guess that means I'll miss my morning *barre*. Let me get dressed before Jeremy gets here."

Jeremy was sitting at the table when she came out of the shower. He was drinking coffee out of a glass.

"Sorry," she said, grabbing clothes out of the dresser drawer and dropping the towel she had wrapped around her to the floor. "I meant to hurry, but I guess I went into a trance in the shower."

"It's okay, take your time."

She threw on jeans and a sweatshirt and sat down. Her jeans felt a lot looser. "So now what? How many cups of coffee have you had?"

"A few. Do I seem a little hyper? I've been waiting for someone to wake up."

"You could have called us," said Biddy.

"I know, thanks. Chief O'Dell called. He has some more questions, though I can't imagine what more we can add."

Biddy gave Lindy a warning look.

"Where does he want us?" asked Lindy.

"Down at the station. I told him we'd come this morning, get it over with. I may sound callous, but my main concern is getting on with this tour, keeping everybody on an even keel."

It was an unceremonious morning. The station was located in the middle of the historic downtown, but it was a new brick building, one story with a flat roof. It looked pitifully small and mundane to Lindy. Of course, her knowledge of police stations came only from mysteries and television; both sources seemed terribly inaccurate.

They were interviewed separately. Lindy told about the boys' pranks, speaking the words into a tape recorder. While they were waiting to sign the typed statements, they compared notes, except Peter, who sat glumly in one of the metal and plastic chairs, a conspicuous distance away from the others.

It had taken two hours, but now they were driving back to the hotel. They had all lapsed into silence. Lindy considered turning on the radio, but decided it would be in poor taste. Instead, she began humming a Noël Coward tune under her breath, "Why must the show go on?"

"Oh, no, the dress."

Lindy slammed on the brakes, pulled the car to the curb, and turned to look at Biddy. Peter and Jeremy were staring at her, too.

"We don't have a dress for Andrea. The police have Carlotta's, and there isn't an extra one."

Lindy sighed deeply. "You just about scared me to death. We'll get Andrea something to wear."

She maneuvered the car back into traffic. Leave it to Biddy to be thinking about a costume at a time like this. Even distracted by murder, she was the consummate professional. The show must go on. Chief O'Dell had given them clearance to use the stage, though they wouldn't be able to use the downstairs dressing rooms. In lieu of the radio, Lindy began to hum again.

"Alice brought the extra fabric. I'll see if she can pull something together," said Peter. "She's probably already at the theater. Very efficient, that one."

It was the first time he had spoken to them that morning. After a curt "hello" when he met them at the car to go to the police station, he had maintained a preoccupied silence. When he hadn't offered information about his interview, no one had pressed him to talk. Lindy would have to talk to him later. She had a few questions of her own.

They dropped Biddy and Jeremy at the hotel to round up the company and bring them to the theater for rehearsal.

"It seems strange that we are being allowed back into the theater so quickly, don't you think?" she asked Peter as the two of them drove toward the theater.

Peter was staring out the passenger window. "Probably finished doing whatever it is they do."

"Do you think they'll let us go on to Hartford on Sunday?"

"No idea. I've never been in this kind of situation before."

Lindy kept her eyes glued to the road ahead. "When Sandra was hurt, wasn't there an investigation?" She heard his intake of breath, but she didn't move her eyes from the white line of the highway.

"How—" He gave up. "Yeah, there was an investigation. It was ruled an accident."

"But you didn't believe that?"

"What are you getting at? You think Jeremy goes around bashing dancers on the head? That's not funny," he added in a harsh whisper.

"Jeremy?" Did Peter actually think Jeremy had killed Carlotta? "If you blame Jeremy for the accident, why did you come to work for him, Peter?"

"Leave me alone. I didn't kill the bitch."

She shouldn't have been so abrupt. It was cruel and counterproductive. She began a more circuitous line of questioning.

"Do you think Alice will be able to finish a dress for Andrea by tonight?"

"Probably. Like I said, she's efficient."

"Jeremy was lucky to get both of you."

"What's that supposed to mean?"

Lindy shrugged. "Just that Jeremy was lucky to lure Alice away from a higher-paying, secure job at the ballet."

Peter looked blank. "He didn't lure her. When I signed on, she asked me if I thought they needed a costume mistress. I said maybe, and that was it."

"Why would she want to leave her job?"

Peter rubbed the back of his neck. "I never thought about it. The costume shop was big there. She probably was stuck with menial jobs. Seniority and all that. She's duller than dishwater, but she's good with fabric. With a smaller company, she gets to be her own boss, I guess."

They arrived at the theater. Peter jumped out of the car as soon as Lindy pulled into a parking place. "I'll find Alice," he said as he slammed the door.

He had outmaneuvered her. She had gotten off on a tangent about Alice and hadn't learned anything that would help her find out who was stealing from the company, or why Peter hadn't returned the invoice to Jack's briefcase. She slammed the door of the Volvo and followed him across the parking lot.

Peter was banging on the stage door when Lindy caught up with him. After several minutes, the door was opened by a policeman, who asked their names before he allowed them to enter.

Lindy stopped just inside the door. She was not prepared for the scene inside the theater. Yellow tape had been drawn over every door. It closed off the entrance to the hallway where all the first-floor dressing rooms were located. It was blocking the door to the prop room, the costume room, and the shop.

Peter strode over to the door of the shop. He was stopped by a policeman, whose frame barred the way in.

"What's going on?" asked Lindy, coming up behind Peter.

"They won't let me in. How am I supposed to set up for rehearsal when I have no access to the sets or props?" Peter threw his hands in the air.

"Sorry, ma'am, but we're still working in certain areas. As soon as we're finished, you'll be able to get back in." The officer looked at Peter. "The sooner you accept that, sir, the sooner I can get this area cleared. And you can thank the president of the university for even letting you continue with the show. It makes our work that much harder."

Peter growled and turned away.

They found Alice at a portable sewing machine set up in the chorus room, which had been used for the interviews the night before. Pieces of chiffon and gold lamé were draped over the benches and the back of the chair she was sitting on.

Alice looked up when they entered and smiled vaguely. "I'm working on a costume for Andrea. I realized that we might not get the, um, other one back, so I decided . . ." Her voice trailed off. "But they wouldn't let me in. That means dirty socks for tonight, I guess. And every time I need a straight pin, I have to ask, and someone brings them to me. It's going to take all day. But I don't mind," she added.

Peter rolled his eyes and left.

"Thank you, Alice. I knew you would have everything under control. Good work."

"Thank you," Alice murmured, looking out the door.

The company arrived a few minutes later. They entered single file through the stage door, each giving his or her name to the policeman on duty. The dancers who had dressing rooms on the second floor climbed wordlessly up the stairs.

"Be onstage in fifteen minutes," called Jeremy. He turned to the others. "Now, to find a place for the rest of us." By doubling up in the usable rooms and commandeering the chorus room, Jeremy and Lindy settled everyone in.

"They can't get to their makeup or the costumes," said Jeremy. "I hope these people step it up."

"Why did they close off all the rooms?" asked Biddy. She looked like she might burst into tears at any minute. "It's just not fair."

"I know it's hard for you to believe, Biddy," said Jeremy. "But life is not fair."

Biddy's bottom lip quivered.

"Pull yourselves together, you two. It's going to take a lot to get through today," said Lindy.

"Sorry, Bid." Jeremy kissed the top of her head.

Dancers began to move past them on their way to the stage. Lindy followed them. Peter was at the lighting panel, throwing on the stage lights.

"I think we'll run the music through the house system today instead of using the boom box. We could use the extra energy, if you don't mind running tape for me."

Peter shrugged. "Might as well, there's nothing else for me to do."

Lindy scanned the faces of the dancers as they warmed up. There wasn't much to read in the concentrated expressions on their faces. But their body language betrayed them. Tense, morose, scared—Lindy saw it all and steeled herself for the hours to come.

"When you're ready," she said to the stage in general and walked to the front. She said a few words. The speech was not thought-out, she was just anxious to get started. Moving was the only way to dispel the gloom.

She had to stop the music three times within the first couple of minutes.

"Come on, this is pretty lame. When the curtain opens, I want to see energy, vigor. You can do it. Take your places. Lift up. Get the weight out of your butts, or you'll end up looking like suburban housewives."

They lifted up. Well, it was a start. Mieko led the girls'

dance with precision. She is unflappable, thought Lindy. We could use a few more like that.

Andrea, however, was a mess. She fell out of balances, missed her turns. She moved through the steps like a somnambulist. Lindy pulled her aside. They started again. It went a little better.

The music filled the theater, louder than usual because there were no bodies in the house to absorb the sound. That helped. The dancers were pulling themselves together, slowly.

"Hold it. Peter, run the tape back to the beginning of the *Sarabande*." She turned to the sextet. "Deep into the music, please. You're skittering along the surface of the notes. It makes your movement look superficial. Make it sensuous, draw it out. Lag slightly behind the beat." They began again.

"That's better, but there's something wrong with the spacing. Hold on a minute." Lindy jumped off the edge of the stage and jogged backward up the aisle surveying the spacing of the dancers. "Kate, pull over to the quarter mark. That's right. Try to make it there by the second phrase. Eric, does that throw your spacing off? No? Then let's try it."

The music started again.

"You're good at this, aren't you?" The voice came from behind her to the left.

Lindy looked back over her shoulder. It was the man from last night, Bill. He was stretched out comfortably in a seat a few rows behind her.

"Getting people to do what they're supposed to do, even under extreme conditions," he continued.

"The theater is one long, extreme condition," she replied. She turned away from him and walked back to the stage.

She hoisted herself up over the edge. What was he doing here?

She gave the dancers a break. She needed to move onto *Carmina*, but she dreaded it. She was sure that everyone else dreaded it, too. Just get them back on the damned horse, she told herself. The cage was released for use by the policeman in charge. Peter and one other stagehand assembled it. The other stagehands had been sent home.

Lindy looked at the dancers; nobody was moving to their places.

"Let's go," she said. They took their opening positions.

Mieko was deposited on the cage. Andrea picked her up without emotion. When Mieko's arms dropped to her side, Lindy saw her give Andrea a reassuring smile.

They managed to get through the piece. It wasn't a superb effort, but it was a hard-won attempt. Lindy dismissed them for dinner.

Bill was still sitting in the audience, slouched slightly in his seat, elbows resting on the armrests.

All right, let's just see what you want. Lindy braced herself and jumped off the edge of the stage. Hey, she thought, I can land on my feet. Not bad for being back to work for a week. She walked up the aisle, a thinner, stronger, more confident Lindy, and sat on the arm of the seat in front of him.

Bill straightened up. He didn't look like a policeman. His hair was short on the sides and in back. Brown with traces of lighter hair, gray maybe, laced through the longer hair on top, too long for a regulation haircut, surely. Did policemen still have regulation haircuts? And his face was too classically defined, and too pleasant-looking, to have spent his days with mayhem and murder. Prejudice, prejudice, thought Lindy as she perused his face. That's like saying all male dancers are raving queens; you should know better. But for so large a man, his features seemed too refined. He looked more like a director than a policeman.

He sat patiently watching her and then asked, "Are you linked up to a computer?"

She must have been staring at him longer than she realized. She felt her cheeks heat up, but knew her complexion wouldn't register the blush.

"Who are you?" she asked back.

"Bill Brandecker." He flashed her a wide smile and held out a big hand.

Lindy's hand disappeared into his. "Lindy Graham, unit leader."

Bill laughed. It was a hearty reverberation.

She waited for him to continue, but he just sat there, an expression of easy humor on his face. The kind of humor a person acquires by always standing a step away from the situation they're in, she thought.

"Are you a policeman?"

"Yes, no."

"Well, that about covers it."

He laughed again. "Yes, I'm a policeman of sorts, but no, I'm not working on this case. Not my, um, field."

Field? Didn't he mean jurisdiction? "Oh." Lindy slid off the armrest and onto the seat. "Just here for the show?"

"If you mean, do I get my kicks from watching other people's pain, the answer is no."

Now she blushed. Anger had that effect, and she was

more angry with him for turning her words around than embarrassed. She tried frantically to think of something nasty to reply, but her mind wouldn't cooperate. "Then why are you watching?"

"Because I'm here. Because Dell has been up all night trying to finish up so that the show can go on, as they say. Because I'm not burdened with finding the facts. Sometimes you learn a lot more just by watching."

Lindy felt chilled. "So you *are* working on the case."

"I'm just satisfying my curiosity. Do you mind?"

Of course she minded. It was the most heartless thing she had ever heard of. But she didn't say so. "Well, I hope we don't disappoint you," she said through clenched teeth.

That smile again. "Oh, I'm sure you won't."

Lindy gave him her best glare and left. That was a bust. In the old days she could have charmed the man into telling her whatever she wanted to know. But this guy seemed impervious to her. Maybe she wasn't in such great shape after all.

She practically crashed into Biddy, who was flying around the corner of the back hallway. Lindy caught hold of her to keep her from falling.

"Jack's back. He's really hysterical. He's going to upset everybody."

"Get everyone on the bus. I'll deal with Jack."

Lindy heard them before she saw them. They were standing in the stairwell. Jack had Jeremy backed into the wall.

"You're a Judas kiss; everything you touch, you destroy."

Jack's voice was shrill and hysterical. His face and lips were drained of color.

Lindy grabbed the man's shoulder. "For the love of God, Jack, control yourself. It isn't Jeremy's fault."

Jack looked at her, unseeing, and shook her hand away.

"It is his fault, and even you can't fix it, can she, Jeremy?" He grabbed his briefcase from the floor and rushed out the stage door.

"I guess I deserved that," said Jeremy mildly.

Lindy shook her head. How much abuse was the man willing to take? She turned away. Brandecker was standing a few feet away. His back was to them, but she recognized his silhouette. And she knew he had heard.

The performance was sold out. Jeremy had even relinquished their seats to the box office to be sold. Lindy stood next to Biddy along the half wall that separated the audience from the standing-room section. Jeremy stood on the other side of the aisle. Jack was next to him, an uneasy distance between them.

"Nothing like a little murder to fill a house."

Lindy turned slowly. "Hello, Mr. Brandecker. I didn't know you were a dance fan."

"Oh, I have all sorts of interests. Have the bosses made a truce?" he asked with a nod toward Jeremy and Jack.

"Biddy, this is Bill Brandecker, a 'sort of' policeman. This is Arabida McFee."

"A pleasure. Call me Bill."

Biddy nodded in some confusion. Bill settled himself next to Lindy. "The only thing I don't really like about live theater is that they don't sell popcorn."

"Well, at least you can get a beer at intermission."

Bill smiled his wide smile. "I'm a wine drinker myself."

Of course, you would be, thought Lindy. The man was infuriating.

"I'm always amazed at the public's thirst for blood," he continued. His voice seemed to carry to the balcony. "This crowd is particularly festive, don't you think?"

Lindy gritted her teeth. Biddy was staring at him in openmouthed disbelief.

"I bet a third of them just came out of morbid curiosity."

"You're wrong." Lindy choked on the words.

"Why else leave their cushy suburban homes, their big-screen televisions, their Surround Sound . . ."

"Oh, God, Glen. I forgot to call him, he'll be frantic." Lindy shoved her notebook at Biddy and ran backstage to the phone.

"Who's Glen?" Bill asked.

The machine picked up the first time she called. "Glen, I know you're there. Pick up, please." She hung up and called again. This time Glen answered.

"Hi, hon." The sound of sirens wailed in the background.

"Glen, I'm sorry I didn't call before, but so much has been happening."

"Hmm, yeow. Gruesome body."

"It was. It was just awful. And the police think it's murder."

"Of course they do, the guy's face was blown off."

"What?"

"Pretty graphic stuff, even for prime time."

Lindy blinked. Twice. How could he confuse a television

show with what was happening to her, here, now? "Glen, I mean here. A murder."

"I told you, you wouldn't like going back to work. Hey, do you mind calling me back when this show is over?"

"No. I don't mind." She blinked again. This time to cut off the incipient tears that stung her eyes. "I love you."

"Love you, too."

Lindy stared at the receiver. What she needed was a big hug and some sympathy. What she got was a rain check. She hung up the phone with more force than was necessary. It clattered around the hook before it finally settled down. She turned on her heel and stalked back to Biddy and Bill Brandecker at the back of the house.

Biddy handed the notebook back. "Things okay?"

Lindy nodded. If Brandecker didn't stop smiling, she was going to hit him. She could see the headlines of the local paper: BRANDECKER DECKED BY EX-DANCER. She didn't find it amusing.

The houselights dimmed, and the curtain opened to a smoke-filled stage. Bill stifled a laugh. Lindy stepped on his foot.

The phone was ringing when Biddy and Lindy opened the door to their hotel room. Lindy grabbed for it.

"Murder? What the hell are you talking about?"

"Hi, Glen." Lindy told him everything that had happened.

"You're coming home right now. Tonight."

"I can't. The police won't let anyone leave."

"Then I'm coming there."

Thank God. He really had been paying attention.

"I can't believe you got yourself into such a mess."

Lindy felt a wave of disappointment. He was coming to bail her out. And he was annoyed.

"Thanks, but I don't think that's such a good idea. One murder suspect in the family is enough."

"That's not funny, Lindy. Surely, they don't think you did it?"

"I don't think so, but you couldn't really do any good. I'll keep you posted, okay?"

"I guess. I do have a pretty important meeting tomorrow, but if you want me to come, I will."

"No, but thanks." She hung up the phone. She could handle this on her own; she was just out of practice. She had dealt with some pretty disastrous tours before. Of course, none of them had involved murder. . . .

"Is he coming?" Biddy handed her a glass of brandy.

"No." Lindy sipped at the brandy and grimaced. "At the rate things are going, maybe we should just buy a bottle of this stuff."

Biddy sat on the edge of the other bed. Their knees were almost touching. "What are we going to do?" Her face was the color of blanched almonds. Her hair stood out at bizarre angles.

"We're going to make a list. We know a lot more background than the police do at this point, and maybe we can figure out what we don't know."

"And do it before Wednesday?"

"Wednesday? Oh, Hartford. Surely, they'll let us go to Hartford. It's only an hour away. They can't expect everyone to stay neatly in place every time they have to investigate a murder."

"Even if we all had motives and opportunity?"

"Oh, Christ, Biddy, this isn't some book. Though if it were, I'd be tempted to turn to the last page and forget the suspense."

"Me too."

"I wish I had read more police procedurals, but they're just so boring. In the books I read, the police are either bumbling idiots or sophisticated, urbane gentlemen."

"Like Mr. Brandecker?"

"Hardly like Mr. Brandecker."

They moved to the table with paper and brandies before them and began to make a list of names and circumstances.

"For now, let's rule out you and me and the dancers on the second floor. That leaves the first floor. Paul."

Biddy wrote down his name. "His father was Carlotta's partner. She was mean to both of them."

Lindy frowned. "Seems pretty insubstantial, but write it down."

"Rebo?"

"Hmm, he did orchestrate those tricks, but leave a blank."

"Eric. Carlotta threatened him with the candelabra."

"Yeah, but, Biddy, the kid was petrified. I can't see him sneaking back and clubbing her with her own weapon. But write it down."

Biddy listed the others. Juan, Kate, Mieko. "Andrea? Ingenues have killed to get parts before."

"Only in the movies, but write it down."

"Jack? If he is stealing the money, and if Carlotta found out about it, then—"

"Exactly, add another column for things to investigate. For example, where is the money going? Certainly not to clothes or cars. That black Buick must be eight or ten years old. And the only wardrobe expense he has is that ridiculous boutonniere. Even out of season freesias can't be that expensive."

"I forgot, Jack was in the city that night."

The image of the parking lot appeared in Lindy's mind. A dark car, pulling out onto the street. It was a black car. She could still see it clearly in her mind.

"Maybe, write it down."

"Peter?"

Lindy considered, swirling the brandy around in the water glass. "He blames Jeremy for his sister's accident."

"What?"

"It kind of slipped out in a conversation we were having."

"But he's always nice to Jeremy. Why would he want to work for him if he hates him?"

"Exactly. And did he return the invoice to Jack's briefcase? I never got a chance to ask him. And if he didn't, why didn't he, and where is it? What if he's skimming the money and not Jack? And who broke into our room?"

"You're going too fast." Biddy was writing furiously. She stopped, pen poised in the air. "But what does all this have to do with Carlotta?"

"Beats me."

"I know, write it down."

"Alice."

Biddy shrugged. "She did leave a good job to come to work here. But I thought maybe she, well, sometimes she seems to like Peter."

"So she followed him here to be close to him? Kind of

pitiful. He hardly knows she exists. And he seems to favor Andrea."

"I think Andrea reminds him of Sandra."

"Sounds more like a soap opera than a murder."

"They do murder each other on soap operas."

"Oh, Biddy, you don't . . ."

"I spend a lot of time in hotel rooms. There's not much else to do. Usually."

"Well, your expertise may just come in handy. That leaves Jeremy."

"No, he wouldn't. I know him."

Lindy waited. Slowly Biddy wrote his name.

Gently and quietly Lindy said, "Carlotta was wrecking his company, but he was planning to fire her today."

"He was? But he didn't say anything."

"He told me not to tell anyone until he spoke to Jack. It was last night during the intermission. I overheard him talking to David Matthews. David was furious, but Jeremy had already decided before that. He would have told you, Biddy, if things hadn't happened the way they did."

"Then he would have no reason to kill her," Biddy said defensively.

"No. But I can't help thinking that it's all involved somehow. Jack comes to him and gets him to start a new company. Part of the deal must have been that he had to take Carlotta, but why?"

"He would never have agreed to that."

"But he did. Maybe not right away, but she was here. And Jeremy obviously hated her. What the hell could that relationship be? He would never have taken her for a lover, even if he weren't gay. Not his type."

Biddy blushed.

"I know, it is a disgusting thought, yuck."

"So now, what do we do?"

"Get some sleep. And tomorrow we start asking questions, subtly. And if the dance pixies stay with us, we'll be on our way to Hartford before Wednesday."

Thirteen

Lindy didn't remember dreaming. That was about the only good thing she could say for the morning. She had hoped for subliminal understanding while she slept, but she only felt confused. Maybe she should stay in bed and watch television. How bad could soap operas be? She rolled over, but years of discipline had resurfaced, and she couldn't drift back to sleep. She got up, walked over to the dresser, hoisted her right foot to the dresser top, and leaned over it, stretching. She changed feet and stretched again. Her mind began to clear.

She concentrated on *pliés*, forcing any thoughts about Carlotta's murder out of her head. Biddy groaned in her sleep. Lindy held her leg out to the side. By her last *grande battement* worry had begun to seep back into her consciousness. She picked up the phone and dialed room service, then lay down on the floor and began her sit-ups, thinking how lucky Biddy was to be able to sleep.

"Twenty-four, twenty-five, okay, that's it." She looked over to the huddle underneath the blanket. "Get up, Sleeping Beauty."

Biddy groaned. "Just a few more minutes."

"Coffee's on its way, another twenty-five sit-ups, and we're going to the mall."

"Shopping?"

"It's good therapy, remember? I think better when I'm spending money. Anyway, my clothes are getting too big."

"You can't have lost that much weight. You've only been here a week."

"If you don't have to struggle to get into your jeans, they're too big. Better a tight eight than a comfy ten."

"Oh, all right." Biddy rolled out of bed.

The mall was new, big, and surrounded by pastures. "It probably replaced some beautiful, old farmhouse," said Biddy as they drove into the parking lot.

"Or several beautiful, old farmhouses," returned Lindy. "Where shall we start? One of the big stores on the ends or the smaller ones in the middle?"

"We might as well start at one end and work our way through."

They took the escalator to the second floor of Neiman Marcus. "Head straight to the clearance rack," said Lindy.

"You still shop the clearance racks?"

"Old habits."

"But doesn't Glen make lots of money?"

"Sure, but anybody can look good in a three-hundred-dollar dress. It takes talent to find a good sale item."

"I doubt if I can even afford the sale items," said Biddy as she stopped in front of two long rows of dress racks marked "Additional 30% off."

She frowned. "The problem with shopping in big stores

is there is so much to choose from, and the clothes are so crammed into the racks that it's hard to see what's there."

"Just like the rest of our life. We've come to the right place."

"How about this?" Biddy pulled a slinky black pants suit from the tangle of clothes.

"No black pants suits and no stretch pants. I didn't wear them when I was twenty and weighed a hundred and five pounds, and I'm not going to wear them twenty-something years, and pounds, later."

"Okay, so we're at the mall, let's think."

"This isn't bad." Lindy held up a floor-length floral dress with a halter top. "It would look great on you. See if you can find it in a size six."

Biddy made a face.

"Too overstated? Maybe . . ."

"Lindy."

"Oh, all right. We have a murder. Nobody liked"—Lindy gulped—"the victim. There are plenty of motives, what about opportunity? It had to have happened sometime after Carlotta's outburst and before we heard Andrea scream. That's intermission, *Holberg*, and a few minutes of notes—less than an hour. I'll stay backstage after the intermission tonight and see who is where."

"That's a good idea, but what if it was an outsider?"

Lindy heaved a section of clothes backward to make more space and started searching through them. "Biddy, I think you had better give up on the outsider theory. I hope the police do catch some psychotic diva-hater that was seen lurking around the theater on Thursday night, but until then, we had better start piecing some ideas together. I don't like it any better than you do, but consider. If we tell the police about the missing money, they're going to blame Jack or Peter. If we tell them about Sandra's accident—well, you get the point, right?"

"I get the point."

"So concentrate on shopping; it will clear our heads."

They carried armloads of clothes into the fitting rooms. "So when we get back today, we'll start conducting our own interviews," Lindy said through the slats of the dressing cubicle's door. She stepped outside. "How's this?"

Biddy stuck her head out of the swinging door. "Too matronly."

"I thought so. What have you got on?"

Biddy stepped out into the aisle wearing a silk striped miniskirt with bolero jacket.

"Not bad, except for the cast. When does it come off?"

"Soon, I hope. I've got an appointment with the sports doctor after Hartford, if there is a Hartford," she added under her breath.

"Buy it. You can wear it opening night at the Joyce." If there is an opening night, she thought.

"Don't you think it's a bit . . . ?"

"Exactly, buy it."

They returned to their respective cubicles and came out in new outfits.

"Wow. That's perfect," said Biddy.

"And a size eight with plenty of room, almost." Lindy tugged at the waist and twirled around. Shots of silver thread sparkled against the muted patterns of gray and pink. The dress was cut high across the neck and plunged to the waist in back where the bias-cut skirt cascaded to the knee. "And I can even wear my new stilettos."

"Better you than me."

"Well, at least there's one advantage to breaking your leg."

They made their purchases; Lindy threw two pairs of size-eight jeans on the counter.

"Don't you want to try them on?" asked the silver-haired clerk.

"They will fit," said Lindy. "I will them to fit."

Biddy giggled. Some of the color had returned to her cheeks.

They stopped on the first floor, browsing at the jewelry counter. "So are you going to save the dress to wear for Glen or maybe wear it for a certain good-looking police person?" asked Biddy as she slowly turned a display case.

Lindy ran her fingers over a pair of dangling earrings, working at keeping the corners of her mouth from turning up. A vision of her wowing Bill Brandecker rose up in her mind. Maybe a new conquest was just what she needed; maybe Glen could use a little competition.

The thought of Glen brought her back to earth with a thud. There was no way she was going to screw up the last twenty years for a temporary fling, no matter how enticing. "Certainly not. I'm a happily married suburban housewife." She plucked the earrings from the rack, giving play to the last of a fantasy that would never be acted on. "I think these earrings are perfect." She bought them. "There goes a week's salary. I can't afford to work."

Biddy's face clouded over. "Speaking of salaries."

"Okay, forget shopping; let's get to the theater. I'll try to pump info out of Peter, and maybe talk to Alice. You take Paul and the boys."

The stage door was still locked. Once they were let inside, they separated. Lindy found Alice folding laundry in the costume room.

"They finally let me back in," she said without looking up.

"Maybe they're going to finish up today," said Lindy. "There seem to be more uniforms but less tape."

"Do you think so?" It was the most animation Lindy could remember seeing from Alice. She sat down on a trunk.

"It must be pretty hard working like this."

No response from Alice.

"Having to make a new dress on such short notice. I wonder why they didn't have an extra one made up already."

"They ran over budget, I think. Anyway, I just added some lamé to the inside of Andrea's robe. There wasn't enough fabric to make a new one. And I constructed a pattern for the dress from one of the corps dresses and adapted it."

"Carlotta must have been hard to work with."

Alice's mouth tightened at one corner. "I didn't mind her."

"She could be really nasty, though."

"She didn't bother me much. Saved it for the others, I guess."

Lindy settled in for the long haul. She watched Alice's face. "She really put it to Andrea, didn't she?"

"She was jealous," Alice said, lowering her eyes to the socks she was holding. She began folding them into a ball, tossed them into a basket, and retrieved two more. "Andrea is pretty and talented, but Carlotta was stupid. The way she treated her only made Andrea seem even better."

That was certainly true. Just about everyone had been ready to throw down the gauntlet for the young ingenue. And pretty astute of Alice to be aware of it. She was always in and out of dressing rooms, backstage, collecting costumes—always around, never noticed. What else could she have observed? At this rate, it would take Lindy all day to get information from the stolid costume mistress.

Lindy leaned back on her hands and tried to look relaxed. "She sure had Jack on a nose ring."

Alice threw another ball of socks into the basket, then her face lightened. "She was horrible to him. The things she called him . . ."

"In front of you?"

Alice nodded. "I didn't mind."

Lindy held her breath. How could the girl be so damned complacent? She willed Alice to keep talking.

"She was always threatening him. 'You'll never get rid of me.' Stuff like that. I mean, if somebody wanted to kill her . . ." She left the rest unsaid but gave Lindy a meaningful look. It was the first time she had made prolonged eye contact with Lindy. It was unsettling. Alice dropped her focus back to the laundry basket. "But then, when I came in and saw Andrea leaning over the body—well, like, that makes sense, too."

"You think Andrea might have killed her?" Lindy asked incredulously.

"Well, I hate to think—you know, but she could be pretty

high-strung, and that's what the police think, isn't it? That it's the person who discovers the body, like?"

God, the whole world was watching prime-time cop shows, thought Lindy, and Alice works nights.

"I have no idea. Well, I better get to work." Lindy walked out of the room, her head spinning. Too many suspects, too many motives, too complicated for me, she thought despondently. I hope the police are better at this than we are.

She ran into Peter in the hallway. He was wiping his hands on a paper towel and looking murderous. His eyes narrowed when he saw her. He twisted the paper in his hands until it was a tight roll and tossed it toward the trash can. It hit the rim and bounced onto the floor. "Now they're fingerprinting everybody in the chorus room. Better get it done."

He walked past her, shoulders rigid, and Lindy felt a lurch of compassion. Stop it, she thought. No favorites, keep your mind objective. She entered the room. Rory looked up from his clipboard and motioned her to a table covered with cards, ink pads, and metal boxes.

Lindy remembered taking Cliff and Annie to the local police station to get their prints taken as part of a Protect Our Children Campaign. She missed them terribly. Annie had cried when they took her fingerprints. She was only seven, and she was afraid the ink wouldn't come off. She didn't want her friends to see her black fingers when she played her cello in the school orchestra.

Glen had laughed and gone to wait in the car, but Cliff had wiped each finger until the ink faded to gray, then took her into the men's room. While Lindy stood guard at the door, Cliff scrubbed Annie's hands until they glowed pink.

Rory rolled the tips of her fingers across the ink pad, pressing each one into the appropriate box on a piece of white cardboard. Ten boxes, ten fingers.

The procedure didn't take long, but her hands were shaking the whole time. She felt guilty. Did she look guilty? And what about the others?

She tossed her paper towel in the garbage and finished wiping her fingers on her jeans. Peter wasn't in the shop or the costume room. She found him in the small storage room at the end of the hall. The room was about ten feet square, dim, and smelling of dust and machine oil. Two walls were covered by rusty metal shelves that held wooden crates of hand props. Each box was labeled in broad black letters: LANTERNS, REVOLVERS, FANS, CANES. A row of stage rifles lined a cabinet on the opposite wall.

Lindy cleared her throat. Peter whirled around at the sound, and she yelped in surprise. He was holding a long military sword; the tip was pointed at Lindy's solar plexus.

"Planning a duel? I think one of the guns would be more effective." She pulled the crate of revolvers out a few inches and looked inside. "Colt forty-five? No, you don't have a ten-gallon hat. Derringer? Only for saloon girls. What's this?" She held up a snub-nosed pistol with a pearl handle.

"Beats me; props aren't my expertise."

"Maybe the sword would be better. More romantic. The sound of metal clanging in the ears of some fair damsel as her lovers fight to the death."

Peter shook his head and slid the sword back onto the shelf. He smiled faintly. "Sometimes, Lindy, you are so . . . so absolutely . . ."

"I know, that's what they all say," she said lightly.

"Have a seat? I know you're going to badger me until you get your way, and I'm getting tired of trying to avoid you." He upturned two truncated stools, the kind used by milkmaids, and they sat down. Peter's knees stuck up by his ears; he stretched his feet out in front of him. "I like this room. Cozy, in its own way, surrounded by the spirits of past plays. I find it comforting."

"Let's cut to the chase, shall we? Who do you think murdered Carlotta?"

Peter's eyes widened, the brown irises dark and arresting and deep. A woman could get lost in those eyes, thought Lindy.

"Not Andrea."

"But who?"

"Jack or Jeremy. My bet is Jeremy. It wouldn't be the first time he had—" He stopped. Lindy watched his Adam's apple twitch spasmodically.

"I know this is hard for you, but you have to help me with some background. Why do you blame Jeremy? Sandra's fall was an accident."

"That's what they finally said. But they suspected him at first. She had to have hit the radiator with such force, somebody must have pushed her or thrown her, but they couldn't prove it, or they didn't try." Peter dropped his head into his hands. His long, pale fingers made tracks through the black strands of his hair.

"But why would he want to hurt her?"

Peter looked up, templing his hands in front of his lips like a child praying. "I don't know. I was on tour in Europe when it happened. He always seemed to adore her. But then she fell in love. She wrote me that she wanted to get married.

Maybe he didn't want to lose his best dancer. She was good, not just a technician. She had such energy, such joy. By the time I got back she was—it was—damn it, Lindy, don't make me do this."

"All right." She dropped to her knees and pulled his hands from his face. "Why didn't you return the invoice to Jack's briefcase?"

"How did you know that?"

"Someone searched our room."

"When?"

"The night after we rifled Jack's briefcase. Wednesday, I think."

Peter stood up and pulled Lindy to her feet. "You and Biddy, be careful. Did you tell the police?" His thumbs were digging into her upper arms.

Lindy hesitated only for a moment. "No, Biddy made me promise not to. She's trying to save this company, but it's just a matter of time. Peter, why didn't you return the invoice?" Gooseflesh had broken out on her arms, and her scalp was charged with fiery fingers of electricity.

"Because I wanted to make sure. Check with Atlantic."

"And did you?"

"Yeah, the company pulled the order during the last tour. Told them that *Carmina* had been postponed, and they wouldn't need the structure. Atlantic returned the specs and took the normal cancellation percentage. Just a few hundred dollars, nothing compared to what Jack or Jeremy made on the deal with Barton. I called them, too. They're a body shop."

"You mean for cars?"

"Exactly. They barely spoke English, and when I mentioned Jack's name, they forgot what little they knew." He seemed to have forgotten that he was holding Lindy by the arms. His grip had drawn her up on tiptoe from its intensity.

"So it was Jack."

"You thought it was me." His face wore an expression of bleak disappointment.

"Not for a minute."

Peter's fingers loosened, but still he held her in front of him. "I wouldn't do that to the company; I care about them. It's Jeremy I hate. Obviously, I had an ulterior motive for working here. I thought if I was around, if I could watch him, he'd slip up, and I'd finally know for sure what happened to Sandra. I don't know why it's so important to me. It won't change anything. Nothing will."

He swallowed. "There's one more thing. Remember the night the batten fell? It—" He glanced past her shoulder and shut his eyes. "Shit." He released her and strode out of the storage room.

Alice was standing in the doorway.

Lindy caught up with him at the prop table. She had forgotten about the rehearsal completely. Dancers were already on the stage; a few were coming out of the chorus room wiping their hands. "Peter, what about the batten? We have to join forces on this. It's everyone's livelihood."

"We're not necessarily on the same side, Lindy." His whole body went rigid. "Onstage, everybody." He brushed past her and headed for the stage.

Lindy turned around and let out an exasperated sigh. "Bill, how nice to see you."

His expression was unreadable, but he certainly wasn't smiling. "Talking shop? Or doing a little amateur sleuthing?"

"Excuse me, I have to start the rehearsal."

"Leave it to the police, Lindy. They know what they're doing. That's why they get paid."

Lindy turned away and lifted her chin. Her back was to him, and he couldn't see her face, but maybe he'd pick up on the body language as she walked away. She heard Biddy come up behind her.

"What's he doing here?"

"Making me uncomfortable, for starters."

"Do you think he's being paid to keep an eye on us?"

Lindy considered. "Maybe when he said 'sort of' policeman, he meant he was a private investigator. That would make sense."

"Yeah. Anyway, I found out an interesting piece of information from the boys."

"Tell me. But look like you're talking shop so he won't try to read our lips."

"Do you think he can do that?"

Lindy shook her head. "I wouldn't put it past him. What did you learn?" Lindy leaned over to cue the boom box.

"The boys think Jack gambles. Juan overheard Carlotta saying to him that his little compulsion had wrecked lives and was going to finish off the company."

"That's something I hadn't thought of. It would explain where the money was going. From the way he dresses, he must lose a lot. What did Jack say to her?"

"Juan didn't stick around to find out."

"Well, that casts a new light on things. Carlotta concerned for somebody else? Do you think she was trying to convince him to stop?"

"Juan said she sounded like she was putting the screws to him."

"That sounds more like Carlotta. But it does add a whole new twist to the problem." She stood up. "Places, please." She turned to Biddy. "All we need is another element to grapple with. We're drowning in too many possibilities already."

Before Lindy had a chance to begin the rehearsal, Jack appeared at her elbow. "Sorry for interrupting, but can I have a couple of minutes with the company?"

Lindy nodded and called the dancers over.

"Some good news in all of this," said Jack in a dry voice. "The bank has cleared our checks, and I have paychecks today. Those of you who have direct deposit have already had your checks deposited."

There was an approving murmur from the group. They all looked a bit haggard; maybe today would turn things around.

"Thank you, Lindy." Jack's eyes were black slits surrounded by puffy skin; his whole face seemed to sag. His jacket hung limply around his rounded torso, and he hadn't bothered to put on his boutonniere. But when he walked away, Lindy noticed there was a spring to his ordinarily frenetic stride.

"Wow, he must be upset," said Biddy. "I think this is the first time I've ever seen Jack without a flower in his lapel."

"Or maybe the florist couldn't—" Lindy stopped in mid-sentence. "Freesias." She was such a dolt. Or maybe it was just a coincidence. That was more likely. "Freesias," she said again to no one in particular.

"What . . . what?" asked Biddy, a look of concern spreading across her face.

Lindy ignored her. "All right, everybody. Give me lots of energy. We'll have a short rehearsal. Give you some time to spend those paychecks."

"What?" Biddy repeated.

"It may be nothing, but you and I are taking a little drive after rehearsal."

Two hours later, having successfully eluded Brandecker, or so they hoped, Lindy and Biddy were driving down Fox Hollow Road on their way to the Hollingwood Gardens Nursing Home. Lindy hadn't explained what they were doing. It was too nebulous at the moment. Ideas, events, relationships were popping around inside her head like hundreds of corn kernels. With luck, they might settle into a pattern that made sense.

Lindy led Biddy through the front lobby.

"Posh, isn't it?" said Biddy. "Do you think Peter pays for it? I don't think they have family left. Maybe insurance?"

"Something else we need to find out."

"Good day, ladies, could you please sign our guest register?" Behind the reception desk sat a wizened lady in a pink floral wrapper. Her eyes twinkled like blue glass, but the effect was spoiled by the crust that had formed in each corner.

"Mrs. Harrell, thank you, my dear, for helping me out. I'll take over again." Mrs. Harrell was replaced by a carefully coifed woman in a tasteful tweed suit.

She turned to Lindy and Biddy with a pleasant smile. "Every time I leave my station, she pops right in. I hope she didn't say anything, well, you know. We have some real characters here."

Lindy had signed the register before it occurred to her to use a false name. If Peter found out she had been back, he would not be happy, and she felt a certain trepidation about provoking him into anger. She guessed that once that nearly implacable facade cracked, the emotions released would be intense and possibly dangerous.

As she and Biddy walked down the hall, Lindy tried to retrace her path from her first visit. All the hallways were painted a pastel blue beneath steel handrails and were covered with flocked fleur-de-lis wallpaper above. Lindy couldn't find any features that distinguished one hallway from another, and she wondered how often patients roamed the halls without a clue as to where they were. She was about to concede that she was lost when she caught sight of Daneeta coming down the hall. An orange-and-black University jacket was thrown over the shoulders of her uniform, and the strap of her shoulder bag hung over the jacket. She must be getting off work.

"Daneeta." The woman slowed as she reached them, then recognition showed on her face.

"You're Miss Angie's friend. If you're looking for Sandra's room, you sure are lost."

"I thought we might be. This is my friend Biddy. She's also a friend of Angie's."

"Nice to meet you." Daneeta began walking back the way they had just come. "Just turn right at this next corridor, then left at the next, and you'll see the nurses' station. Keep going straight, and her room's on the right."

"Would you mind terribly taking us there? We're pretty

bad at directions. I know you must be in a hurry to get home, but I'd really appreciate it."

Daneeta didn't answer but led them down the corridor to the right. The nurse on duty looked up as they passed. "People to see Sandra Dowd," Daneeta said.

"Oh, her brother's here. I think he took her down to the solarium. It's such a nice day."

Daneeta nodded. "You can see the solarium from her window. Save you the trouble of chasing around after them."

"Would you mind going with us?" Daneeta must think she was an idiot, but Lindy needed to talk to her alone.

Daneeta shrugged and led them down the hall.

Lindy's heart began to pound against her ribs. Please don't let us run into Peter, she petitioned to no one in particular. Biddy's face was blotched with pink patches. Like the Cowardly Lion meeting the great and powerful Oz, she looked like she might bolt and run at any moment.

Lindy slowed as they reached Sandra's door, then peered inside. Empty. She stepped inside. The bowl of flowers sat on the bedside table, an enormous arrangement of yellow and white freesias. She touched Biddy's arm and indicated the arrangement with her head.

"What?" whispered Biddy. "I don't understand."

They moved inside the room. Daneeta seemed to have lost her urgency to get home.

"What?" she asked.

"Daneeta, does the nursing home provide flowers for their, um, guests?"

"No. Oh, you mean these? They're beautiful, aren't they. He sends them every couple of weeks. So thoughtful. You wouldn't believe how many folks here are just out of sight, out of mind. He's a good man, Mr. Peter. He takes care of his own."

"Her brother sends them?"

"I guess so. No one else visits her."

"How could we find out?" asked Biddy.

Daneeta's face screwed up. "Why do you want to know?"

Lindy waffled for a second and said, "It's important. It's hard to explain, but something is going on in our company, and we think it has to do with the flowers."

"Why don't you just ask her brother?" Daneeta moved to the window. "They're out there now."

Lindy looked past Daneeta. The solarium was about twenty feet away, glass-enclosed and planted with potted shrubs and drifts of spring flowers. Peter and Sandra sat in full view, separated from them only by the plate glass of the solarium wall. She shrunk back. Biddy stared mesmerized by the scene before her. Peter was sitting in a white wrought-iron lawn chair, leaning forward toward Sandra's wheelchair. He held her limp hands in his. His thumb moved gently across the knuckles of her sculpted fingers.

"We shouldn't be watching," cried Biddy. "I didn't know. How awful."

Lindy dragged her away from the window. Tears had sprung into her eyes and trickled down the groove between her nose and cheek.

Daneeta handed Biddy a tissue and said gently, "Why don't you just wait here for them? It's her dinnertime. They should be coming back in a few minutes. You could ask about the flowers then."

Lindy fought with the unreasonable panic growing inside

her. "Look, Daneeta. We don't have much time. Someone who works with us, with Peter, has been murdered."

"I read about that in the papers. That was you?"

"Yes, and we need to know who sends those flowers. It could be really important."

"You mean they think that Peter might have killed that woman? Never." Daneeta's face screwed up again. She seemed to have only two expressions, benign smile and distorted worry.

"We don't know what the police think, but we have to find out before they do."

"Then come with me." Daneeta was out the door before Lindy could grab Biddy and follow.

She was standing over a computer, fingers running rapidly over the keyboard, by the time Lindy and Biddy caught up to her. The computer took up the entire space of the records office, which seemed to be a converted storage closet.

"Armstrong Florist. It's local. But no name of the sender is listed." Daneeta turned abruptly and screwed up her face at them. "I hope you're not up to something bad. Those two people have been through enough."

"We're trying to help," said Biddy.

"That's all right, then." Daneeta's face returned to its smile. "Let's get out of here before someone sees us and starts asking questions."

Lindy grabbed a pen and copied down the number of the florist on her palm. "You've been a great help, Daneeta. Just keep your fingers crossed. Now, where can I find a pay phone?"

The pay phone was placed unobtrusively in an alcove off

the main lobby. An arrangement of silk flowers sat on a small telephone table; beneath it were a pen and a writing tablet bearing the name of the nursing home. Lindy dialed the number. This time she remembered to use a false name.

Her cousin was a patient at the Hollingwood Gardens Nursing Home. She had just come from Indiana (well, why not) to visit her, and she was wondering who sent those lovely freesias. She wanted to thank them for their thoughtfulness. Sandra Dowd. Yes, I see. Yes, he's always been so kind to the family.

Biddy shifted from one crutch to the other as she listened to the one-sided conversation. Her head darted from side to side as she kept watch for Peter, who would have to pass them as he left the nursing home.

Lindy hung up the phone. "It's Jack. He has an account there."

"That's really . . ." Biddy searched the air. "Kind?"

"Weird is more like it," said Lindy with forced patience. "Doesn't it strike you as a little ritualistic? He sends her freesias, and he always wears one. Like some lover's symbol."

They stared at each other. Was it possible?

"That's pretty farfetched," said Biddy, shaking her head. "I can't see Sandra in love with Jack. I mean, he's nice but not exactly the type that young, beautiful girls go for. And, anyway, what could this possibly have to do with Carlotta? Unless, she was in love with Jack. No, impossible. He doesn't fit the image of—"

Lindy raised her finger to her lips and closed her eyes. "Don't move." She mouthed the words at Biddy.

Biddy froze.

It would only take a few seconds for him to pass from their view. But time had slowed down as it tended to do in bad dreams and embarrassing situations. Peter passed the reception desk moving in freeze-frame slowness. Lindy held her breath. Why were they sneaking around like this? She should have just told Peter what they were doing. He probably would help them. If he could be trusted. But could he?

Peter's movements and Lindy's thoughts snapped back into real time as the figure of Daneeta appeared, her body blocking the view of the pay phone. She chatted animatedly to Peter as she led him to the door. She waved him a friendly goodbye, then turned and wiggled her fingers in the direction of the phone and left by the front door.

"Thanks, Daneeta, we owe you."

The house was sold out again that night. Instead of staying away, the audience packed the theater, and there was a definite "festive" mood in the air. Though Lindy was loath to use Bill's description, she had to admit that Carlotta's death had been good for business. So far, anyway. Hopefully, the whole sordid affair would be cleared up without doing permanent damage, except to Carlotta, of course.

She rushed backstage while the dancers took their bows for *Carmina*. She watched as they filed off the stage, deposited the candelabras back onto the prop table, and went through the door to the hall and back to the dressing rooms. The police tape had been removed, and everyone was back in their original rooms. Carlotta's room was still taped, and a padlock had been added to keep everyone out.

Everyone was where they should be. Dancers dressed for the next piece. Toilets flushed. One of the boys called for

Alice. She shuffled into their dressing room with a pair of socks and exited, tossing a used pair into the garbage can next to the door.

Peter was overseeing the demolition of the cage. It would be completely dismantled so that it could be loaded into the truck the next morning for the move to Hartford. The night of the murder it had just been removed to the back of stage right, out of the way of entrances and crossovers.

Jeremy wasn't backstage. Lindy had left him talking to Biddy in the back of the house. On Thursday night, he would have been in his office with Eric. But Eric would have had to leave to dress for the next piece. Lindy looked through the door to the hall. From where she stood, she could see the door of Carlotta's dressing room and part of the opening to the boys' room.

Across the stage, two stagehands stood along the rail. They began to pull the ropes of the counterweight system, hand over hand like sailors hoisting a sail. The backdrop for *Carmina* rose into the fly space above the stage, and the scrim for *Holberg Suite* lowered to replace it.

Peter had returned to the lighting panel and was speaking into a headset to the follow-spot operators in the booth located at the back of the balcony. He would call the show from the board, while two lighting men ran the cues next to him.

None of the equipment in the theater was computerized. Old-fashioned, unwieldy, and slow, it would take everyone's full attention to get through each piece. So who would have time to leave their station and kill Carlotta?

Peter called five minutes. Dancers began to take their places for the next dance. Lindy moved out of the way to the far side of the light board. A stagehand readied himself at the front curtain, waiting for his cue. Two others manned the light board. The others drifted back into the shop to wait for the end of the piece when they would be needed again. The hallway was empty; everyone was focused on the beginning of the *Holberg Suite*.

"Places, please." Lindy heard Peter's steady voice give the cue. "Warn on blackout. Warn on curtain. Blackout, go." All light went out onstage. Only a small lamp on the light board illuminated the panel. The rest of the backstage area, as well as the stage itself, was engulfed in darkness. "Curtain, go."

Lindy heard the curtain being pulled. The stage was effused with a bright, warm light. At the same time, the music began, the sound of violins bouncing into action. Backstage became even darker and then gradually came back into shadowy view as the stage lights spilled into the offstage area.

Lindy had to pull her attention from the stage; it was such a beautiful effect. Lights, music, costumes, graceful bodies. It was mesmerizing. Backstage, everything appeared as it had before the blackout. There had been time for someone to sneak past the door and enter Carlotta's room without being seen. But who?

All the dancers were in both pieces, except Carlotta. The memory of a Tunisian vacation popped into Lindy's mind. She and Glen had been sitting at the horseshoe bar in the hotel when the lights suddenly went out. When the emergency generator had finally restored them, Glen swore that the people sitting across from them were not the same people as before. For the rest of the night, they had made up stories of innocent tourists being shanghaied from the bar during power failures.

But everything here was just as it had been before. No one could have moved that fast. It must have been someone out of the stage area. Only Jeremy was unaccounted for, but maybe he had already gone back out front. That's what he would have normally done, but had he done so that night? He hadn't returned to his seat in the theater, and he hadn't joined her at the back. There was only one way to find out. She would ask him as soon as the performance was over.

And then what? She refused to think about it. He had to be innocent. She couldn't make herself imagine Jeremy bludgeoning Carlotta to death. And there hadn't been any blood on him, had there? She would have noticed. He would have had time to enter Carlotta's dressing room during the brief blackout, but he would have had to come out after the lights were back on, and someone would have noticed. Lindy looked around her. Everyone was intent on their job. Peter watched the stage, his voice calmly giving cues into the headset.

The music changed tempo; the *Gavotte* had begun. Lindy caught snatches of flowing costumes as the dancers passed from her view. She moved toward the back of the stage, slowly trying to see things in a new perspective. Catch any little thing that wasn't quite right, just like in rehearsal. It was usually just a misplaced hand, weight shifted to the wrong foot, a step taken a second too quickly. The smallest quirk could throw off an entire movement, or a stage full of performers. But nothing here caught her eye. She was at the prop table when she noticed someone standing in the wings.

The music had changed to the *Air*. The melody was bewitching. The men were lifting Andrea, handing her from one to another in a floating reverie, passionate, yet serene. Like the choreographer, thought Lindy, classical structure with a longing romanticism just below the surface. Lindy wrenched her gaze from the stage and looked at the person in the wings. The blue smock flared out over Alice's ample bottom.

Lindy moved up beside the costume mistress. She was standing with her arms folded in front of her, one of the robes from *Carmina* draped over her elbow.

"I love this music," said Alice, staring dreamily toward the stage.

"Me too." It couldn't have been Jeremy. No one who could create such beautiful movement would be capable of destroying a life. In the back of her mind, she knew that wasn't true; great artists were often selfish and destructive, but not Jeremy. She wouldn't believe it.

She took a few steps backward, trying to detach herself from the spell being woven by the dancing. Peter had slipped off his headset; it rested around his neck. His head was turned toward the stage.

Lindy walked toward the door to the dressing rooms. No one seemed aware of her presence. She turned around abruptly, shooting one arm into the air. One of the lighting people glanced up briefly but then looked back to the board. Anyone could have walked right past.

Peter popped the headset back over his ears. "Warn on cue seventeen. Warn on curtain." In a minute or two the curtain would come down on their last performance at University Theater. The *Rigaudon* music was bouncing to the end. Everyone was in action. The music ended, the curtain closed, and the dancers got ready for the curtain calls.

The entire cast lined up across the width of the stage for the first bow. After bowing, they split center and exited to both sides of the stage. The demi-soloists, then the soloists took their bows, and finally the entire cast again. The curtain flew in and settled in a pool of fabric.

"Houselights, stage lights. Thanks, everybody." Peter dropped his headset onto the light board and left the stage.

"Do you want to talk to us?" Kate was one of the first dancers offstage.

"Uh, no, but I think Biddy might have taken a few notes. Hang on." Lindy took the time to watch everyone as they began leaving the stage, where they went, who was talking to whom. Was it like this on the night Carlotta was killed?

Biddy came backstage, Jeremy walking beside her.

"Have any notes for the cast?" Lindy prompted.

"Uh, no," said Biddy, looking surprised.

"All right, you guys, you're cut loose. Good show." Lindy watched the path that everyone took. It had been several minutes before they had heard Andrea's scream. Everyone but Andrea had been onstage.

"Was I supposed to take notes?" asked Biddy.

"Huh?" Lindy shook her head without taking her eyes off the retreating dancers. She followed them into the hall and watched as they disappeared into dressing rooms, closing doors behind them.

It was no use. Carlotta must have been dead by the end of the piece. Lindy stood in the empty hallway. Empty, except for her and the yellow tape that stretched across Carlotta's dressing-room door.

Fourteen

A hotel lobby had never looked so inviting. Lindy had filled Biddy in on what she had noticed backstage during the last part of the performance, carefully editing out her fears about Jeremy. She could feel the tension that emanated from her friend, and she knew she would have to be very careful when she finally broached the subject.

"Guess who's here," Biddy said in a voice that underscored her tiredness.

"Oh, God, why us?"

Bill Brandecker, the ever present, was walking toward them. Lindy readied herself with several bons mots to hurl at him while she continued slowly forward.

"He does look kind of elegant."

"For crying out loud, Biddy. He's wearing jeans and a flannel shirt."

"Maybe he's lonely."

"Then he should go home and start looking for another poker game." Lindy braced her shoulders, fixed her eyes on the ground, and decided to walk past him without acknowledging his presence.

"Good evening, ladies."

"Good evening," they both mumbled. They even sounded

guilty. Lindy looked up with the most dazzling smile she could muster. It wasn't very effective. She was sure the expression was more like a razor cut than a smile. She showed more teeth.

"Why, Mr. Brandecker," she began, then gave up the pretense. "What do you want now?"

"I thought I might buy you a drink."

Right, if he thought he could weasel information out of her—but then, the game did work both ways. "We'd love to have a drink with you." She smiled sweetly—she hoped.

Biddy looked at her in amazement. Her eyes widened; warning emanated from them like lighthouse beacons in a storm. "Not me, I'm really tired tonight. Thanks anyway." She moved around him so quickly that she barely missed hitting him in the shin with her crutch.

"Some other time, perhaps." He gave Biddy that disarming smile. Lindy braced herself. "And you?"

"Actually, I'd love a drink, thank you."

Biddy had stopped behind Bill and was pantomiming to Lindy, slicing her index finger across her throat. Lindy ignored her.

Biddy gave up and retreated toward the elevator.

Bill led her into the bar, which was surprisingly quiet for a Saturday night. He stopped at the booth where she had sat with Jack just a few days ago. Lindy walked past it and said, "How about here?"

Bill shrugged and sat down, watching as she slid into the upholstered bench across the table from him.

"Mr. Brandecker . . ."

"Call me Bill, please. 'Mr.' makes me feel a little anti-quated. And what shall I call you? Belinda, Lindy, Haggerty,

Graham? Do you have any other names I should know about?"

"Sacco, Vanzetti? You can call me Lindy."

"It's an odd world, the theater. Everyone's name seems to end in a y or ie, or some other diminutive. Or they use something totally fictitious. Doesn't anyone get called by their real name?"

"Hardly ever, and then, like children, only if you're really mad at them."

Bill laughed. It was disarming, like his smile. But Lindy wasn't fooled by it. Brandecker, she was sure, could indulge in conversation complete with witty comments and apparent charm, while taking mental notes, complete with crossed t's and dotted i's. She would have to be careful.

"Take Carlotta Devine, for example." Well, he had moved onto that subject smoothly enough. "Do you know what her real name was?"

Lindy shook her head. "I've never thought about it."

"Carol Schwartz."

"You're kidding. Well, that's appropriate."

Bill looked puzzled.

"Isn't *schwarz* German for black?"

"That bad, huh?"

"Oh, yes." Lindy tried to survey the minefield that lay ahead. "She was a hideously nasty person, but I'm sure you've heard that from everyone. I suppose I'm sorry she's dead, but I find it hard to work up any compassion for her. She made everyone's life miserable when she was alive, and she seems to be continuing the tradition now that she's dead."

"So, everybody hated her?"

"No," she said a little too quickly. "I wouldn't say 'hate.'

There's one like her in every dance company, probably in every secretarial pool, too. You just learn to cope and say really catty things about her behind her back."

"What did people say?" Well, so much for trying to lighten the conversation.

" 'Divine Swine' was my favorite." She smiled in spite of herself.

Bill smiled. Thousands of tiny alarms went off in her head. Don't be cute. Pay attention.

The barmaid interrupted them. Lindy ordered a glass of white wine, which Bill immediately changed to a bottle of French chardonnay. He thinks I'll get drunk and confess, she thought. She changed tactics.

"Since you obviously invited me here to talk about the murder, do you mind if I ask why?"

Bill leaned back and looked at her, but didn't speak.

"If you're just 'sort of' a policeman, and this isn't your 'field,' why are you going to all this trouble? Are you a private investigator?"

"Do you remember everything people say? Pretty observant."

"I'm trained to be observant. It's my job. Are you a private detective?"

"No."

"Look, I don't feel like playing twenty questions tonight. Can you just tell me why you are doing this?"

"Because I'm here. I used to be a policeman. Now, I teach at John Jay."

It took her a second to assimilate what he said. "A professor?"

"Yeah, don't I look like one?"

She looked at his flannel shirt, opened at the collar. She tried to study his face, but the lighting in the bar was too dim. "But you used to be a policeman."

The barmaid returned with the bottle of wine and set it in a standing ice bucket. She made a show of pouring it out, carefully turning the bottle to keep it from dripping. It was probably the most interesting thing she would have to do all evening, and she was making the most of it. "Enjoy," she said and walked away.

Bill watched her leave, his eyes focused on the hem of her black satin miniskirt. "I used to be a policeman, but now I teach criminology. I got sick of the violence and the gore and the pain."

"So now you just deal with theories instead of criminals?"

Bill leaned forward and crossed his arms on the table. "I now try to look at the reasons people turn to violence, maybe someday add my little bit to prevent violence instead of always cleaning up after it. Maybe even train a few people to go out and do a better job than I did. You think that's a, pardon the pun, cop-out?"

"Not at all," said Lindy, startled by the chink she had so easily stumbled upon. "I think it's very altruistic and a bit idealistic. Decent qualities in a man. Do you think it's a cop-out?"

He started to speak, then changed his mind. Then slowly he said, "What I think is that you have a pretty nasty situation here. Dell is good, but he hasn't had much experience with artistic types. Most of his cases revolve around drunk drivers, domestic disputes, and burglaries. There's a surprising lack of murder or art, here, even for a college town."

"And do you have experience with artistic types?"

"I've known a few. I'm not just some flat foot with a degree. I can tell the difference between Puccini and Mozart, *Swan Lake* and 'Slaughter on Tenth Avenue.' "

She had annoyed him, and she felt smugly elated. Some other time she would have loved to delve into the inner workings of the man, but she needed other information from him now. There were more serious matters at stake.

"So you've graciously volunteered to kibitz on the investigation. I thought policemen were fanatically territorial."

"They are, and I am not kibitzing."

"Oh? Then why are you showing such an interest in all of this? Deriving a new theory at our expense?" Her tone was aggressive. She couldn't help herself. "And on your vacation. Isn't that taking your work a little too seriously?"

He laughed. "That's the same thing my ex-wife said when she showed me the door. Though she didn't state it quite so sympathetically."

"Sorry." Why was he telling her this? He didn't strike Lindy as the type of man who spilled his guts to every woman with whom he drank wine. He must be leading her somewhere specific.

Bill seemed to realize the subtle shift in her attitude. "It was a long time ago. Police work, at least mine, and family don't seem to mix. And you?"

His question had caught her off guard. With two words he had subtly regained his control of the conversation.

"What about me?"

"Does your work and family mix?"

Lindy blessed the dim lighting and her olive skin. If she had Biddy's complexion, her ambivalence would have colored her face.

Bill's eyebrows rose. He was waiting for a response.

"I'm really retired; I've just been back a week. Biddy asked me to help her." She stopped talking abruptly. She had almost told him why Biddy had asked her to come back. She had to be more careful. Her glass was almost empty. "It was hard for her with her broken leg. I wasn't busy, so I came to help them out until the New York season. It's a good company, and I was glad to help. They're good people; they're just caught in bizarre circumstances."

She was talking too much, clumsily trying to lead the conversation away from the details of Carlotta's death. She was out of her depth. God, what an amateur; she just hoped she wasn't digging herself into a hole. She concentrated on her wineglass, twirling it around with her fingers. "They're emotional and self-indulgent sometimes," she said without looking up. "Tempers flare up quickly, and then it's over. They're supposed to be dramatic. People who express their feelings all the time don't have the energy left over to do really terrible things. Even in the real world, isn't it always the bottled-up types who go on a rampage?"

"Don't you consider this life the 'real world'?"

That was not the question she had anticipated, and it took her a second to answer. "Some people do."

"But not you?"

She stared past him, her eyes following the pattern of gold squiggles on the mirrored wall tiles. "I did once. Maybe I will again."

"Maybe living in this make-believe world of fairies and princes has warped somebody's sense of reality."

"We don't do fairies and princes. We're a modern-dance

company." Lindy heard her own words, how she had shifted from "they" to "we."

Bill's face was blank. He topped off their wineglasses. She realized that he had been goading her.

"You have a devious mind."

Bill lifted his wineglass and took a sip. It was a peculiarly refined gesture from a man of his size.

"Why don't you people look outside the company? She probably had a private life; most people do."

"I'm sure the police are considering all options."

"Don't you know?"

"I'm not privy to confidential information, even if my brother-in-law is the chief of police. I'm strictly unofficial, as I keep telling you."

"But what kinds of options?" She threw subtlety to the wind.

"Well, it's an old saw, but usually true."

"I know—lust, greed, and I forget the other one."

"Revenge." He tilted his head.

Revenge? Bill's eyes seemed to penetrate right through to her stomach. Her face felt clammy, and for one dizzying moment, she thought she might pass out. His words droned on. "I'll tell you one thing. The police are looking into her finances as a possible motive: bank accounts, insurance policies, inheritance."

Lindy relaxed slightly.

"But I think it's closer to home."

She tensed again. "You're wrong."

"You've told me that before."

"I'm sorry. But you were right when you called it 'home.' It *is* like a family. This kind of work consumes your life. It becomes your entire world. Dancers make terrible salaries, when they're paid at all. They're constantly being squeezed between management and the unions. We depend on each other, support each other . . ."

"Protect each other?"

Lindy fought with the growing lump in her throat. "When we have to. But not like you think. I know it sounds melodramatic. That's just the way we express ourselves."

"You're not their mother, Lindy."

"No, that's Biddy's job. I'm the Dutch uncle." She smiled. He poured out the last of the wine. "And don't try to get me drunk. I never get drunk. I always fall asleep first. And I'm not going to confess to being a mass murderer with bodies buried all over the state of Connecticut."

"Personally, I don't think of you as a serious suspect. Not very objective thinking for a policeman, I realize. But Dell will not be so easily swayed."

"Then why are you being so nosy?" To hell with it. She took another sip of wine.

He smiled. He smiled a lot. Only this wasn't his usual variety. It seemed more gentle. It was also fleeting. His voice became more direct. "Because I think you're interesting. I also think you're holding out on the police. If you know something, Lindy, tell them. Withholding evidence is not only a crime, it can be very dangerous."

"I don't know who killed her."

"But you know something. What is it? Who are you trying to protect?"

Lindy felt herself wavering. Bill was leaning across the table; his right hand was resting close to hers. His eyes were penetrating. She felt flustered. She tried to pretend he was one of those two-dimensional fictional detectives, easily out-foxed. But she felt herself succumb to his intensity. It was tempting, but dangerous. His hand moved slightly. It was close enough to grab hers.

She moved her hand back. "I just know that I didn't kill her. Trust me. If she caused me that much trouble, I would have jumped into my station wagon and headed back to my comfy home in the suburbs. I wouldn't have bashed her head in."

"But someone did. Someone beat her to a bloody pulp with a prop, for Christ's sake. Someone who is willing to sacrifice the rest of you, to save himself."

"It isn't one of us. It can't be. No one would do that."

"Lindy, you've got a brain. . . ." He left the rest unsaid.

"Anyone could have come into the theater. The stage door was open. There were sixteen candelabras sitting on the prop table in full view. Even a stranger would have seen them. And anyway, how do you know it was the candelabra?"

Bill shrugged lightly, or was it a twitch?

"I thought you weren't privy to confidential information."

"It's obvious," he said, looking into his wineglass.

Lindy felt every muscle contract. They'll think it's Rebo. He had said they would, but revenge? Brandecker was trying to confuse her. She could feel that. How much of what he was saying was the truth, and how much was fabrication? She couldn't trust him. Too bad; she needed his help.

"Well, wouldn't the killer be covered with blood if that were the case? I mean, doesn't it spray all over the place, leave traces or whatever?" She felt queasy. "Listen to me, nobody was covered in blood. I would have noticed. That's not something you could miss."

"You were all pretty upset. A person doesn't always notice details under those circumstances."

He didn't move away. His voice was gentler but his body held its intensity.

Lindy felt smothered by his closeness. "I do. I'm always astonished by the kinds of detail that jump out at you when you're under pressure. I know they didn't find blood on anyone. Did they." It wasn't a question, but a demand.

"Not that I have knowledge of, but consider what happened after Carlotta's body was discovered. Jeremy sent everyone back to their dressing rooms. Most of them had changed into street clothes before we arrived."

"That's why they taped off the dressing rooms? They were looking for—" She couldn't continue. Bill's hand moved closer to hers but didn't touch it.

"What did they find?" She could barely make the words audible. He didn't answer, and she thought that he must not have heard her. "What did they find?" she repeated. She didn't care if she sounded hysterical, and she was sure she must. Bill's face loomed before her; the rest of the room went out of focus. Maybe she was drunk after all.

He wasn't going to answer her. "You're full of shit with your 'busman's holiday' and 'not privy to,' Bill Brandecker."

Bill pulled his hand back. His mouth had tightened into a straight line across his face. The interview was over. Police had a way of indicating that without saying a word, and Bill was still a policeman at heart, even if he called himself a professor.

He pulled some bills out of his wallet and plunked them on the table. "I'm sure they will cover all the angles. I'll walk you to the elevator."

He led her across the lobby to the elevator, holding her rigidly by the elbow. He pressed the up button with his free hand and turned her toward him. Her elbow was beginning to throb, but she didn't try to free it from his grasp. He leaned down, his face inches from hers. For one terrifying moment Lindy thought he was going to kiss her.

"Be very careful, Lindy. And if you ever decide you can trust me—" He shoved her abruptly into the elevator, and the doors closed. She leaned back against the rail, relieved and just a little disappointed.

Fifteen

Lindy awoke to the buzzing of her travel alarm and the blinking message light on the phone by the bed. She slapped off the alarm and ignored the light. She needed to talk to Jeremy.

She found him in the weight room in the basement of the hotel. Surrounded by computerized exercise machines, Jeremy was the sole human occupant. She stopped at the observation window and peered in.

He was sitting at the pullover station on the Universal circuit. Dressed in baggy sweatpants and a loose-fitting T-shirt, cut away at the neck and sleeves and truncated above the waist, he lowered the weight-encumbered bar to his lap. She could see his abdominals ripple as he slowly released it upward. His biceps strained with the effort, but his face was impassive. A dancer's training. Never let the work show in your face. The audience doesn't want to see the exertion, just the magic. Jeremy was perfectly disciplined.

And, of course, he would go to a gym. She had never seen him exercise, except for occasionally demonstrating to the dancers how a step should be executed. She had tried to imagine him in his hotel room, dressed in tights, giving himself a *barre* while he corrected his placement in the hotel mirror. She couldn't picture it. In fact, she never really thought of him as a dancer. He had been good in his day. She had seen him onstage a few times during her own career. But he had retired early to take over the directorship of an established company, and he had clothed his dancer's muscles in street clothes ever since. He even rehearsed in slacks and collared shirts. It was a smart move. It separated him from his peers, who, at first, were not much younger than himself. He had an instinct for the nuances of leadership.

Now watching his bare arms straining with the effort of weight lifting, the sweat trickling down into the waistband of his sweats, she was struck by his vulnerability. She even felt a little embarrassed watching his enforced regimen. He was in great shape for someone who must be well over forty. It inspired her to watch him, reminded her to stick to grapefruit for breakfast when her taste buds cried for pancakes and bacon. She stood by the door admiring his physique unabashedly, until he finished and motioned her over.

"Staying in shape is hell," he said from underneath the towel he had thrown over his head. He scrubbed his hair and slipped the towel around his neck. "Getting old is a bitch."

"I know," she said. "I've let myself go pretty badly in the last few years."

"I did, too. Now, I'm paying the price." He set up at the next station, impaling several, different-size weights onto a metal pin and straddled the bench. He curled the weights upward. She watched the sweat trickle down his forearms and drop off onto the floor. It suddenly struck her what a solitary figure he was. Of course, he would keep in shape by working with weights, competing with the machines, with his own weaknesses, alone. Always in control, never breaking down in front of others. He hadn't really asked for her help, only said that Biddy needed her. What did he need, she wondered.

"The local police seem determined to keep us here for a few days," he was saying. "Even though I imagine the state police will be taking over the investigation. They are probably more equipped to deal with something like this."

He was carefully avoiding that one word: "murder." They both knew it was just that. *Murder.* No way to get around it. To ignore it. Carlotta wouldn't be getting up from her pool of blood to take her curtain call. But he was loath to say it. And so was Lindy.

"What do you want to do in the meantime?" she asked. She sat down on the plastic cushion of some machine that reminded her of an obstetrician's table, padded braces for feet and knees. She crossed her legs.

"I talked to Angie Levinson this morning. Offered to do a lec-dem for her students tomorrow morning," he said between grunts. "Figured we might as well keep the kids busy. Better for their minds to be occupied with their work and not with this stupid tragedy. Peter's left the sets and floor at the theater. No need to load up and wait around for someone to rip off the truck. The sponsors in Hartford are a little anxious about us making it in time, but ticket sales have skyrocketed." He laughed harshly as he dropped the weights for the last time and threw his leg over the seat. "I've assured them we will be there by Wednesday at the latest. God, I hope I'm right." He walked toward her until he stood above her, looking down. "Who the hell could have done this, Lindy?"

Lindy swallowed and said as calmly as she could, "I was going to ask you the same thing."

He looked at her for a few seconds without answering. She felt uncomfortable. She didn't think he had done it, but she thought that he thought she did. His cheeks were flushed from the exertion of exercising; he looked vulnerable, not sinister.

She jumped in. "I've been doing some snooping, for a good cause, I hope. Peter's sister is in a nursing home nearby; I went to see her."

Jeremy rubbed his face with his towel, hiding whatever reaction he had to her statement.

"I can't help thinking that Carlotta's death is tied up to what happened in the past. Can that be possible, Jeremy? What exactly happened to Sandra?"

Jeremy turned from her without a word, walked through the door to the waiting room, and sat down on the Naugahyde couch. Lindy followed him and sat next to him.

"You want the whole story, I suppose."

"That would be nice," she said encouragingly.

"I despised Carlotta. She destroyed my life. I'm glad she's dead."

Lindy tried not to let her jaw drop.

"But I didn't kill her, if that's what you're thinking."

"I wasn't thinking that," she mumbled. She wished he'd elaborate, but he sat staring at a coffee spill on the carpet, and she knew she would have to drag the story out of him piece by piece. "Then why did you keep her on?" she asked.

Jeremy shrugged. "Jack."

"What does he have to do with it?"

"I'm not sure. He wasn't forthcoming, but he insisted that I hire her, so I did."

"But why?"

"Jack pulled me back from the lunatic fringe. I was killing myself—drugs, booze. He stepped in and badgered me into pulling myself together, starting over. He got the funding, the bookings, everything. I owe him."

"Jeremy, what happened that made you quit in the first place? I know it isn't really my business, but the police will find out, and they may get the wrong impression. They don't understand us. If it could have anything to do with Carlotta's death, please tell me."

"I don't want to remember it, Lindy. It's taken a long time for me to forget it."

"Jeremy."

He cradled his head with his fingers, digging the heels of his hands into his eye sockets. When he finally spoke, it was to the coffee-stained floor. "Sandra DiCorso. She was a promising young dancer in the company. So talented, so beautiful. I liked her . . . a lot. You know what I mean?" He looked at Lindy over his fists.

"You mean like . . . ," she stammered.

"Yeah, like . . ." He began to massage his forehead with his fingers. The only sound in the room was the buzzing of the fluorescent light above them. Then Jeremy let out a deep sigh. "I know everyone thinks I'm gay because of the way I look and because of my profession. They just assume, and I never tried to dissuade them. It's good for business, or at least a good cover. I just never got into other guys. Well, a couple maybe, but I never needed sex enough to die for it."

Lindy nodded, knowledge of what he was saying dawned on her slowly.

"Anyway, she didn't care for me, that way."

Lindy wondered why he couldn't say it. He had loved Sandra DiCorso. Did Peter know? Did Jack? And, more importantly, had Carlotta?

"I was supposed to rehearse her in a new role after the rest of the company had finished for the day. We had a fight. She told me she was quitting dancing; getting married. But not to me. I went berserk, stormed out, and she went on rehearsing alone. She must have fallen, hit her head. She's never recovered. I visited her once, but I couldn't stand it. She's locked in some world that no one can reach. I just couldn't take it." His voice cracked, and Lindy realized that if he hadn't been so well trained, he would cry, and she ached for him. But she pressed him to continue.

"If I hadn't been so self-indulgent, if I had stayed . . ." He shook himself and steadied his voice. "But I didn't. Instead I went out to a club and drank myself under the table. Carlotta showed up. She always had a way of finding you at your most vulnerable and putting the screws to you. She came on to me. She was disgusting. I said some horrible things to her, I think. I was pretty out of it."

"So, crippled with guilt and feeling sorry for yourself, you quit and went on a binge of self-destruction," Lindy continued for him.

"You make it sound so—"

"It just doesn't sound like you."

He glanced at her from the corner of his eyes. The rest of his body was immobile. "There's more." He lifted both feet to the couch and hugged his knees.

Lindy focused on the ragged ends of his shoelaces. She hoped she could handle this. You should never try to get people to face things they don't want to face unless you're equipped to deal with their reactions. It was too late to worry about it now. She waited.

"It was finally declared an accident, but first there was an investigation. It was questionable whether someone could hit her head with such force without being pushed or thrown. Something like that. I was the prime suspect for a few agonizing days. I had an alibi; Carlotta was all over me at the club; she wouldn't take no for an answer. But when the police talked to her, she denied having been with me."

Lindy's stomach shriveled to the size of a walnut. "Didn't anyone else see you?"

"You know how those places are. Everyone loaded on something or on the make. People thought they remembered seeing me, but they weren't sure when."

"God, Jeremy."

Jeremy didn't acknowledge her. He didn't even seem aware of her. He was now citing facts as if reciting a litany. Lindy guessed that he must have repeated the story, asked himself the same questions, day after day, night after night, and getting no answers, except that he had been betrayed, and his life was in shambles.

"I tried to get back to work, but the looks, the innuendoes, my own guilt. I couldn't hack it. I finally opted out."

"Until Jack kicked you back in?"

"Right."

"And Jack insisted on Carlotta?"

Jeremy nodded.

"And she wanted this job to punish you for rejecting her."

Lindy was thinking out loud, but she thought Jeremy needed to hear it. "That's just like her. And you kept her on, not just because of Jack, but because you wanted her to keep punishing you, because you can't forgive yourself."

Jeremy dropped his head to his knees.

She was being cruel, and she hated it. But it was time to get things out in the open. "And you don't let everyone think you're gay because of the image. It's to keep everyone confused. Men think you're being discreet, and women think you aren't attracted to them. That way they won't get close to you. So you can't hurt them—"

"Stop it." Jeremy's voice was ragged with pain.

She had gone too far. He wasn't ready to face it yet. She touched his hair and watched his body tense. "Okay, so what about Jack?"

Jeremy turned his head to look at her. "What about him?"

"It's hard to believe that Carlotta orchestrated all this. She may have taken advantage of the opportunity to get back at you, but Jack really needed a job for his own survival. He approached you, made you feel obligated to him; he needed you in order to save himself. He was accused of embezzling, in case you've forgotten. And now, the same thing is happening again. The company isn't paid on a regular basis . . ."

"Cash flow or something. I let Jack handle the money. It's a relief not to have to deal with everything."

"Get a grip, Jeremy. You know as well as I do, if a sponsor doesn't pay, you don't perform. I've sat through hour-long intermissions waiting for final payment before continuing to the last act."

"Only in Italy or Mexico, maybe. It isn't the same in the States. We don't usually have to resort to such extremes."

"But we always get paid in advance. We looked at the books, Jeremy."

"What?"

"Biddy and I looked through Jack's briefcase, the day Carlotta fell. He left it behind when he took her to the emergency room. Peter was there, too. Jack hired an unknown company to construct the cage, instead of the one Peter had recommended, at twice the fee. Jack is skimming, and you had better face it."

"Why would he do that? If he needed money, I would have given it to him. I owe him everything. He kept me from killing myself."

"Do you pay any attention to the books?"

"No. That would be admitting that I didn't trust him. When he wants me to sign, I sign."

"I'm not blaming you."

"But it's another of my little failings."

Lindy ignored his self-contempt. "Some of the dancers think he gambles."

"Jack? Ridiculous."

"Juan overheard a conversation between Jack and Carlotta about his 'little obsession.' "

"No, I don't believe it. Surely, I would know that at least. Oh, God. I've made such a mess of things. Maybe I should disband the company."

"And go back to drinking and drugging? You can't disband. You won't. You're tougher than you think, Jeremy. We'll see this through."

An involuntary shudder passed through his body. "I suppose. But, Lindy, we'd better hurry."

* * *

Hurry. She knew she had to, but part of her recoiled at the thought of what she might find. There was nobody she was willing to sacrifice in order to find the truth. Jack, maybe. She didn't really like him. He would also be the easiest person to replace. But life didn't usually work out that way, and she felt guilty for being so willing to throw him to the dogs.

Jack was taking the money. She was sure of that. But what was he doing with it? Carlotta must have known. How else could she have gotten so much control over him? Maybe she was threatening to expose him. That might be a motive for killing her. Maybe she was even demanding some of the take. She couldn't have afforded that ostentatious fur coat on a dancer's salary. If she had known about his original stealing—could prove it—she could have forced him to hire her when no one else would. That would make sense, but was it possible?

If Jack had killed her, the company could continue without too much disruption. It was too convenient, maybe. And how did the freesias fit into it? Why would he continue to send flowers all these years? Initially, he might have sent them as an official company gesture, but for five years? That seemed a bit extreme.

All she had were questions. She needed some answers, but she had no idea of how to find them. If the police found out how Jeremy felt about Carlotta, they would arrest him for sure. He was alone in his office, once again without an alibi. History repeating itself. He even admitted that he hated her. Maybe he had been waiting for years to get back at her. That's the way the police would see it.

She had left Jeremy sitting on the couch. She needed to think, to hurry, but instead she wandered aimlessly across the hotel lobby. She stopped to look into the darkened gift-shop window. The shop was closed. Maybe Connecticut had a blue law. Who would want to buy this stuff anyway? University sweatshirts, stuffed animals, key chains, the flotsam of a weekend spent in a hotel.

"Ms. Graham." Lindy jumped. The desk manager motioned her over. It was the same young man that had been on duty the day she had arrived. He had been gracious then, had welcomed her with a smile. He was churlish now. Having possible murder suspects in your hotel couldn't be good for business. Policemen, even in plain clothes, would be upsetting to the guests. The staff probably looked at each of them as possible murderers. This man certainly had that look on his face.

"Yes?" She walked over to the counter.

"Messages for you." He barely looked at her as he handed two memo sheets across the registration desk. As soon as she took them from him, he turned and began straightening the keys in the room boxes behind him.

"Thank you," she said to his back. She looked down at the messages: "9:15 A.M. Glen Haggerty. Call home"; "10:05 A.M. Bill Brandecker. Meet him at the theater as soon as possible." Lindy crammed the message from Glen into the pocket of her jeans and headed for the parking lot.

Strange. Why would Brandecker want to meet her at the theater? Why would he want to meet her at all, after last night's conversation? Maybe he had found something. Would he actually share it with her?

She turned the Volvo out of the hotel parking lot. Please

let it be good news, she thought. Her mind was racing. She arrived at the theater without being aware of the drive.

There were no cars in the lot. She realized she had never seen Bill's car, but he must have one. The company truck wasn't even there, but the stage door was held open with the pig iron.

She went inside. It took a few moments for her eyes to become accustomed to the darkness after the brilliance of the daylight outside. She walked to the shop. The door was ajar, but no one was there. The cage had been dismantled and was packed in cases stacked near the loading-dock door. Rolls of Marley lay against the wall, ready to be loaded into the truck.

"Bill?" she called tentatively. No response. Well, really, why was he being so enigmatic? Where was he? Did he have something to show her that could only be seen at the theater? Had he really found something? More questions—where were some answers?

She called again. Her voice echoed down the hall, but still, there was no answer. For a man who has no respect for theater life, thought Lindy, he sure has a flare for the dramatic. She walked down the hall to the dressing rooms. They were all locked. She didn't go near Carlotta's; the tape was still in place. She went through the door to the stage. It was even darker, and she hit the side of the prop table with a thud. Holding her aching hipbone, she oriented herself in the direction of the light board and walked carefully forward.

The back of her neck began to prickle. She had been in dark theaters hundreds of times and felt totally comfortable, but she had also read hundreds of mysteries. If she had been reading this one, she would be screaming at the heroine: "Go back, you ninny." But this wasn't a book. She groped her way to the lighting panel and threw a lever.

A deep-blue light washed across the stage from the side lights, blinding her momentarily. The curtains seemed to waver as bright light sliced through the darkness surrounding the stage.

She looked out across the stage and called, "Hey, Brandecker. Is this a remake of *The Phantom of the Opera?* Do I have to sing?" There was still no answer. She couldn't see anything past the lit stage. Shadows thrown by the light across the stage dissolved into total black. She walked onto the stage.

It lay bundled up in the middle of the floor. At first it looked like a body, draped in a piece of curtain fabric. She rushed forward. It seemed too small for Bill, but who? She knelt down and reached toward it. The material sank underneath her touch, just a pile of fabric. It slipped through the gaping hole in the floor. The trapdoor had been lowered.

"What?" She hadn't heard anything. The push came totally without warning. Not strong, just enough to throw her balance forward. Instinct took over, and her arms stretched out before her. Her elbows hit the edge of the opening, sending sparks of pain all the way to her teeth. The flesh beneath her sweater tore as her weight hurled her into the darkness below. Her fingers clutched at the edge, barely breaking the momentum of her downward fall. Her body automatically landed on both feet absorbing the shock with a deep *plié*. She curved into a backward roll, off to one shoulder to protect her spine.

I did a lift like this once, she thought. Then blackout.

* * *

She heard her name, over and over, from down a long corridor. She was missing her entrance. She couldn't get to the stage on time. She tried to sit up. Heavy material was draped around her body, and the more she tried to move, the more tangled she became. The sound of her name was louder now, but it still had an echo effect. She'd wake up soon. It was just one of those nightmares where you heard your music but couldn't find your way to the stage. Those happened all the time. She couldn't move. No matter, it would be over soon, and then she would wake up. Breakfast maybe.

"Lindy!" This time the sound was loud and right above her. She tried to look up; her shoulder hurt like hell. She didn't usually feel pain in a dream. A head appeared in the sky, surrounded by a square halo of blue. The gods speak from the heavens. As a Greek god, Bill looked kind of funny, and his costume was terrible. She started to giggle.

"For Christ's sake, don't try to move."

It really was Bill.

"Bill." They should have done better dialogue. This wasn't very clever. Her body ached everywhere, dull pain accented by sharp.

"Don't move, I'm coming down."

"Not this way, we haven't got the kinks out yet. Try the stairs."

Bill's head disappeared, leaving only the shining blue box. Pretty good special effects, she thought drowsily and drifted off.

The next thing she knew, Bill was kneeling beside her. It wasn't as dark now. He must have found the light switch.

She hurt everywhere. This was no dream. Someone had pushed her through the trapdoor. She jerked up and let out a groan.

"Don't move."

"You said that already. Where the hell were you?"

His hands were running along the length of her body, her arms, and her legs. It would have felt good if she didn't hurt so much. "Ouch!"

"Of all the stupid . . . what did you think you were doing?"

"I came to meet you; where were you?"

"What are you talking about? You probably have a concussion."

"I got a message to meet you here. Wasn't I supposed to meet you?"

"No."

"Then why are you here?"

"I was following you. And it's a good thing. You're impossible. Is anything broken?"

"I don't think so. Somebody pushed me."

"Obviously. I didn't think you jumped down on purpose."

"You don't have to be so mean."

"See if you can stand up." Without waiting for her to move, he pulled her to her feet. She meant to stand up, but her knees buckled and she slumped against him. Strong arms caught her. She leaned into his body. She felt safe, but her head hurt. She could feel his heart beating through his windbreaker. For a second she forgot that she was a happily married suburban housewife. Then her brain cleared with frightening speed. She pulled away. "Thanks. I'm okay."

"Yeah, right."

"Are you annoyed with me?"

"Yes." He looked like he wanted to finish the job someone else had started.

"Why?"

"Because I can't believe you fell for such an obvious trick."

"I fell down the hole, didn't I?"

His eyes closed and he shook his head like a father who had just been told his kid had screwed up again. "Let's get you cleaned up. You're bleeding all over my jacket."

He helped her toward the stairs. The storage room made her skin crawl. Dust and cobwebs covered everything. The single lightbulb that hung from the ceiling didn't cast much light, and for that, she was grateful. Years of discarded objects littered the surface of the floor, and cardboard boxes were stacked in haphazard piles along the walls. Cleaning buckets, broken chairs, mildew-covered rags vied for space. Lindy kept her eyes focused on the rickety stairway and the open door above her.

Bill led her into the shop, pulled a folding chair over to the industrial-size sink, and eased her into the chair. Lindy touched her throbbing cheek and pulled away sticky fingers.

"It's just a scrape; face wounds always bleed a lot. It'll look nasty for a few days, but probably won't scar." He cocked his head. "Do you want to go to the emergency room?"

"No." He thought she was vain. Well, she didn't care what he thought. It was clear to her that she would need his help, regardless of how he felt about her or the rest of the company. And he had said he was following her.

"Why were you following me?"

Bill held a not-too-clean towel under the tap, then wrung it out. He dabbed it gently at her cheek. Big hands, light touch. The towel felt rough, but cold and soothing.

"Because you need following, obviously," he said, continuing to clean her face. "I knew you would get yourself into trouble. After you gave me the slip yesterday afternoon, I figured I'd better get serious. I've been camped out in the hotel lobby all morning. I saw you go into the weight room; I saw you leave the hotel." He handed her the towel. "And now I want some answers. Everything."

She had no choice. She needed his expertise. "Okay, but promise you won't jump to any conclusions, keep an open mind."

"Damn it, Lindy. I always keep an open mind. I'm the professional, remember? Now, start talking." He pulled another chair across the floor; its metal tips screeched across the concrete. He swung it around so the back was facing her and straddled it, leaning on his arms across the back.

"I'll make a trade," she said, nestling her cheek in the wet towel. "I'll tell you what I know, and you tell me what you know."

"When is it going to sink into that pea brain of yours, that this is serious. It's not some stage show. There won't be any applause at the end, and you won't forget the plot when you leave the theater." His voice thundered across the space between them. It made her head pound.

"You don't think much of us, do you?"

"What I think is that you're all a bunch of self-indulgent, pampered children that live in a dreamworld. Somebody in your little family has lost their grip on reality, what little they had in the first place. And I'm going to find out who it is. Do I make myself perfectly clear?"

"Perfectly," she said calmly and then added, "I bet your wife was in the theater, right?" She looked at him blandly and knew she had hit the mark.

"Actress," he said. "Now, I've told you something; it's your turn."

"My arms hurt." Lindy began to pull her arms gingerly out of the sleeves of her sweater.

"Stop stalling. I'm beginning to lose my patience."

She started with Biddy asking for her help, about searching Jack's office. "We think he's stealing from the company, and Carlotta knew it."

"He was accused of embezzling before," he said.

"How did you know that?"

"The police know a lot more than you imagine. They've done a background check on everyone involved, including you. They also know that Jeremy was investigated over the injury of a young girl in his former company. That makes him a prime suspect in this case."

"No. He didn't cause Sandra's accident or this one."

"Carlotta's death was not an accident. It was plain, old, unadulterated murder. No one saw him during the last part of the performance that night."

"But he had decided to fire her. He told me."

"Who else did he tell?"

"No one. He didn't have time."

"That won't help him much. It's hearsay."

"It's not hearsay. I heard him. Unless you think I'm lying," she challenged.

"It doesn't matter what I think. Keep talking."

"The girl who was injured, Sandra DiCorso, is Peter's sister. She's in a nursing home near here. Jeremy would have never hurt her. He—" She stopped herself before blurting out that Jeremy had loved her. Somehow that fact might make Jeremy even more suspect. "It's Jack who's been sending her flowers ever since."

"Sullivan? Why?"

Lindy shrugged. "I don't know."

Bill pulled out a notebook and pen from the pocket of his windbreaker.

"I did bleed on you." Lindy nodded toward the spots of blood across the right side of his jacket. Bill ignored her and scribbled into the notebook. "Bill," she said slowly. "Wouldn't there have to be blood on the killer, on his clothes? The police must have found something, if it really was one of us."

Bill looked up from his writing. His eyes were a pale blue, or maybe not. It was hard to tell in the light; the lighting seemed to be dim whenever they were together. She couldn't even describe his features; they were always partly in shadow. She felt an urgent need to see his face in daylight.

"Come on, I've been doing all the talking. It's your turn." She waited.

"I can't tell you."

"But why not? How are we going to figure this out if you're not honest with me?"

"*We* are not going to figure this out. It's a police matter, and you're going to butt out."

"Then I'm not going to tell you the rest." She threw the wet towel at his head. It settled on his shoulder. She shouldn't have done it, but it was a gesture of her frustration. She waited for his temper to explode.

But it didn't. He smiled. "See? Self-indulgent." He tossed the towel back to her.

She pressed on, ignoring his sarcasm. "If they found the clothes, why haven't they arrested someone?" Fragments of ideas darted across her mind. "Because they don't know who they belong to." She was thinking out loud, but she had nothing to lose. "A costume. No, they all have the dancers' names in them. Something of Carlotta's. Her coat, maybe." She looked for a response from Bill. Nothing. He was waiting for her to figure it out. "It would have to be big enough to cover the person, but then they would have to have had time to put it on and then hang it up again. Or at least throw it over . . . the candelabra? It would absorb any spray of blood. Right?" She sank back in the chair. "But if the candelabra was covered, it wouldn't be hard enough to kill her or cause blood. Bill?"

"Stop guessing. Do you have anything else to tell me?"

Lindy shook her head.

"Then you'd better get back to the hotel and a hot bath. That's what you people do for stress and strain, isn't it?"

He drove her back to the hotel in her car. The sun was shining, and Lindy took the opportunity to memorize his face. Brown hair streaked with blond and gray. Eyes, definitely blue—a light, clear reservoir of blue. And he didn't seem so big outside. Not over six feet two and rather thin. It was his manner and voice that were so overpowering.

"I'll see you to your room. Just to make sure you don't try to sneak away again."

They were walking through the lobby, when Paul, Eric, and Rebo came out of the restaurant. They separated, and Rebo walked toward the front door.

"I think I'll just have a talk with that boy," said Bill, setting off in the direction of Rebo. "Go upstairs."

Lindy followed him toward Rebo. "Don't call him 'boy.'"

Bill stopped. "I didn't mean it like that."

"I know, but he takes it like that."

"Jesus, what happened to you?" Rebo stared at the side of her face.

"Where have you fellows been for the last two hours?" Bill countered.

Rebo stepped forward. His normally rich-chocolate complexion had an ashy gray tint to it. Must have had a wild night last night, thought Lindy. "Self-indulgent" echoed at the back of her mind. Time for another little lecture.

"Having lunch." He was being surly. Lindy narrowed her eyes at him, and he took the hint. He lightened his tone. "For the last hour, and hanging out before that."

"All three of you?"

Rebo nodded. "What happened to Lindy?"

"Someone pushed her through the trapdoor at the theater. Knowing your penchant for pranks, I thought you might know something about who did it—"

"Bill," Lindy interrupted.

"Shit, no, I'd never hurt Lindy; you know that." He appealed to Lindy. "Or anyone else," he added to Bill.

"I know that, Rebo. Mr. Brandecker is just a little edgy." She knew it was the wrong thing to say before she had finished speaking, but it was too late. She *felt*—more than *saw*—the change in Bill.

"Maybe not Lindy, she's so lovable," Bill said through gritted teeth. "But you did threaten to kill Jack Sullivan. Maybe you settled for Carlotta instead?"

Rebo looked at Bill incredulously. He turned on Lindy. "Is that what you told him, Lindy? I'd expect that attitude from a lot of people. But not you."

"I didn't."

"Thanks for the vote of confidence. You want to arrest me? Go ahead. If not, stay out of my way." Rebo pushed between them, shoving Lindy to the side, and headed to the door.

"That was real professional."

"Go upstairs, Lindy," Bill said wearily. "You throw me off my game."

Sixteen

It was a long afternoon. The bath didn't help, only made her abrasions sting more. She pulled on sweats, limped down the hall to the ice machine, and had barely eased herself onto the bed when Biddy walked in.

"The grant proposals are finally ready to be mailed. I hope a murder won't shed unfavorable light on our—Good Lord, what happened to you?"

Lindy looked out from under an ice-filled towel. "Fell in a hole."

Biddy threw her crutches on the opposite bed and sat down next to Lindy. She pulled the ice pack away and cringed. "Aloe. I've got some in the bathroom." She pushed herself off the bed and started dragging her leaden leg toward the bathroom. "Oh, damn. I hate these crutches." She leaned back at a precarious angle to retrieve them. "I feel so useless."

"I know just how you feel." Lindy closed her eyes.

Biddy returned from the bathroom and gently spread the cream on Lindy's battered cheek. "Tell me what happened."

Lindy told her about the note, about going to the theater and being pushed down the trapdoor. Biddy's eyes ballooned with each new fact, growing larger and larger until they looked like they might burst. "Then Bill found me, and . . ."

"Bill?"

"You know, Brandecker. He's been spying on us. I told him what we knew."

Biddy's eyes grew even wider. "Not about the books!"

"Yes, I'm sorry, Biddy. I had to. We're in way over our heads. We need his help."

"Do you trust him?"

"Not for a second, but he's the best we've got. He doesn't like us much, probably resents the fact that we ruined his vacation, but he's smart. I also told him about Jack sending the flowers."

"Do you think Jack pushed you? He might be getting desperate if he thinks we're onto him."

"Possibly. We have to be careful. The police probably already know a lot about his finances, and with what I told Bill, they'll want to talk to Jack again."

"Brandecker's going to tell the police everything, isn't he?"

"I'm pretty sure he will. He doesn't have much of a choice. I made it clear that some of the things I told him were in confidence, but I don't think that means diddly to him. He's like a hound on the scent. Not very attractive."

She continued with the details of her conversation with Bill, carefully editing out the parts about Jeremy. She felt uncomfortable about considering the possibility of Jeremy's guilt in front of Biddy. She couldn't protect her forever. She might have to face losing Jeremy soon enough. Biddy's loyalties ran deep, had always run deep. She was loyal to the company, but more than that to Jeremy. It seemed to be her lot in life to be attached to someone who couldn't commit as much to her. First Claude, and now Jeremy. But then, Jeremy wasn't gay. Well, Biddy didn't need to know that yet.

Lindy felt tiredness numb her mind. She couldn't juggle a murder investigation and everyone's emotional involvement at the same time. "There's one more thing, Biddy. Bill knows about Sandra's accident. I guess the police have checked everyone's background." She yawned. It hurt her jaw. "They know that Jeremy was suspected of causing it."

Biddy began to protest.

"I know," said Lindy as her body plunged toward sleep. "It may get nasty before this is over. We've got to be strong."

"I've always been strong. It isn't much fun."

Lindy placed a heavy hand on Biddy's and fell asleep.

It was dark when Biddy shook her awake. Her body felt incredibly heavy and sluggish.

"I've been to see Jack."

Lindy sat up. Jolts of pain shot out in every direction. "Are you crazy? He's still here? I haven't seen him since he yelled at Jeremy in the theater."

"I couldn't stand it any longer. We have to push him into making a move. He must be the murderer."

"Yeah, and he could kill you next."

"I'll take the chance. I told him I had looked at the books; I didn't tell him that you and Peter were there. And I didn't mention the trapdoor."

"What did he say?"

"He denied everything, of course. He tried to blame

Peter for the over expenditures. But I didn't buy it, and he knows it."

"So you set yourself up as his next victim, is that it?"

Biddy lifted her chin. "I'm not afraid. I'll do what I have to do to save this company. And you'll have to do what you can to save me."

"Oh, Biddy, I was bored in the suburbs, but I didn't need this much excitement."

"But you do need something to eat. I'll call room service. Some soup, maybe?"

"The hell with soup, how about a bacon cheeseburger?"

"What about your diet?"

"To hell with that, too."

It was delicious. Lindy knew if she were ever to face a firing squad, however unlikely, her last wish would be a bacon cheeseburger. They sat across from each other at the table by the window.

Biddy pointed a French fry at Lindy. "It used to be that after a show, we'd come back to the room and paint our toenails and talk about boys." She took a bite and pointed again with the remaining half. "Now we just talk about murder."

"All the boys are younger than we are now." Lindy took a bite of burger.

"Jeremy didn't do it."

Lindy's mouth was full, and she couldn't cut Biddy off. She waved her hand. She wasn't ready to deal with this, but Biddy continued before she could swallow and guide the conversation away from Jeremy.

"I know you're trying to protect me. You don't think I

can act rationally because of my loyalty to him. It's not like with Claude. I was really in love with him; I thought in time, he would love me, too. Jeremy is talented and sensitive, and I respect him a lot, but I couldn't stand it if you thought I was just, you know, some fag hag. The dancing is what's important to me. Maybe, because I came from a family of eight children, getting married hasn't been too appealing to me. Nor that kind of emotional commitment. But I'm not perverse." She shoved another fry into her mouth.

How could she eat after a speech like that? Lindy forced her mouthful down with a large gulp of seltzer. "Biddy," she began, and that was as far as she got. Biddy had guessed exactly what she had been thinking.

"I just wanted you to understand," said Biddy matter-of-factly.

"I do, I really do. After a few years of marriage, commitment changes to a kind of peaceful coexistence. *Your* life is a lot more creative. I just worry about your retirement."

Biddy laughed high in the back of her throat and stabbed a pickle with her fork. "I won't have a job long enough to retire from if we don't solve this murder." She chewed slowly and swallowed. "The thing I keep wondering about is, well, there was a lot of blood on the floor, right? Wouldn't the murderer have blood on him? That's the way they catch them on TV."

"Carlotta's coat."

"Her coat?"

"I kept asking Bill about the blood. He wouldn't tell me, but he let me keep stabbing around until I came up with the idea of the coat. The murderer could have worn it; the blood would be on it, not his clothes." Lindy stood up and looked around her. She pulled the plug on the table lamp and wrapped the cord around the base.

"Oh, no, you don't," said Biddy.

"Where's your bathrobe?"

"In the bathroom."

Lindy went into the bathroom and returned wearing the robe. "Something just isn't right, Biddy. So, in the tradition of famous detectives, all of whom were smarter than we are, we're going to 'reenact the crime.' Stand up, please."

Biddy popped another fry into her mouth and stood up. "Which one am I?"

"Carlotta. Come out into the middle of the room. Turn around."

Biddy turned away from her, and Lindy touched the lamp to the back of Biddy's head. "So I hit you with the candlestick, and you fall. . . ." Lindy started laughing.

"Forward." Biddy lowered herself to the floor. "Onto my face, but Carlotta was on her back."

"So I bash you a few times and turn you over." Lindy demonstrated. "But that would still leave my hands and face exposed. Or, what if I bash you on the head, turn you over, throw the coat over you . . ." She took off the bathrobe and threw it over Biddy.

"Be careful," said the muffled voice underneath the robe.

Lindy picked up Biddy's head and carefully touched it to the carpet several times. Biddy wrestled out from under the robe.

"The coat would cover everything," said Biddy excitedly. "And it also takes care of the fact that the candelabra isn't heavy or sharp enough to draw blood, but the concrete floor would be."

"Exactly." Lindy helped Biddy to her feet. "But how does that help us?"

There was a light tapping at the door.

"Jack?" asked Biddy.

"Maybe," said Lindy, picking up the lamp from the floor. "Oh, this is stupid." She put the lamp back onto the table and went to open the door.

Paul, Eric, and Juan stood side by side. They stared dumbfounded at Lindy's face. She stared back at them, relieved.

"Oh," said Paul. "We shouldn't have come."

"Well, you did, so come in." Lindy opened the door wider, and they entered single file, lined up again, and stood mutely waiting.

"This looks like your rendition of bad ballet," quipped Lindy.

No one laughed. They turned to Biddy.

"Rebo's gone," said Paul.

"What do you mean 'gone'? He has a lec-dem tomorrow. You mean 'out'?"

"Out, but he said if he didn't come back, just to throw his stuff in his suitcase and put it on the bus."

"I'm going to beat him senseless when I get my hands on him," said Lindy, and then she cringed at her own words. So did Biddy. "Tell us everything."

Juan began. "He was really upset when he came back to the room this afternoon. Said you had told that cop that's been hanging around that he killed Carlotta."

"I hope you don't believe that."

"Of course not, you know how he gets. He's complicated. Like he can't decide whether to get famous or kill himself, instead. He just sort of flipped, raved about how they were going to blame Carlotta's death on him, 'cause he was an easy make. That nobody really cared about him, all that old shit."

"Do you think he went back to the city?" asked Biddy. "They'll just find him, and it will be worse for him."

"No, some guys we met came to pick him up."

"What guys?" asked Lindy.

Juan looked at Eric, who inhaled deeply and took up the story. "Last night these guys came backstage. They knew some people we know and invited us out after the show."

"Go on."

"They drove us into New Haven to a bar."

"You went all the way to New Haven for a drink?" asked Biddy.

Eric looked at Lindy. "A gay bar. It was the closest one. Rebo got really wasted and was ready to hang with these guys all night, but we made them drive us back."

"So do you know how to get in touch with these guys?"

"No. We kind of only remember their first names, but they seemed to be regulars at this place, and we thought maybe they might go back there tonight."

"On a Sunday?" asked Biddy.

"And we thought, maybe, you would loan us your car," said Juan, ignoring Biddy. "We'll be really careful, and we could get him back before he gets into more trouble."

"And he thinks nobody cares, poor thing."

"We know he's a jerk sometimes," said Paul. "But he just can't seem to reconcile his various lifestyles. Black, but from the Midwest; rich, but black; gay, but . . ."

"I get the point," said Lindy. "I'll go with you."

"You don't have to. We'll be really careful with the car."

"I'm going. Biddy, you'll have to go down and distract Brandecker if he's still in the lobby. Tell him anything you want, except what we're doing. Just give us time to get away. And then come back and lock yourself in. *Capisce?*"

It took more than forty-five minutes to find The Grind. The boys were a little vague about its location, and it wasn't exactly the kind of place you could ask directions to from a gas station's attendant. They were cruising the warehouse district when Juan pointed to an old diner. "There it is."

Lindy pulled the Volvo into the parking lot. The faded silver facade of the bar looked dull in spite of the colored floodlights that focused upward from the ground. The windows had been painted over, and the door was a black hole, no illumination marking its entrance.

"You'd better wait here," said Paul.

"Not a chance," she returned.

"Maybe you both should wait here," said Eric.

"I know how to say 'no,' " said Paul huffily and got out of the car.

Eric and Juan gave Lindy knowing looks. "He's so straight. How did he ever get into this business?"

It took a little convincing before the bouncer let Lindy in. She had thrown on a pair of jeans and a shiny shirt. Her face was bruised and ugly, but she tried to look jaded and seductive at the same time, showing her best profile, in this case, the undamaged one.

The music was deafening; it throbbed into every corner of the crowded space. The original counter served as the bar, but all the booths and tables had been removed to make room for a dance floor and dark corners where other things went on.

They moved slowly along the bar, looking for Rebo. Men stood three deep, pressed together, arms entangled, hands resting on denim butts. It was impossible to tell where one body left off and another one began.

Lindy received more than one appraising look, and Eric was fondled by a pair of pudgy hands attached to a man who looked like he had just arrived on his Harley. Maybe he had.

Rebo was on the dance floor, a glass in one hand, his arm draped over the broad shoulders of a tall blond. For a frenzied second, Lindy thought it was Jeremy, but when the man turned to nuzzle his head into Rebo's shoulder, the similarity vanished. He was young and handsome, but not healthy. Lindy's stomach constricted.

"Get him out of here."

Juan sidled across the dance floor, hips swaying, until he was next to the couple. He put his arms around Rebo's waist and separated him from the other man.

Lindy saw him whisper into Rebo's ear, then Rebo's eyes met hers. He swayed slightly. Juan kept one arm around his waist, caressed his chest with his other hand, like a lover come to claim his own, and led him to where the others were waiting.

The lights and music were pounding. The heat of too many, too needy bodies stifled the air.

"The bouncer's watching," warned Eric. He laced his arms around Paul and Lindy and started slowly toward the door, laughing. Juan followed with Rebo, who let himself be led away.

Just as they reached the door, Eric slipped his tongue into Paul's ear and groped him erotically. Paul stood bolt upright. "Fresh, but cute, isn't he?" Eric winked at the bouncer, who looked bored and turned to peruse the room. Juan and Rebo had slipped through the door.

"God, that was disgusting," spat Paul as soon as they had reached the parking lot. He threw Eric's arm from his shoulders.

"Sorry. I've always wanted to do that. Won't happen again. Forgive me?"

"I guess."

"It was for a good cause."

"Oh, all right. But never, never do that again."

"Methinks the boy doth protest too much." Rebo grinned. His eyes were glazed. That was obvious even in the dim light of the parking lot. His body leaned on Juan in rubbery abandon.

"Get him in the car," said Lindy. "And don't throw up on my backseat."

They stopped at the first McDonald's they came to, and Lindy ordered large coffees for everyone, two for Rebo, at the drive-through window. He was about halfway through the first cup when whatever he was on started to wear off. "You shouldn't have bothered," he whined from the backseat.

"And leave you there to wallow in self-pity? You have a lot of nerve. Your life just isn't that bad."

"I thought that you—"

"Bullshit. You know I didn't tell Brandecker that you killed Carlotta. It was just an excuse to go off on a binge. Kill yourself if you want to, but not on my time."

"You're really pissed at me, aren't you?"

"Yes." She screamed the word. "I'd like to . . ." She had had enough of violent expressions. "To . . . spank you."

"That would be yummy."

Lindy's anger dissipated into laughter. It was impossible to stay mad at him. "Well, I just might. Especially if I thought it would keep you home."

"Home," Rebo repeated.

"Lindy," said Paul. "There's a car following us."

"Ignore it. Brandecker probably eluded Biddy. I don't feel like adding a chase scene to an already overloaded night. Just don't talk to him when we get back."

But the car continued straight when they turned into the hotel. They hauled Rebo, who had fallen asleep during his second coffee, out of the backseat and through the lobby. The night clerk glanced up, but returned to the paperback he was reading with a look of disgust.

She left them at the door of Juan and Rebo's room. "Don't let him leave. And make sure he's on the bus for the lecdem at nine-thirty. I hope he feels like shit in the morning."

Seventeen

Rebo was not the only one to look under the weather on Monday morning. Lindy's face was purple, scraped and swollen on one side. The contrast of the untouched skin on her other cheek only made it look worse. Biddy's complexion was blotched from restless sleep. The dancers filed gloomily onto the bus. Dark clouds hovered low above them, but rain refused to come. Wind swept around in little cyclones without managing to find a single dried leaf or stray piece of trash to kick about.

"I think it's time for a company meeting," Lindy said quietly to Biddy as they watched the others embark.

Biddy rolled her eyes.

"Company dinner?"

"That's a better idea, but I'm so tired. I don't think I can stand an 'angsting' session."

"We'll keep it light. Want to drive over with me?"

"No, I think I should go on the bus."

"Then I'll go, too."

It had been a long time since Lindy had been on a tour bus. She stopped by the driver and looked down the row of seats. It was like peering into a diorama, the kind school-children made for book reports. Seats made of folded cardboard. Paper people pasted to the front of each one. *Belinda Graham Goes on Tour* would be the title. It would be about a young girl whose dream in life was to be a ballerina. After a few earth-shattering problems, which would be cleared up rapidly before the final pages, the girl would be the star of the show and have gotten her man, as well.

But these were real people. They may be called kids, but they were full-fledged adults with their own sets of dreams and disappointments. Headsets had come out; faces were buried in paperbacks. A few dancers were already dozing. It didn't matter if they were going five miles or five hundred, they were at home.

And what about her? Was this her home, too? An old, familiar feeling gurgled up from some hidden recess inside her. It was just like the old days: when she was at work, feeling guilty about leaving Glen and the kids; and when she was at home, feeling guilty about not concentrating on her work. Some things didn't change. Where the hell did she belong?

Biddy nudged her from behind. "Are you going to stand all the way to the lec-dem?"

Lindy sat down in the first seat. The high back of the seat cut off everyone else from her view. For the first time since leaving New Jersey, she felt utterly alone.

Biddy stood in the aisle, counting heads, then dropped into the seat beside her, clutching her crutches in both arms. "I'm sorry I got you into this."

Lindy dragged her attention back to the present.

"I just thought you could help me deal with Carlotta. I didn't know she was going to get murdered. We were in New

Jersey, and I automatically thought of you. You always knew exactly what to do when things got tough."

"Biddy, you didn't get me into this. I wanted to come. I thought I was perfectly content until that night at the Endicott. It kind of jostled my perspective of things. I didn't realize before how much I missed this. Silly, isn't it?"

She had given up her career because it was too hard to juggle work, husband, and kids. "I'd already retired as a dancer before I left."

"But you were a great rehearsal director. Still are."

"Yeah, but I wanted to be a great wife and mom, too."

"You are." Biddy squeezed her hand.

Lindy squeezed back. "I guess." God knows she had tried hard enough. While she attempted to shape and mold and enhance the lives of her husband and children, her own life had flown by like a giant desert sandstorm, leaving Lindy in its wake.

Sitting here on a bus in Connecticut, it seemed to her that once she had settled them into the house of their dreams, it was Glen who had taken off. Now, Cliff and Annie had taken off, too. And where did that leave her?

It left her right here, and it was about time she got her act together.

"Really, Biddy, except for the murder and getting pushed down the trapdoor, this has been the most fun I've had in years."

A few minutes later, the bus pulled up in front of the Movement Education Building. A few comments wafted toward her as she gathered up her dance bag.

"Wow, the twentieth century."

"My kingdom for a dressing room with lights that work."

"Cushy."

"The theater in Hartford has been totally renovated," Biddy said primly over the tops of their heads.

The dancers filed off the bus. They moved sluggishly. Well, no one really loves an early-morning call, thought Lindy, but she felt uneasy. Things were beginning to fall apart. Jeremy had removed himself from everyone, like he was waiting for the final blow. This was no time for vacillating. She needed to take control.

"Definitely in need of a company dinner," she said to Biddy. "Where is Jeremy? I'll ask him if it's okay."

"He and Peter came earlier with Angie. Peter has to teach a Stage Craft seminar. He was not thrilled. Talking for a whole hour is not exactly his style."

Angie met them in the upstairs hall. She looked distracted. "Hi, everybody. Girls' dressing room is here, and the boys' is down on the left. Yell, if you need anything." She turned to Biddy and Lindy and led them farther along the corridor.

"The police are here. They took Jack in for questioning this morning, and now they've asked Jeremy to come to the station. There's more than one of them, and they look pretty serious. I hope things aren't getting worse."

Biddy gasped. Jeremy was walking down the hall between Detective Williams and another officer. His face was completely drained of color, but he appeared calm and not surprised at being led away.

A group of girls came out of the door and stopped abruptly, their conversation dying midsentence. They all watched the procession move toward them. Jeremy slowed as he reached the group of worried faces.

He nodded slightly to Biddy. "You'll have to do the lec-

dem. The tapes are in the studio. Peter will be here soon."
And then they were gone.

The girls disappeared back into the dressing room. Lindy could hear their frantic whispers through the closed door. It wouldn't be long until everyone had heard. There would be another round of suspicion, fear. The company was disintegrating. She was failing Jeremy, and Biddy.

"You shouldn't have told him, Lindy," Biddy sobbed. "He'll destroy us. It's your fault." She spun around and hobbled into the studio.

Angie put her arm around Lindy. "She didn't mean it. I don't know what's going on. I stayed away because I knew you'd call if you needed me. She'll be all right."

Lindy choked back a sob. She was a stranger again. Jeremy had turned to Biddy to carry on. He had cut her out of what she loved most. She skulked down the hall feeling like the traitor Biddy thought she was. She groped her way around the corner and pressed her forehead to the wall. Do not fall apart on me now, she begged.

Crying is a great catharsis—witness the popularity of tragedy in the theater—but Lindy knew she didn't have time to cry. That would come later. Tears of relief or wretchedness—at this point she didn't care which. She just wanted it to be over. She'd go home to New Jersey, where she belonged. She wouldn't complain if Glen watched television all night. She'd even watch it with him. She banged her forehead on the wall. No, she wouldn't. Pathos. Really, Lindy. No, bathos, it's even worse. Let's try the stiff-upper-lip routine. She straightened herself up and marched down the hall and into the rehearsal studio.

*   *   *

They made it through the lec-dem, answering the usual questions at the end, like, "What do you eat for breakfast?" and "What's touring like?" Not like this, Lindy thought bitterly.

She took her place on the bus; Biddy moved to the back. It was Peter who sat down beside her. They stared out at open fields, new growth bending in the wind, as the bus carried them back to the hotel.

"Now, what?" asked Peter.

Lindy looked at him. His cheekbones stood out like ledges over the hollows of his cheeks.

She leaned her head back against the seat and closed her eyes. "I don't know."

"I've hated him for so long. Now I just want it to be over."

"Me too."

Lindy lingered in the lobby until she saw Biddy go into the elevator. She didn't have the energy or the courage to face more incriminations. There was no news from Jack or Jeremy. She followed the last group of dancers into the elevator and rode up to the third floor.

Biddy was lying facedown on the bed. She made no sound except for an occasional shudder, but her back heaved with silent sobs.

Lindy threw her bag on the floor and sat on the edge of the other bed. And waited.

After a few minutes, Biddy lifted her head from the bed. "Glen called. The message light was on when I got back. I thought it might be word from—" That was as far as she got before she broke down again.

Lindy reached for the phone and pressed the numbers mechanically. Glen answered on the first ring.

"Where have you been? What's going on there? You never return my calls."

Lindy glanced at the top of the dresser and the pile of message slips that had accumulated there. "Yes, I do. Eventually."

"You sound really depressed. Are you okay? Did they arrest anyone yet? Are you safe?"

"Yes, no, yes. I'm just really tired."

"Good. No, I'm serious. Tired is better than a lot of alternatives I can think of. Remember that meeting I told you about?"

"No."

"It was the night of your murder. Anyway, it's definite. They've offered me an overseas consultant position. What do you think?"

Overseas. Like in international travel. More days and nights away from home. Lindy mentally kicked herself. This was a great step-up for him. He deserved it.

"Well? What do you think?"

What did she think? She was . . . envious. "That's great, Glen."

"Big pay increase. A lot of travel, but you can come with me, sometimes. I'll be really busy at first, but after that, we can mix business with some pleasure. What do you say?"

"If it sounds good to you, it sounds good to me."

"Then, I'm going to accept it. I wanted to talk to you first."

"I'm really proud of you. Congratulations."

"Gotta go. Love you."

"Love you, too."

Biddy had raised herself onto one elbow. "What was that all about?"

"Glen just got a promotion. Overseas consultant, whatever that is. Lots of travel. That will be fun," Lindy said without much enthusiasm. A string of lonely nights with only Bruno as company stretched before her. A nice, warm, hairy body that snored, shed, and had doggy breath. Great.

"You'd be traveling with him?"

Lindy shrugged. "Sometimes. It will be nice to go back to all those places I never got to see the first time around. The inside of a theater looks the same in any country. Dark. I'll enjoy being a tourist for a change."

"Oh."

"What?"

"I was kind of hoping that you might stay on."

"Biddy. You're the most changeable creature I've ever met. I thought you hated me."

"I'm not changeable," said Biddy. "I'm just resilient. There's a difference. Anyway, I don't hate you. I was upset. I lashed out at the safest person. I knew you'd forgive me. Right?"

Lindy moved over to Biddy and gave her a hug. The telephone rang.

"Glen," said Lindy as she picked up the receiver. "Hello." A pause. "What do you want?"

Biddy sat up and mouthed the word "Who?"

"Listen, Mr. Brandecker. I don't need to talk to you. I don't want to talk to you. You've got what you wanted, now leave us alone." She slammed the phone down. "The nerve of the guy." The phone rang again. "Don't answer it."

It kept ringing. They sat, unmoving.

"How long do you think he'll keep this up?" asked Biddy.

Lindy shrugged. The ringing stopped. She grabbed the receiver and shoved it under her pillow. "This should take care of any more phone calls." They sat on Biddy's bed, staring at Lindy's pillow, nerves on edge.

Biddy squeaked when the banging on the door began.

"Don't answer it," commanded Lindy.

"Lindy, he could keep pounding on the door all day."

"Then I'll call security."

"You think security is going to tangle with a policeman, and one that big? Maybe you should hear him out and then get rid of him once and for all."

"You get rid of him. I'll hide in the bathroom."

Biddy erupted into giggles. "It's a ridiculous idea."

"It worked in Brussels, didn't it? Oh, all right. But I'm not going to be nice."

Bill Brandecker had no intention of being nice, either. Before Lindy had the door open, he pushed his way through and slammed it behind him.

"I know you think this is my fault," he bellowed at her. A vein in his temple pulsed. Veins always pulsed noticeably in fiction. Lindy had never actually seen one pulse in real life, and she found it fascinating.

Not getting any reaction, Bill stopped yelling and looked at her. "What are you looking at?"

"The side of your head."

A growl rolled from deep in his throat. He turned to Biddy, who cowered back against the headboard. "How can you stand her?" He turned back to Lindy, who still stood by the door. "If you ever—could get control of your wandering thoughts, even for a second—you might—just might—organize them into an ordered thought process." The sentence had taken several breaths and had ended in a near roar.

Lindy knew this trick. Attack before they have time to attack you. She'd wait him out and then let him have it.

"Are you finished?" she asked calmly. "If you are, I can recommend a good theatrical agent. You need a little fine-tuning, but a few lessons should do the trick."

She very methodically opened the door. "Good day."

Bill looked stunned. He eyed her intensely for a few seconds and then walked out the door.

Lindy leaned back against it. "I've always wanted to do that exit. Just like in the BBC version of *Pride and Prejudice* where Eliza gives Lady Catherine the boot."

"I feel a little sorry for him," said Biddy. She pulled the receiver from under the pillow and replaced it on the table.

"I can't believe you. Just a few hours ago, you were saying he had destroyed our lives. And now you feel sorry for him?"

"He doesn't seem so bad in person. He's so loud and big. But I think he, well, respects you."

"Just remember that he ratted on us."

"He didn't really have much of a choice."

"I know. I shouldn't have confided in him. I just didn't know what else to do."

"I didn't mean all those things I said. You did the right thing."

"So what *are* you saying?"

"Maybe you should talk to him if he calls again. Maybe he'd be willing to help if you ask nicely."

Lindy bared her teeth. "Like this?"

The telephone rang.

It was the "I'm sorry" that did it. Lindy wasn't used to men apologizing, straight out with no extenuating reasons tacked on. They usually turned it into being your fault: "Sorry, but you know I had to work late . . . Sorry, but all the other moms . . . But if you had only—I would have . . . Sorry, but you always . . ."

That simple "I'm sorry," period, nothing else, had left her momentarily nonplused. And before she could recover, she had agreed to meet him downstairs.

Bill was sitting in one of the overstuffed club chairs in the lobby. He rose when he saw her. He seemed to tower over her. He didn't look contrite, and for a second, Lindy wished she had sent Biddy in her place. She had expended the last of her energy in the confrontation upstairs. She felt claustrophobic.

"I suppose it's too early for a drink?" he asked.

"Let's walk. I can't stand it in here." She headed toward the front door. Bill stuffed his hands into the back pockets of his jeans and followed her out.

"There's an access road down on the left," he said.

She turned to the left. The day was still overcast, but the clouds had lifted and the sky had turned a light gray. Still no rain, but the air was chilled. She crossed her arms in front of her.

"Cold?"

Lindy shook her head. Bill seemed to have shrunk to normal size in the outdoors. Open space was a better background for him, she thought. He was more approachable.

She felt sorry for his students, who probably cowered in their seats during his classroom lectures.

"The police knew everything. Nothing I told them had much bearing on their decision to requestion Jeremy."

"I thought you would help us," she blurted out, her anger making a brief resurgence.

"I'm trying. But what do you care more about? Saving your friend or finding the truth?"

"He didn't do it," she snapped, but her voice lacked the conviction she wanted to feel. "What about Jack?"

"They've released him for now."

"Why?"

"He admitted to skimming the books, but he implicated Jeremy in that, too. He said that Jeremy forced him to take the money, and out of loyalty, he did."

"That's a crock."

"I think so, too."

"You do?" She looked up at him expectantly. His eyes were definitely blue. "Then are you going to help us?"

"It isn't that simple. You know absolutely nothing about the way an investigation is carried on, do you?"

"No. I've never even had a parking ticket. Well, except once when—"

"Don't get started." He smiled.

She shut up.

Bill took her arm and steered her down the access road that skirted the parking lot and led to the back of the hotel.

"Let me explain a few things," he said pedantically, and Lindy braced herself for a big dose of condescension. "I shouldn't tell you anything. I wouldn't know anything about the case myself except Dell sees me as some kind of expert on the waywardness of arty types."

Lindy started to speak, but he stopped her. "Jeremy has means, motive, and opportunity. Carlotta refused to alibi him for this previous accident. It's all in the records, if you have access to them. Then his life falls apart. You can see how that might fester until he was driven to get his revenge."

"Circumstantial, right?"

"Alone, but coupled with the fact that he can't account for his whereabouts at the time of the murder, that the choreographer was pressuring him to fire her, and his fingerprints were on the candlestick . . ." Bill turned his hand, palm up, in a gesture that said fait accompli.

"But he picked it up after Carlotta threatened Eric with it. Everybody saw him."

Bill nodded, but Lindy knew there was more coming. "They're hoping they can get a confession."

"Even if he's not guilty? You make it sound like a police state."

"They don't torture people, Lindy, just manipulate them into telling the truth. I shouldn't have told you this, but I owe you one for being honest with me yesterday. You can send cookies to my jail cell if they find out I've talked to you."

He had made the last statement casually, but Lindy didn't miss the enormity of its implication. "You were a lousy cop, weren't you?" she asked gently.

"Yeah." He looked over her head into the distance. "You get caught up in people's lives, then go about systematically destroying them. It wasn't so bad with the hardened criminals, but you'd be surprised how many homicides are committed by normally decent human beings."

They had cut off the access road and were walking down a heavily overgrown dirt track, an abandoned tractor path that was no longer needed since the surrounding fields no longer supported working farms. Shoots of new grass mixed with the dried stalks of old, their height virtually blocking out the view. Only the top of the hotel was visible.

Lindy felt her head begin to clear, her body relax. Fresh air had a way of doing that. "What if Sandra's accident really wasn't an accident?"

"That would make it worse for Jeremy."

"No. Not Jeremy, but someone else." She had been wrestling with an idea for days. It was out of reach still, but maybe the two of them could ferret it out. "What if, say, Jack was involved, and Carlotta was blackmailing him?"

"Go on."

"I mean, Jack has been sending flowers all these years, every two weeks. That seems a little extreme unless, maybe, he was responsible for the accident."

"An interesting idea, but it doesn't help with the current murder. Jack didn't return from New York until the next day."

"But he did."

"What? How do you know, and why didn't you tell the police?"

"Hearsay."

"You're getting your terms mixed up."

"Everything is all mixed up, but I know he was back. I saw his car leave the parking lot. It was late, around three in the morning. I couldn't sleep. I was staring out the window and I saw his car drive away. I didn't make the connection at first. I was preoccupied with everything else, and I didn't expect to see his car because I thought he was in New York. It was a dark car. But now that I think back, I'm sure it was Jack's. Old, big, black. That would mean he was here and could have murdered Carlotta."

"I think you're stretching facts to fit into the scenario you want."

"Are they sure Jack was in New York all that night? Maybe he came back, then left and came back again."

Bill looked amused. "I'll see if I can find out, let's turn back."

"I know you're just humoring me," she said as they began retracing their steps. "You think I'm totally dizzed-out, but I'm not. It's more instinct than intelligence, but I know I'm right."

He reached for her shoulder and swung her around. "You may be right, and I'll help you if I can, but do not act on this yourself. I don't want to investigate your murder." He pulled her toward him and kissed her. A major kiss, arms enfolding her. A wave of fascination, then something stronger, rushed up her body. Heady stuff. It had been a long time since a man had come on to her so abruptly and so ... thoroughly. She had no choice but to respond. For a minute.

She broke away. What the hell was she doing? "Don't."

Bill gazed out over the tops of the surrounding grasses. "I know. But I figured it was the only chance I'd get."

She felt the blood rush up her neck and into her cheeks. How could he stand there with that distracted half smile on his face? *She* probably looked awkward and embarrassed . . . and eager. She looked away.

"We'd better get back." Bill shoved his hands back into his pockets and began walking toward the hotel. She fell in step beside him, neither of them breaking the silence.

They returned to the access road. The pavement felt hard and secure beneath her feet. "Can you find out if Jack was really in New York?" Her voice only sounded a little shaky.

"I'll try, but I have to get back to the city. They'll probably release you to go on to Hartford tomorrow with or without Jeremy. But you and Biddy had better start thinking about what to do with the company. Jack will be arraigned on embezzling, if Jeremy files charges. If they have enough on Jeremy, it will go to trial. Somebody will have to deal with the business end."

"Biddy can handle that if she has to." She was ridiculously close to tears. "I'll handle the rest, but . . ."

"I'll contact you in Hartford if I find out anything."

"Thanks. I'm sorry we ruined your vacation."

They finished the walk back in silence.

"He kissed me."

"I knew it," cried Biddy triumphantly. "And on a scale of one to ten?"

"Biddy, it's not funny."

"Lindy, if you're going to get back out in the world, you've got to be prepared for men falling in love with you. They always did, remember?"

"But it was fun then. This wasn't fun."

"But was it good?"

Lindy shot her a menacing look. Biddy stood with one

hand on her hip, that saucy "tell me every detail" expression on her face. One lift of her eyebrow, and Lindy was ready to confess. She sank onto the bed.

"Delicious."

"Oops." They both started to laugh. "So what are you going to do about it?"

"What any red-blooded American girl would do—forget it ever happened."

Biddy frowned.

"We've got too much to deal with already without adding adultery to the pot. But, oh, Biddy."

"So what did you learn?"

"That you sleep in the bed you make."

"About the investigation."

"Oh." Lindy straightened up. She ran through the conversation with Bill, explaining her dawning ideas about Jack.

"Wow, that makes perfect sense."

"If only it were true. Bill also said that they'll send us on to Hartford tomorrow, and we'd better be prepared to carry on without Jeremy."

Biddy didn't even flinch at the suggestion. She had readied herself for the fight. Lindy felt a sudden surge of hope.

Eighteen

They moved on to Hartford the following morning without Jeremy. Biddy rode on the bus; Lindy followed behind in her car.

The bus maneuvered down the narrow city street and double-parked in front of the hotel, a building dating from the 1920s, which was flanked by two rows of smaller boutiques. Lindy pulled up behind the bus and was relieved of her suitcase by a waiting bellboy, and of her car by a parking valet. "If you need your car, call the front desk, and it will be driven around. The parking garage is around the corner and very secure." He drove away.

She walked through the double wooden doors, held open by a uniformed doorman. The lobby could have been used for an F. Scott Fitzgerald set. Tall potted palms rose on each side of the chestnut registration desk; the entire lobby was paneled in the same polished wood. The atmosphere was warm and rich, and evoked the insouciance of another era.

Lindy could have appreciated the ambience if she hadn't been so preoccupied. She longed for the serenity that her surroundings promised, but knew there would be no peace for any of them until one of them was declared a murderer and removed from this life forever.

She shuddered involuntarily and followed the bellboy up the curving staircase to her room.

"I've called a company meeting for six o'clock. The hotel can put us in one of the banquet rooms," announced Biddy as she pulled clothes out of her suitcase and tossed them haphazardly into drawers. "We'll feed them, but we'll have to let them know what's going on."

"And what is going on? I saw you talking to Detective Williams at the hotel this morning, but I didn't want to interrupt," said Lindy.

"They haven't arrested Jeremy yet. Just held him overnight for questioning. I guess they have to arrest him or let him go."

"And how are we going to find that out?"

"When he shows up in Hartford, or doesn't."

"Then, we'll just have to stick it out. In the meantime, you have some nervous sponsors to meet."

"In two hours. I hope you'll come with me. I think I can convince them not to cancel, that we can carry on. There'll be a lot of loss on both sides if we can't deliver."

"We'll deliver, and, of course, I'll come."

The rest of the afternoon was spent reassuring the Hartford Arts Association. They met at the theater, which was only a block away from the hotel. It wasn't an easy meeting. There were a few members with extremely cold feet, but Biddy was convincing, and even Lindy was swayed by her seeming confidence.

There was a telegram waiting for her at the desk when she and Biddy returned to the hotel.

"I haven't gotten a telegram since my last opening night." She tore open the envelope. "It's from Bill. Quaint, but more private than leaving a message."

Lindy read it through and then crumpled it in her hand. "Jack's clear. He charged gas at ten o'clock going north on I-ninety-five."

"I'd still like to ask that rat a few more questions," said Biddy.

"So would I, but I doubt if he'll make another appearance. I wouldn't dare show my face if I were in his place. It's your baby now."

They barely had enough time to shower and change before meeting the dancers downstairs. They mulled over how to approach the meeting while choosing what to wear. They discussed what to say, and more importantly what not to say.

"I guess we've seen the last of Bill Brandecker, too," said Lindy.

"Are you sorry?"

"No, not really. But it doesn't seem like him to just walk away. Though he's spent more time on us than we have any right to expect." She pulled a pair of shoes out of the armoire that served as the closet.

"Maybe you should have encouraged his advances."

"It was not an advance, more like an experiment."

"Maybe you should have encouraged him to experiment more." Biddy finished pulling a green velour sweater over her head. "All right. Sorry. I was just trying to make a joke."

"Laugh so we won't cry. Nice try."

"Oh, come on, Lindy. Married people play around all the time."

"Not me."

"I know, not you. But don't you miss it?"

"Not until now."

"Well, it wouldn't be the worst thing in the world. People do it all the time."

"And we know what happens to those people. Marriage is like that finger in the dike thing. Relax your vigil for a second even, and you might drown in the results."

"Sounds too complicated to me."

"Like the war on drugs, you just say no." Lindy slipped her arm over Biddy's shoulder and they hurried downstairs.

The company was assembled in the smaller of two banquet rooms, tastefully refurbished like the rest of the hotel. The waitresses and busboys seemed happy enough to accommodate the group at the last minute. Lindy wondered how long it would take before she saw suspicion in the faces of that well-trained staff.

Peter looked up from a huddle of dancers. Lindy noticed that Andrea was among them. Could anything good come out of this mess? Peter, if no one else, deserved some respite. "We've loaded in, floor's down," he said as Biddy and Lindy approached the group. "Is it a go?"

Lindy watched Biddy assume her "business face."

"Yes, it's a go." She turned to the rest of the room who had stopped their conversations in order to listen. "We're continuing on. Jeremy has been delayed in order to clear up a few loose ends, but he'll be joining us soon. You're all free to leave as far as the police are concerned, but I hope you'll stay on. It's been a frightful experience, and, unfortunately, it isn't over yet. We've been through more than a lot together, but we have something good here. I can feel it. I know you can feel it. Let's not lose it now, when we're so close."

"But, Biddy, what if they arrest Jeremy? Are we still going to have jobs?"

She turned in the direction of the voice. "We're contracted through the Joyce season. That gives you a paycheck through May. Beyond that, I don't know. It will depend."

"What's going to happen to Jack? We heard what he's been doing. You're not going to let him back, are you?"

"Jack won't be working here any longer. I don't have the authority to fire him, but I'll make sure he doesn't touch another penny of the company's money."

"But he signs all the checks," said someone else.

"Not without Jeremy's accompanying signature, or in Jeremy's absence, mine."

Lindy looked at her in astonishment. When had she managed all of this?

"I want you all to take time to consider before you make any decisions. I hope you'll decide to stay. Now, let's eat."

Talking broke out again as the dancers moved toward the tables.

"I'm staying." Rebo's voice resounded from the crowd. "I don't have to think about it. If you want me, I'm staying."

"Thanks, Rebo." Biddy's voice was tremulous. "We want you."

Lindy sat next to Biddy. "When did you get the power to sign checks?"

"I've always had it, in case we needed a check and one of the two signers wasn't available. It's a normal formality."

"Oh," said Lindy, impressed.

They proceeded through dinner: salad of field greens with balsamic vinaigrette, a main course of above-average chicken Marsala with julienne vegetables. It was not the lively affair that most company dinners were, but at least they were together. Nothing like breaking bread to put things back on an even keel.

The room was set up banquet style, tables pushed together to form a U. Lindy and Biddy were sitting at one of the sides. Lindy watched Rebo spread his arms in front of his dinner companions. Jesus at the Last Supper, she thought and bobbled her wineglass. There was a burst of laughter, and the image faded.

She had regained her composure and was half listening to Biddy recounting some tale of tour when Mieko and Kate burst into the room.

Mieko looked wildly around until she zeroed in on Lindy. "He's here, that bastard," she exclaimed breathlessly. "Jack. We saw him in the lobby. We were coming back from the bathroom. He looked like he was checking in. I can't believe it."

"Biddy, what are we going to do?" asked Kate. "Should we try to stop him?"

"We'll take care of Jack." Rebo sprang from his chair. Paul, Eric, and Juan started to rise, but Peter already had his hand on Rebo's shoulder.

"I'll take care of it." He pushed Rebo back into his seat and started toward the door.

Alice jumped up, turning her chair over, but Andrea had

already followed Peter out. Lindy and Biddy followed her, with the rest of the company behind them.

Peter had stopped Jack on his way to the stairs. The desk clerk was looking on nervously.

Jack's voice was low and spiteful. "You're wasting your energy, Peter. There's not much you can do at this point."

"I can keep you away from the company, and I will."

Jack snorted and turned away; Peter's hand caught him by the shoulder. Jack responded by swinging his briefcase into Peter's ribs, doubling him over. Andrea was knocked down by the impact of Peter's weight hitting her.

Biddy rushed past them. "You're finished here, Jack. You can wrap up whatever business you think you have tomorrow and then leave."

"That's exactly what I plan to do. There is no company. They'll arrest Jeremy for Carlotta's murder, and that will be the end of this little travesty." He pushed past her and rushed up the stairs.

"You can't stop us, Jack," cried Biddy to his retreating form. "We're going to make it."

The faces behind her had plunged once more into hopelessness. Lindy was glad that Biddy was staring up the stairs. "Let's get back to dessert, shall we?" The group moved back into the banquet room. Andrea was attempting to help Peter, but he pushed her away and lunged for the stairs.

"Peter, no." Biddy's voice stopped him at the foot of the stairs. He seemed to waver, then turned and strode across the lobby, out the front door, and into the street.

Andrea stared after him. Lindy put her arm around the girl. "He just needs some time to cool off. He'll be back."

Andrea bit her lip and quietly shook her head. "I don't want to go back in there."

Lindy led her over to one of the paisley-covered love seats that sat at each side of a square glass coffee table. The front door was hidden from their view by a large potted palm; a few of the bottom fronds were turning brown.

"Why can't he open up? Trust someone?"

Lindy watched the girl twist the tails of her knit shirt into a ball. She wasn't prepared to give advice to the lovelorn. She felt terribly out of her league. "I don't know."

"Alice says he's completely devoted to his sister and never looks at another woman."

"Well, he doesn't look at Alice, anyway."

Andrea laughed softly. "I almost miss Carlotta. When she was mean to me, he always stood up for me. I thought that maybe . . . but I guess I was wrong."

"I wouldn't be so sure." Lindy looked furtively around. If Peter would just make an entrance, she could wrap this up. But Peter wasn't accommodating.

"When I found the . . . when I found . . . her, he was so gentle. He told me what to tell the police, and how to—"

"He told you what to say to the police?" Lindy interrupted.

Andrea nodded. "He said, if they pushed me, to tell them I heard a noise, and that I went in to see what it was."

"And did you?"

Andrea looked at her blankly. "Did I what?"

"Did you tell the police that you heard a noise?"

"No. I couldn't lie. I know Peter was trying to protect me." She sighed deeply, a shiver running across her shoulders. "At least, I thought he was. But now he hardly even speaks to me."

"So you didn't hear a noise?" Why hadn't she questioned Andrea more closely?

"No. I went in to tell Carlotta what a bitch she was and to leave us alone. I had had enough. When you took everyone back to the stage at intermission, Peter followed her. She said the most awful things to him. Said he was useless; that he couldn't even help his own sister. I could have killed her when I heard her. And stuff about Sandra, vicious things. She was insanely jealous of everybody, even a poor girl who will never dance again."

"Did you see him leave?"

"What?"

Lindy grabbed the girl by her shoulders and faced her directly in front of her. "Was Carlotta alive when he left her?"

"Of course. He stormed out and back to the light board, and she slammed the door."

Lindy let out a momentary sigh of relief. "And did you see Jeremy then?"

"No. He was still in his office with Eric."

Lindy released Andrea's shoulders and jumped up. "Look, I'm sure things will work out. Peter just needs some time to figure it out. So much has been happening. Why don't you stay and wait for him?" She practically ran across the lobby in her rush to find Biddy. As inconspicuously as she could, she dragged Biddy away from her coffee and cheesecake and led her to the stairs. Andrea was sitting where she had left her. Lindy hoped she wouldn't have too long to wait.

"What—what?" asked Biddy as Lindy closed the door to their room.

"Peter saw Carlotta alive during the intermission after the fight, a little tidbit, he forgot to mention, at least to me. Andrea just told me. I didn't even think to ask her. I am such a dolt."

"But how does this help Jeremy?" Biddy held up her hands. "I know, write it down." She grabbed hotel stationery and a pen out of the desk drawer and plopped onto the bed.

"Carlotta was alive during the intermission, and after I released everyone, there was a rush to get ready for the next piece. People were all over the place. So it had to happen during the *Holberg Suite* or during notes afterward."

"So we've narrowed the time down about ten minutes. What now?"

Lindy sighed with disappointment. "We keep narrowing, eliminating possibilities until we get it right. I want to talk to Peter." She picked up the phone and rang the front desk.

"Andrea's gone. What are the chances that she and Peter . . ."

"And if they are, should we interrupt them?" added Biddy.

They were interrupted by a knock. Exchanging glances, they both went to answer the door.

Not Peter, not Jack, but Jeremy. Smiling.

"Thank God, how did you—what did they say?" Words tumbled out of Biddy's mouth in an avalanche of relief.

Jeremy responded by gathering her up, crutches included, and giving her a hearty hug.

Hmm, thought Lindy, and then she was gathered up, too.

Their levity didn't last long. Jeremy pulled away. He looked tired and disheveled. He had changed clothes, but

Lindy could tell he hadn't paid much attention to what he had put on. She could see tiny lines of fatigue around his mouth and eyes.

"You look beat. Sit down and tell us what happened, if you can stand to."

Jeremy moved away from them, shrugged out of his jacket, and threw it across the bed. He sat down in the boudoir chair next to the window. He was much too big for the chair, and it took a few seconds for him to find a comfortable position. Biddy and Lindy sat next to each other on the end of Biddy's bed facing him.

"The upshot is they had to let me go, momentarily at least. They didn't want to; we're now in somebody else's jurisdiction, but they couldn't put all the 'maybes' together enough to actually arrest me. And I wouldn't oblige them by confessing to something I didn't do." He looked from Biddy to Lindy and back again, waiting for a reaction.

It was Biddy who spoke. "You big idiot. Don't you dare look at us that way. We know you didn't do it."

Jeremy looked down at his hands, then at Lindy. She shook her head slightly. Men, she thought. Jeremy was worried that she had told Biddy about Sandra and him. He was sitting here, suspected of murder, and he was embarrassed about an old love affair.

"Jack's here."

Jeremy vaulted to his feet. "Him, I could kill. He implicated me. Told them that I had made him steal the money. What an imbecile. All they had to do was look at our bank accounts to know that was a lie. What's he up to, I wonder."

"I'm going to find out right now." Biddy heaved herself off the bed. Her crutches clattered onto the carpet.

"Sit down, both of you." Lindy was exasperated beyond endurance. "It's worse than the opera around here. Comic opera, if it weren't so tragic. No one is what they seem. Skeletons in every closet. Misguided lovers. Threats and chases and trapdoors." Biddy and Jeremy were staring at her, eyes round. "Sit down."

They sat down.

"Now, we're going to start again. Take it one step at a time." She felt like a schoolteacher facing two dull students. "Jeremy didn't kill Carlotta. Biddy didn't kill Carlotta. I didn't kill Carlotta."

She was interrupted by a knock on the door. "Oh, God, not again. It's worse than New Jersey." She dropped onto the bed and threw her arms over her head. Jeremy and Biddy broke out laughing.

"No, stay where you are, I'll get it," offered Jeremy, still laughing. He looked at Biddy, and she broke out into a new round of giggles.

Peter was not laughing. "I heard you were back." He looked at Jeremy, but didn't step inside.

"Come in, Peter. Welcome to Bedlam." Jeremy clapped him on the shoulder and moved him through the door.

The realization hit Lindy like a bolt of proverbial lightning. Jeremy had no idea of how Peter felt about him. She could hardly believe it, but Jeremy seemed entirely comfortable with the other man. Was it possible that they had spent this much time together without him picking up on how Peter felt? It seemed incredible. Well, maybe it was time he found out. The action in the room continued without her. Doubt fought with certainty in her overloaded brain.

She took the chance. "Jeremy, Peter thinks you injured

Sandra." She was vaguely aware of Jeremy stopping, his arm still around Peter's shoulder. Peter stared at her, eyes blazing. Biddy turned to her, face frozen in an unfinished laugh. Gee, people really do move in slow motion, she thought.

"I think it's about time the two of you had a little chat." She turned to Jeremy, who still hadn't absorbed her outburst. "Everything, Jeremy." She turned to Peter, who hadn't moved. "Hear him out. And don't do anything stupid. Biddy and I are going for a walk, a long walk, maybe we'll find an all-night grocery store. Peruse the cabbages. Take as long as you want, but get it done."

She walked to the armoire and grabbed two jackets indiscriminately off the hangers. "Come on, Biddy." Biddy scrambled for her crutches and followed her out.

There were no all-night grocery stores. There were no all-night anythings. The neighborhood was dark and deserted. She didn't want to talk to Biddy, and Biddy, for once, didn't seem inclined to ask any questions. They stopped in front of a jewelry store, staring through the plate-glass window at empty velvet display cases.

Lindy couldn't calm her ragged nerves. She stared at the velvet until it began to dance in front of her unfocused eyes. She felt deflated, alone, and she missed . . . Bill. Damn Brandecker. Why did he have to kiss her? But it was more than that. It was the camaraderie, the working together. Well, at least the promise of it.

She did a quick edit. Glen—maybe she should call Glen. But unlike Bill, he would never understand what was going on. How could he? Everything in his life worked perfectly to schedule. All the way up the corporate ladder, he had never had more than minor setbacks, quickly overcome. She envied him in a way. He was comfortable with his life, with their life. After all, they had spent eighteen years building a marriage—or maybe she had been doing the building. He never seemed to have to work at anything. And once Lindy had agreed to marry him, he didn't even have to work at that.

She felt a tear slide down her cheek. Not now, she thought. She never felt comfortable anywhere. Her life was all over the place, the highest highs, the lowest lows. Never anything in between. Why couldn't she just be satisfied with the way things were. Another tear joined the first.

"What's the matter?" asked Biddy without turning to look at her.

"Life is so stupid," she croaked.

"Don't I know it."

They continued to roam the empty streets for an hour. They had passed by the hotel three times when Lindy turned into the door. "That should do it."

Their room was empty. "Well, no sirens. Maybe they worked it out." She still hadn't told Biddy what it was all about.

Nineteen

The next morning, Lindy and Biddy walked to the theater. Almost a week had passed since Carlotta had been found dead in her dressing room, and they were still no closer to finding out who had killed her. Every day had brought new possibilities, new suspicions, and then had dead-ended. Jeremy still wasn't in the clear, as far as the police were concerned. Jack was gone. Maybe they should have found a reason to keep him around for a few days. If he had killed Carlotta, he would walk away free, and they would never know for sure.

The sun beat down, warm and reassuring. Lindy listened to the one-two rhythm of Biddy's crutches along the sidewalk. A new theater. Maybe the change would help, but there could be no going back, no attempt to reconstruct the time sequence, no looking into unexplored crannies for clues that had eluded them. They hadn't even been admitted into Carlotta's dressing room to pack her things. Only Alice had been allowed to retrieve those items belonging to the company, signing for them. The rest had been packed away and taken by the police.

Hawthorne Theater had been part of a massive regentrification of downtown Hartford. Not the new high-rise district, but the picturesque, dying old town. Constructed of brick and stone, its Federal-style facade stood out hopefully among boarded-up shops and storefronts waiting for renovation. Across the street, two restaurants accommodated the theater patrons; one, an Italian coffee bar, the other, a nouveau bistro. They were closed now, not opening until late afternoon.

Biddy and Lindy had used the main entrance for the meeting with the Arts Association. It had taken place in an office, which still smelled of new carpet. Now they turned down an alley on the side of the theater toward the stage entrance. The sun immediately gave way to a cool, dark passage. The theater rose several stories on their right; the old savings and loan building, soon to be a shopping mall, matched its height to their left.

The alley was narrow, and they had to walk single file past the newly painted fire escape, which reached to the upper levels of the theater. Lindy paused, her eyes following the black iron grids upward.

Biddy pulled up short behind her. "Let's stick to trapdoors, okay?"

"My exact thoughts." Lindy brought her attention back to the alley. She intended to memorize every detail of the walk; she planned to scope out the entire theater. If something was going to happen, she would be prepared. But what was she expecting?

They had reached the metal stage door; it swung open. A shiver ran through her. She walked inside.

"Mornin', miss." An ancient, frail man wearing a security uniform was sitting on a rickety stool. He looked up from a clipboard that lay across his lap. "Name's Sal, and you are?"

He finished the question by squinting his eyes at them, glinting eyes encased in a landscape of deep wrinkles.

"Graham and McFee."

His fingers scrolled down the list. "Right." He nodded them in.

Security guard, noted Lindy. Phone on the wall behind him. Outside line. She reached for the inner door. There was a buzz, and it opened. She looked back at Sal. His hand was touching the wall to his right. She began to feel easier.

They walked into a hallway and through another metal door to stage right. Brand-new curtains separated the wings. She walked onto the stage and peered out into the house. The houselights were dimmed, and an enormous crystal chandelier created a halo of light over the red velvet seats. Fabric covered the walls of the auditorium; it would wreak havoc with the acoustics. The ceiling was covered by painted scenes in the Rococo style: helmeted gods riding on clouds; reclining women, with Greek gowns draped suggestively around their voluptuous figures.

"Wow," said Biddy, her head tilted back regarding the scene.

"Let's see the rest."

The dressing rooms were upstairs behind the stage. Directly underneath them were the shop, costume and prop rooms. They climbed the concrete stairs to a landing, then took the turn up another flight.

"You'll get your exercise here," said Lindy as she watched Biddy rattle up behind her.

"Another week and I'll be out of this darned thing, I hope." The sentence bounced out as her crutches hit each step.

They turned down the hall to the left. Lindy made a note of the fire exit to their right. The dressing rooms had been unlocked. They were plain, but sparkling clean. New plumbing had been installed. She hit the light switch inside the first room, and bright makeup lights outlined nondistorting mirrors. The walls had been stripped to the brickwork and shone with a layer of polyurethane. A full-length mirror was attached to the wall next to the tiny window that looked out over the street behind the theater.

"Very nice. Now I think I'll check out the rest of the theater before everyone else gets here."

"Not me." Biddy dropped into a chair. "I think I'll just take a rest before making the descent."

Lindy returned below and peeked into the costume room. Alice was on her knees, steaming the chiffon *Holberg* dresses. The dresses were lined up on hangers like empty doll clothes. She continued on. Open space doubled as the shop and loading dock. To her left, sunlight poured through the half-raised door. She looked to her right. The wall behind the stage was mounted on rails so that it could be opened to move scenery directly from truck to shop to stage and then closed again. Very efficient use of space, she thought. Smaller metal doors on each side led to backstage. The backstage extended all the way to the outside wall. She went in the stage-left door.

Peter was on headset, setting lighting cues. He nodded to her. "I could get lazy in a theater like this," he said between instructions.

She smiled. He seemed relaxed. She wondered if he and Jeremy had come to an understanding. She doubted if she would ever know what they had said to each other.

She wandered onto the stage. The pit was up, but it was

separated from the audience by a brass rail. She went offstage and through the door to the house. She slipped through the curtain that hid it from view by the audience and sat down in the first row, center. It was quiet, except for the occasional clank of metal as the crew unpacked sections of the *Carmina* cage. Lights popped on and off, faded and grew brighter, then changed as Peter tested the next cue.

This was her favorite time in the theater, when everything was still before you. Planning, focusing, imagining the reviews. If she concentrated, she could forget the turmoil of the week before. But it wouldn't go away: images of Carlotta's hair stinging Jeremy's face; the fall from the cage; Carlotta lying contorted on the floor, mixed with scenes of gay bars and hotel bars; Jeremy walking between two policemen; Biddy crying; Jack's briefcase knocking Peter off balance; Alice, standing backstage, saying, "I love this music." They were all wound in a tangled mess in her head. If she could just find the thread that would unravel it, like the thread that when pulled released the hemline of a dress, it would all fall into place, wouldn't it?

The sound of dancers entering the stage door brought her back to the present. She got up wearily and went to show them to their dressing rooms.

The rehearsal started off brightly. Everyone seemed to have pulled together in spite of Jack's brief resurgence last night. Spacing for *Holberg* went quickly since the University and Hawthorne Theaters had standard-size stages with the same number of wings. Lindy called out her corrections from the house. After an hour, they changed over to *Carmina*.

Jeremy stood at the side of the stage, looking on. They

began the run. Andrea threw the cloak open, and he stepped forward motioning to Peter in the wings to stop the tape.

"Do you mind, Lindy?" He turned to where she was sitting in the audience.

"Not at all," she replied in mild surprise. It was the first time she had seen Jeremy take an active part in a rehearsal since she had arrived.

He walked over to Andrea and spoke to her. She flashed him a huge smile, then closed the cloak around her and opened it again, this time with more flourish. "Better, try it again and this time . . ." He moved behind her and wrapped the cloak and his arms around her, holding her by the wrists. "Now." He curved his body over her, making her contract to the right and then threw her arms open. The train of the cloak swirled around her feet, entwining them. The lamé lining shone brilliantly on each side of her willowy body.

He looked out to Lindy for confirmation. She leaned back in her seat. Perfect. She nodded happily. Maybe they were on their way back.

Jeremy stayed on stage, maneuvering groups, shaping individuals, repeating sections. Lindy sat back watching. He was really good at this, and he was finally free to work again. And then the feeling came back. It wasn't over. She had to make it right. There was no one to depend on but herself.

Jeremy gave the dancers a ten-minute break. Lindy walked backstage. Jeremy was talking to Peter, head cocked slightly to the side. She could sense the new understanding between them.

She felt a bright future hanging precariously before her, but danger seemed to be lurking in every wing. Melodramatic, she thought disgustedly. Get a grip. Think logically. She surveyed the backstage area intently as if by looking hard enough she could draw the answer from the walls. But these were new walls with no memory of what had happened. She gave it up and went back to her seat.

Biddy joined her. "I heard that Jeremy was taking rehearsal this morning. I hope I haven't missed it. He's good, isn't he?"

Lindy nodded.

The dancers took their places. Jeremy was back onstage; he was having a great time. She and Biddy watched in silent admiration until Lindy felt someone slide into the row behind them. She turned around.

"Bill, where have you been?"

He looked tired and rumpled, and he was wearing a suit. His shirt was unbuttoned at the neck, and Lindy could see the end of his tie hanging out of his coat pocket. She had never seen him wearing anything but jeans before. A suit, even a wrinkled one, gave him an air of . . . competency.

"We thought you had deserted us," Lindy began.

"Don't give me a hard time, Lindy. I've just spent two days and nights badgering New Yorkers, and I'm tired and—"

"Cranky," she finished for him.

"And cranky. I didn't desert you. I was doing some research."

"What kind of research?" Biddy turned around in her seat.

"Looking at records from Sandra's accident report, what little there was of them. Picking the brains of anybody who was still around who had worked on the investigation, and spending half of last night in search of Sandra's old boyfriend."

"Wow," said Biddy.

Lindy just stared in amazement. "You're a genius," she finally murmured.

He smiled slightly, looking at her with sleep-deprived eyes. "Thanks, but actually, it was just legwork. His name was mentioned in an otherwise useless report, and I figured he might just remember something that would help. A bartender," he snorted. "It took a few bars before I could locate him. He works all over the place. I finally found him in a neighborhood dive on East Ninety-third Street. What I don't get is, why you girls keep falling for the pretty-faced, vapid types."

"Bill, please keep to the subject. What did he say?" Lindy hunched on her knees, facing Bill over the back of her seat.

He crossed his arms and leaned back with a complacent yawn. "What would you say to a love triangle?"

"What?" Biddy and Lindy gaped at him.

"Sandra, Jeremy, and Jack," he said slowly.

"But Jeremy's gay," said Biddy, unbelieving.

"He wasn't then, if what Devon"—Bill enunciated the name, rolling his eyes—"says is true, and I think it is." He brushed Biddy's stuttering aside. "Jeremy and Sandra had been lovers, but then Devon came along. They were planning to get married, but she was having a hard time breaking it to Jeremy, who was still in love with her, according to the boyfriend. In the meantime, she was always telling him, Devon, about how Jack was coming on to her, trying to give her things, and being generally slimy and whining, saying he loved her, asking her to marry him, et cetera, et cetera."

Lindy glanced at Biddy, who was staring into her hands. "But Jack is gone. He showed up last night for a hideous moment, but—"

"Jack hasn't checked out of the hotel yet. And he'll be stopping by here before he leaves town."

"How do you know?"

He smiled. "I left him a note."

"You didn't."

"Yep, only I signed Jeremy's name. Told him I wanted to talk after the rehearsal. Maybe we could come to an agreement. I think he'll show."

"But there's a security guard at the door."

"I left Jack's name with Sal."

"You *are* a genius."

"A genius in deep shit if this doesn't work."

"I'll bake you cookies every week, I promise." Lindy wanted to hug him, but she didn't.

They sat through the rest of the rehearsal: Lindy grinning; Biddy staring at her hands; Bill snoring lightly.

As soon as Jeremy dismissed the dancers, Lindy woke Bill, roused Biddy, who had been sitting like a statue since Bill had dropped the news about Jeremy's sexuality, and hurried them backstage. While Bill apprised Jeremy of his plan, Biddy and Lindy cleared the theater of dancers. The stagehands had left immediately to grab a bite somewhere nearby. Hopefully, Peter would be with them. Alice was the last one out, and Lindy breathed an audible sigh of relief as the door closed. "Do you go on break now, Sal?"

"No, I get a dinner break at five-thirty, then I'm back. Then I'm gonna watch the show."

"We're expecting someone."

"I know, I'll be sure he gets in, and I'll send him upstairs." Sal shifted his bony bottom on his stool and prepared to wait.

Lindy returned to the others. Jeremy and Bill were deep in discussion like two boys in a football huddle. Biddy leaned against the prop table, pulling absentmindedly at a strand of hair.

"Everyone's gone. I didn't see Peter. He must have gone with the stagehands."

"Let's hope so," said Bill. "The man's a loose cannon. We don't need him screwing this up."

They climbed the stairs and left Jeremy in the first dressing room, door ajar. They took their places in the next room and pulled the door closed, but not latched. And they waited.

"I feel ridiculous," mumbled Bill. "Even if it was my idea, especially, since it was my idea."

"Just think of it as a stakeout," whispered Lindy. She was beginning to worry about Biddy.

Bill put his finger to his lips. Lindy had heard it, too. Someone climbing the steps. Crepe soles on concrete. They moved closer to the door.

"You wanted to talk?"

"Come in, Jack." Jeremy's voice was as mellow as ever. "I thought we should have a little chat."

"There's nothing to say. They'll arrest you soon enough. You can try to sue me from jail."

"I think not. The police know that Carlotta was blackmailing you, not me. And when they find out why, I think they'll manage to get around that receipt from a gas station. Perhaps you'd be interested in making a little deal."

Jack's response was cut off by the sound of the door banging into the wall. Bill sprang into the hall, with Lindy right behind him.

"Oh, shit," said Bill, stopping just inside the door.

"Oh, shit," echoed Jeremy.

Oh, shit, is right, thought Lindy, looking around Bill and into Peter's furious face.

"What deal, Jeremy?" His voice started low, strangled, barely enough air escaping to sound out the words. But it was rapidly growing in pitch. He turned on Jack. "Why was Carlotta blackmailing you?"

Jack backed away from him.

Peter advanced on him. "Tell me, you simpering, little toad." He accented each word with a shove that finally landed Jack sprawled against the costume rack. "What did you do that gave Carlotta such power? Everyone knew you were a filthy embezzler, so it couldn't be that." One hand had slipped around Jack's neck. With his free hand, he lifted the man up and pinned him to the wall.

Jack was turning red. "Help, somebody, get him off me."

Lindy started to move. Bill's arm thrust out across her, blocking her way. She looked up at him, shocked. Sweat trickled down his temple from his hairline past his ear. He was staring at the two men.

"Why?" Peter knocked Jack's head against the wall.

"It was an accident, I swear it." Jack's tongue was protruding between purpling lips.

Peter loosened his grip slightly. "What was an accident?"

Jack lurched aside, but Peter brought his head up against the wall. "Tell me, while you still can."

Bill's arm was still rigid across Lindy. She watched impotently.

"Sandra. It was an accident. I only wanted to talk. She was so beautiful."

Peter reeled, but didn't loosen his grip. "What happened?"

His voice was ominously low. His knuckles grew white as his grasp tightened, and Jack made a horrible choking sound.

Lindy felt Bill stiffen, but still he didn't move.

"Keep talking, or I'll break your neck."

Jack looked wildly about him. No one moved to help him. Jeremy was leaning against the makeup table with an air of detachment.

"It was an accident, I tell you."

This time the blow was harder.

"I just wanted to talk to her. She wouldn't stop dancing. I just wanted her to stop. To pay attention to me. I grabbed her arm, but she broke away and hit the radiator." His confession ended in a gurgle. "Jeremy, for the love of God." His plea was barely a whisper.

Jeremy didn't budge. "You let me take the blame, let everybody turn against me. Carlotta must have known it was you. You destroyed Sandra, and you nearly destroyed me."

"I've been trying to make it up to you ever since."

"Peter can kill you as far as I'm concerned."

Peter took the cue and tightened his grip. Bill lunged forward and pulled him away from Jack, then shoved him toward Jeremy, who surrounded him with both arms, part restraint, part consoling.

"So you left her there to be found by a custodian." Bill's voice was grim, and for a moment, Lindy was afraid that he was going to strangle Jack himself.

Bill turned to the door. "I think you can make that call now, Sal."

The old man stood in the doorway, unruffled. "Already did, sir. Soon as the yellin' started."

Bill pushed Jack into a chair and stood guard. Jack buried his face in his hands sobbing. "It was an accident."

"And was Carlotta an accident, too?"

"Carlotta?" Jack blubbered. "I didn't kill Carlotta. I didn't kill her."

It was a long five minutes before the sound of sirens split the air. Peter had pulled away from Jeremy and was sitting on the windowsill. Jeremy watched Peter from the makeup table. Biddy watched Jeremy from where she clung to the door frame. Bill stood over Jack, his hand firmly on the man's shoulder. Lindy leaned against the wall watching them all, the scene etching itself permanently in her memory.

Then she heard the rush of feet on the stairs. Two uniformed officers were taking Jack away. "You have the right . . ." Another man wearing a suit walked over to Bill.

"Brandecker."

"Monroe." Bill returned the greeting.

"O'Dell called me this morning, but what exactly are you doing here, Bill?"

"Getting a little culture."

"Like hell. I'll have to get statements from all of you. But after that, you'd better keep a low profile. Go home if you can tear yourself away from the ballet. You'd better hope we get a confession from this guy."

And then he was gone. No one else moved. They sat where they were, in the charged atmosphere, incapable of leaving. Then Peter slowly got up and walked out of the room. They watched him go.

"Is it too early for a drink?" asked Biddy quietly.

* * *

"But what I don't understand is why the police didn't figure out that it was Jack's fault in the first place," Biddy said. They were sitting in the bistro across the street, the first customers of the day. Looking for Peter, Jeremy had gone once more to the pay phone to call the hotel.

"Who knows? We probably won't. Maybe they investigated Jack, as well. There didn't seem to be that much emphasis placed on Jeremy's involvement from what I could find out. It was probably what happened in the company afterward that led to his defection. What you people do to each other." Bill shook his head. He was drinking scotch. He looked like he needed it.

"Not just us people," said Lindy, looking directly at Bill. "All kinds of people hurt each other, not just dancers and actors."

Bill returned her look with a stony stare, but his reply was interrupted by Jeremy's return. "Still no answer. Maybe he's back at the theater. I'll go check."

"Not yet," said Bill. "In spite of the vast entertainment I've enjoyed in your presence, I'm going to have to leave you. There are a few things you need to be prepared for."

Jeremy sat down.

"Jack will probably try to worm his way out of this. He was rather coerced into confessing his involvement with Sandra's accident, and he still denies killing Carlotta."

"But he did kill her, didn't he?" Biddy's voice was soft but imploring.

Bill shrugged. "Probably. But they'll have to drag it out of him. I think he'll talk, eventually. You'll all have to make a statement. Peter did attack him, and Jack might just have the wits to bring charges against him." He stopped their questions with an abrupt gesture. "It shouldn't come to much, but Jeremy, Peter does need some serious therapy. His nerves are stretched to the limit. Arresting Jack is not going to make that fact magically go away."

"I'll take care of him."

"Professional therapy." He shot a glance at Lindy. "He won't get this behind him with hugs and kisses and 'we love you' from his coworkers."

Lindy glared back at him. He was making them sound like idiots, but she bit back her reply. She recognized that tone of voice; she had heard it often enough. He was goading her, and he knew she wouldn't retaliate; they owed him too much. Okay, Bill, she thought. Get it out of your system.

"But it is over, isn't it?" asked Biddy.

"For you. The police will take care of it from now on. You'll have to sign some papers, appear in court, possibly. But I think you can start 'picking up the pieces,' so to speak. And I have to get back to my classroom." Bill pushed his chair back and stood up.

"I don't know what to say." Jeremy stood up also. "How can I—"

"You can buy my drink." They shook hands formally. "Ladies."

Lindy watched his retreating form with a growing agitation. "Bill, are you coming to the theater tonight?"

"Thanks, but I think I've had enough culture for one vacation."

Twenty

Some secrets are hard to keep, and the news of Jack's arrest was common knowledge by hour call. Shock and dismay gave way to acceptance and relief. Music again blared from the dressing rooms. Corps girls ran in and out of each other's rooms trying new shades of lipstick, making plans for after the performance.

Lindy strolled down the hall and stopped at each door to smile and chat. She felt a little guilty at her immense relief. Jack would go to jail. A terrible thing, but he had done it to himself. Why shouldn't they celebrate at being released from his destructive grip. She took the stairs slowly, letting the last of her pent-up tension pass from her body out into the air. She pushed open the metal door leading to stage left and went backstage.

Less than an hour to curtain; the first time since she had been back that the curtain would rise on a company free of suspicion and guilt. She looked out onto the stage, where stagehands were putting the last bars of the cage into place.

Peter was standing in position just off the first wing. He removed his headset and hung it on a peg on the podium, where his cue book was placed.

Lindy eased up beside him. "How are you?"

"Okay." His shoulders tensed, his mouth tightened, and he looked deep into her eyes. She hugged him. Okay, it wasn't professional therapy, but it *was* a start. "I feel a little sick," he said. "I think I could have killed him."

"I don't think so."

"I'm leaving after Hartford."

Lindy pulled away. "Why?"

"I've found out what I came to find out, and I doubt if Jeremy will want me hanging around reminding him of the past. She never told me about Jeremy. I was really wrong."

"But why leave now? You and Jeremy have worked things out, right? I know you can make better money elsewhere, but you've got a life here."

"Some life, built on deceit and hate."

"What about Andrea?"

Peter turned away. "I guess she'll have a great career."

"You and Andrea. I mean, it's a little obvious how she feels about you."

"It is?"

"I'd say so."

"She's appreciative. I just tried to keep Carlotta off her case." He turned suddenly. "She acts like an air head sometimes, but she's really sensitive and intuitive. And young."

"Not that young. How old is she? Twenty? Twenty-two?"

"Twenty-four."

"Old enough to know what she wants."

"And she wants me, right?"

"Why not? You're intelligent, caring, good-looking, especially if you'd smile a little."

Peter's lips tightened to a thin line.

"That's a start."

He grunted.

"But you'll have to work on the laugh."

Then he smiled. His face transformed, and Lindy felt a little twinge of titillation herself.

"She's going to be noticed; she'll have her pick."

"I think she's already made her choice. Stick around long enough to find out, okay?"

"Yeah. Now let me get back to work."

Lindy sat contentedly in the audience, her notebook and pen resting in her lap. *Carmina* looked great, even for a revival of an already overused ballet. Jeremy's hand was evident in the vitality of the dancers, the nuances of the movements. Andrea handled the cloak with confidence. Each detail that Jeremy had worked on added a new depth to the interpretation. Biddy and Jeremy sat next to her. Theirs was another relationship that would have to work itself out, but Lindy knew they would handle it. Life was looking pretty good.

The boys were romping through the quartet. They were having fun. Andrea reappeared onstage. She had shed the cloak and was clothed in wisps of silky gold chiffon. Her golden hair reflected the light as she turned. The cloak.

Lindy jerked in her seat.

Biddy's head turned toward her. Lindy shook her off. The cloak. Carlotta's cloak hadn't been returned by the police with the rest of the company's possessions. Alice had had to adapt Andrea's cloak in its place. Why? Carlotta was still wearing the dress, so they had to keep that; it was probably ruined anyway. But why keep the cloak? She wasn't wearing it. She only wore it for the beginning of the piece and didn't put it on again.

Lindy made herself picture Carlotta's dressing room on the night of the murder: Carlotta lying on the floor; Andrea leaning over her; Alice coming from behind the door. Carlotta's fur coat was hanging on the dress rack. She could see it in her mind. And the cloak was, where? She couldn't recall. It must have been in the room, because it was gone. The police had kept it, or had they?

Lindy's mind was racing. Had they kept the cloak because it had been used in the murder, or was it missing?

Bill could have told her, but Bill was gone.

A growing uneasiness replaced Lindy's relief. She looked at Biddy and Jeremy. Relaxed. The bitterness of years erased from his face. The fear of loss gone from Biddy's. She couldn't bear to break their happiness by telling them of the doubt that had suddenly leapt into her mind. If only Bill had stuck it out one more night, but he had had enough of art . . . and of her. She was back on her own, like always.

As soon as the curtain lowered on *Carmina*, Lindy rushed backstage. Biddy and Jeremy headed to the lobby.

She slipped through the curtained arch to backstage and pounded on the door. Peter opened it; she rushed past him. Andrea's cloak was lying on the prop table, just like Carlotta's would have been. She slowed down; she would wait and watch. She leaned back against the wall. Intermission passed. The dancers took their places onstage. The cloak was still lying on the prop table.

The lights went to black. She tried to focus on the table, but she couldn't see anything. The music started. The lights popped on. The cloak was still there.

And next to it stood Alice.

She was staring at the stage. "I love this music," she had said the night after Carlotta's death when Lindy had stayed backstage. It had been during the *Air*. She was watching from the third wing with the cloak—Andrea's cloak—folded over her arm. But before Carlotta died, it would have been Carlotta's cloak that she was holding; her job to take it back to the dressing room and hang it up. And halfway through the *Holberg Suite* she still had the cloak.

Lindy stood paralyzed by the understanding that whirred into her brain, like the fragmented pieces of a kaleidoscope suddenly made clear—painfully, violently clear. But why had she done it? That didn't make any sense at all.

Alice picked up the cloak, her eyes still riveted to the stage. Then she turned and shuffled away.

Lindy looked wildly around her. Peter was calling cues. Everyone was either onstage or waiting for an entrance. All attention was directed at the dancing. No one had noticed anything unusual the night Carlotta was murdered. *No one ever noticed Alice!*

Fear constricted her throat, but Lindy forced herself to follow Alice out the back door. She saw her feet round the landing and go up the second flight of stairs. She followed. Her heart was pounding so loudly that she was sure that Alice would hear it and turn around, but Alice was disappearing into Andrea's dressing room when Lindy reached the second floor.

She needed just a peek to be sure. Hugging the wall, she crept toward the door of the dressing room. The music of the *Sarabande* was playing through the intercom. Mieko would be beginning the girls' adagio. She looked inside.

Alice was hanging the cloak on an oversize hanger, smoothing it with deft fingers. She would have been in Carlotta's dressing room that night, during the *Holberg Suite*, just like tonight. Lindy pulled back, but Alice had seen her reflection in the mirror.

Stupid, she thought, and she poked her head back inside the door. "I've lost my notebook. Thought I might have left it here when I was talking to the girls." The blood was roaring in her ears.

Alice glanced at the table covered with makeup, dance clothes, and soda cans. "I don't see it."

"Oh, well, maybe I left it backstage." Lindy started to back away.

"Why are you following me, Lindy?" It was said in the same mild tone in which Alice always spoke, but Alice's eyes were fixed on hers.

"I wasn't—I lost my notebook."

"I saw you, you know." Alice stepped forward, her eyes unwavering. Her gaze was mesmerizing.

Lindy stopped. "Saw me, where? In the mirror?" What was the girl talking about?

"In the prop room. With Peter. He was holding you."

Lindy thought back desperately. In the prop room? "Oh, you mean with the sword."

"He was holding you."

"He was helping me to my feet," Lindy said, not understanding. Sweat began to roll down her armpits.

"Carlotta said you would try to take Andrea's place. I didn't believe her until I saw you. First Andrea, then you. You couldn't leave him alone, either of you. But he isn't interested in you. He only cares about Sandra."

"I'm sure you're right, Alice." Lindy stumbled backward over the doorjamb.

Alice pulled at the ribbon that hung around her neck, her eyes boring into Lindy's. "You shouldn't have tempted him. I'm the only one who understands him. Carlotta knew that, and she was jealous, jealous of me."

Her hand continued to pull the ribbon until the orange-handled scissors slipped out of the pocket of her smock. "She was ruining everybody's life. She deserved to die." She caught the scissors in her right hand; her fingers gripped the handles.

Lindy backed into the corridor; Alice was only a few feet away.

"It's all right, Alice. I understand. It wasn't your fault." She tried to recall scenes like this from those hundreds of mysteries she had read. There was always a scene like this, but her mind couldn't retrieve a single one.

The *Gavotte* began in the background. Four minutes had gone by. Lindy backed away slowly, trying to think. She could scream, if she could scream, but no one would hear her. She made a frantic calculation. Another twelve minutes for the piece to end. A few more minutes to take the bows and get offstage. Could she keep Alice occupied for another fifteen minutes? She backed farther along the corridor. Maybe she should just run like hell.

"I thought she liked me. She seemed so understanding. She said she would help me."

Lindy's eyes were held by the glint of the scissors.

"I should have killed you when I pushed you down the trapdoor, but I thought I could scare you away. Why didn't you go away and leave us alone, Lindy? With Carlotta dead, we could have been happy." Alice lunged forward, stabbing the scissors at Lindy's face. Lindy barely managed to jerk her head away.

"I love him." Fat tears coursed down Alice's face.

Lust, greed, revenge. Love? This wasn't love. Alice had gone round the bend, and no one had even noticed.

"I'm sure he cares for you, too." Lindy managed to whisper the words.

"He did. When he left the ballet to come here, I followed him. But then Carlotta came and began destroying everything. At first, I didn't realize what she was doing. She was supposed to be my friend. But she kept attacking Andrea so that he would feel sorry for her. Pushing her at him and laughing about it the whole time, laughing at me with those big, yellow teeth." The tears were coming faster now; Alice's eyes, pools of desperation. "And then you, throwing yourself at him. Carlotta knew, she saw you. She told me and laughed. Didn't you think I knew what you were up to?"

Lindy's mind was reeling. Alice in love with Peter? She certainly hadn't shown it. There was the way her eyes followed him whenever he was around. But her eyes seemed to follow anything that caught her vision.

Now, those same eyes held Lindy's trapped in their terrible gaze.

"Alice, believe me. I don't want Peter. I'm sorry if you got that impression. I assure you, Peter doesn't want me, either. We're just friends."

Alice shoved the scissors at Lindy's chest. Lindy stumbled backward until she was against the wall. Alice was blocking the stairs to her left. The fire exit. If she could just get to the door. It must only be five feet away. It would swing outward onto the fire escape. She could make it to the alley and back into the theater, with Sal and the telephone.

"That night when she went after Eric with the candelabra—Andrea ended up in his arms. And then when I took the cloak back, it was sitting there on the floor. Just waiting for me. I knew what I had to do. But it didn't kill her. She started moaning. Looking at me with that face, that ugly face. I couldn't stand it. Why did she do it, Lindy? I had her cloak. It hid that horrible face."

Lindy wanted to cover her ears, shut out Alice's garbled confession. Oh, God, please don't let me be sick. She inched along the wall. The *Gavotte* music was still playing. Surely, it had been close to three and a half minutes. She was almost to the fire door. Only a few more feet.

"It felt good, Lindy. Once I started bashing her head into the floor. Over and over. I couldn't stop. I didn't want to stop."

Alice lunged toward her. Lindy sprang toward the door and threw herself against the release bar. Alice fell against the wall where Lindy had been. She staggered a few steps before she regained her balance.

It gave Lindy just enough time to get out onto the fire escape. But not enough time to shut the door. Alice was outside, too.

Lindy turned and ran down the metal steps two at a time. She had made the first landing, when Alice slipped off the stairs above her and fell, knocking her against the rail; the scissors shot past her ear. She pushed against Alice's unwieldy body, but the girl was heavy, and struggling to get another try with the scissors.

"Lindy!" It was Bill's voice. To the rescue again! The man

had an incredible sense of timing. Through the iron rails she could see him running down the alley from the street. She gave Alice a violent push; Alice fell back against the rail. Lindy fled down the stairs.

Bill had already started up the steps of the fire escape. Lindy was racing toward him, when she realized Alice wasn't following her. She looked up in time to see the ends of the blue smock vanish inside. "Use the door," she shouted to Bill and followed Alice back up the fire escape.

The final notes of the *Gavotte* blared down the empty hallway. Ten or so minutes to go. Lindy was breathing hard; she was scared, but the thought of Alice attacking unsuspecting dancers drove her on. At least Bill was here. On cue, Bill reached the top of the stairs.

"God, you're good."

"I may kill you myself. Where did she go?"

"I don't know. Is Sal calling the police?" She followed him down the hall as he pushed doors open and looked inside. The *Air*'s haunting melody filled the air.

"Sal wasn't there. Probably watching the damned ballet."

"Then how did you get in?"

"Don't ask."

They were at the end of the hall where the second stairway led down to the stage. They took it at a run.

"Go call." He shoved her forward. She began to run across the open shop to the stage door. She got as far as the costume room. The door was open. Alice was leaning over the trunk where valuables were kept. Her hair had come loose from its clasp, and it hung limply over her profile. Then she stood up, leaning on the edge of the trunk for support. She held a tiny pistol in her hand; she pointed it at Lindy.

Bill had caught up to her. He stopped abruptly.

"You're not going to fall for that old trick," said Lindy. "It's just a prop. She probably took it from the last theater. Peter and I were looking at them. She saw us."

Alice fired. The bullet hit the metal wall with a deafening clang and ricocheted. Bill threw Lindy against the wall, covering her with his body and driving her breath out of her. She felt her ribs creak under his weight.

"Deadly prop," he said.

Peter bolted through the door to their right. "What the hell was that?"

"Alice has a gun. She killed Carlotta. She's in there." Bill indicated the costume room with a nod.

"Alice?" He took a step forward.

"Call the goddamned cops, Peter, and take Lindy with you."

"Sal's calling."

"Who's calling the show?" Lindy's voice was muffled under Bill's body.

"Screw the show." Peter moved toward the door of the costume room. "Alice, what are you doing?" He spoke calmly in the same voice he always used with the dancers when they needed to be calmed down. "Put the gun down, Alice. I won't let them hurt you."

Alice moved through the door into the hallway; she seemed to waver, but kept hold of the gun.

"Move back, Peter," she said in a flat voice. "It's too late now. I killed her for you. She wouldn't let us be happy."

"Bad dialogue," whispered Lindy. Bill pushed her farther into the wall.

"What's she talking about?" asked Peter, staring at the tip of the gun.

"She's in love with you," Lindy managed to say around Bill's shoulder.

"You're kidding."

Alice moved forward, backing Peter to the wall. "I have to leave now. It won't work out. I see that now. I'll have to go."

The final movement of the *Holberg Suite* was drawing to an end. Bill lessened his weight against Lindy. He was about to make a move. But Alice swung toward him, aiming the gun at Lindy. "Move back. Lindy will have to go with me."

Bill moved out of the way. "Just do what she tells you, Lindy."

"No!" Peter yelled. Alice turned at the same time. The gun was aimed at his chest. In blind terror, Lindy leapt from the wall and aimed her best *grande battement* at the hand holding the gun. Alice yelped as Lindy's foot hit her hand; the gun flew into the air and clattered to the floor.

Bill grabbed Alice. The music ended. Uniformed men came through the door, and the audience broke into applause.

Peter laughed, more like a squawk. "No one would ever believe this."

"And I, for one, am never going to tell them," said Bill.

They were sitting in the waiting area of the train station. Jeremy and Biddy had picked them up at the police station when they finished giving their statements, and Bill had insisted on being dropped off instead of taking a room at the hotel. It was after three in the morning, and the station was deserted except for one black custodian pushing a broom between the rows of benches.

"I can't believe you kicked the gun out of her hand." Biddy's voice echoed around the air. Lindy noticed that she had combed her hair.

"Pretty ridiculous, I know."

"Effective, anyway," mumbled Bill, looking like he might nod off at any minute.

"But in love with Peter? I never had any idea. How can we live with someone that closely and not know them? It's really awful."

"We get so caught up in our own little worlds, Biddy," said Jeremy. "Oh, hell, no one ever noticed her. That doesn't say much for her, or us."

"I certainly didn't notice," said Peter.

"She told me that you had liked her before you left the ballet," said Lindy.

"I hardly ever talked to her. I'm sorry I brought all this on you, Jeremy. I should have confronted you at the beginning. None of this should have happened."

"Bullshit, Peter. You can't take the responsibility for everybody's actions; leave a little guilt for me."

Biddy shook her head. "Boys, let's leave the guilt for Carlotta, Jack, and Alice, though Alice, poor thing, can't be in her right mind."

"No," said Bill. "Obviously not in her right mind. I suppose as long as she thought Peter only cared about Sandra, she could keep her fantasy intact. But once he showed interest in Andrea, and then Lindy came along. . . ."

"But I—"

"I know, but in Alice's warped perception, she saw you as a threat."

"And Carlotta reinforcing her fears and making fun of her . . ." said Lindy.

"She cracked. She just couldn't juggle it all anymore."

"Thank you, Dr. Freud. I told you it was the repressed types who always went off."

He only nodded but gave her a look that made her tremble. "I should have seen it earlier," he said slowly. "The police had their suspicions. No one could really pin down her movements for the night of the murder, though her story was pretty convincing. She had access to Carlotta's dressing room, but they hadn't come up with a plausible motive yet. If someone had bothered to mention how she felt about Peter—" He shifted in his seat. "They would have arrested her eventually."

"Even if I hadn't bungled my way into that last confrontation," said Lindy. Why did she feel so uncomfortable? "I didn't mean to, and if you had been there, I would have told you what I thought, instead of running after her like an idiot."

"Right."

"But thank goodness you did show up," said Biddy. "And in the nick of time, like the cavalry. That was incredible. How did you manage it?"

Bill shrugged. "I was just coming to say goodbye when the show was over. I guess I was a little early."

"With timing like that, you should be on the stage," said Jeremy.

"Lucky for us, he wasn't," said Lindy. "I do appreciate it, Bill." He wasn't looking at her. "But you let me think it was the fur coat. You must have known that they kept the cloak. Why didn't you tell me?"

"Because you can't stay out of trouble, Lindy. You're exhausting. Dell only let me in on all of this because he thought I could better cut through all the drama and get to the truth. And before you get huffy, no, I was not working for the police. I just got caught up in the melodrama."

Was that all it was to him, a melodrama? "Could you tell me just one more thing?"

"Just one?" He smiled.

She ignored her reaction to his question. In a few minutes, he would be gone. It would all be over. It would be better that way.

She cleared her throat. "How did you get into the theater if Sal wasn't at the stage door?"

"I think it was a ballet step."

Lindy grinned. She felt like crying. "I don't know why you did all this," she began. A train whistle moaned the approach of the 3:24 to New York.

"Yeah, you do." Bill got up. "That's my train. Back to the grind. I've already missed three days of classes."

Lindy felt a familiar jolt of panic. It was just like coming to the end of a successful run. That letdown after the final glorious curtain. The emptiness that replaced the excitement.

She missed the goodbyes, the handshakes, the hugs. She was too busy trying to relax her mouth; it was threatening to twitch. And if she allowed that, she *would* cry. She knew the signs.

She followed Bill across the waiting room. He was walking out of her life as easily as he had walked in.

They stopped at the base of the stairs that led to the platform. "I've done a lot of stairs since meeting you," he said.

Lindy looked at the ground. So this was it.

He lifted her chin with his knuckle. "Maybe in some other lifetime."

"That would be nice."

And then he was gone.

Twenty-one

The New York season was met with rave reviews, an adoring audience and the interest of several potential sponsors. Peter had stayed on, they had a new costume mistress named Rose, who "took shit from no one," and had hired a new corps girl to fill the spot left from Andrea's and Mieko's promotions.

Biddy appeared opening night wearing a tailored pants suit and sneakers.

"Free at last, free at last," she sang. "Not a great fashion statement, but I'm on my way."

"I'll miss you clunking around in that cast. It was becoming part of your persona."

"Well, I won't. Wow, Lindy, you look great."

Lindy was wearing the gray-and-pink dress from Neiman Marcus. The waist was loose, not a bulge marred its shimmering surface.

The first person they met on their way to the audience was Carlton Quick. He pecked Biddy on the cheek and congratulated her on her recovery and then turned to Lindy. "You look marvelous. You must have dropped two dress sizes since I saw you last. Nothing like a little murder to kick start a diet."

They made their escape.

"I thought Glen was coming tonight," said Biddy.

"A last-minute meeting. Another evening with an empty seat beside me."

"Well, don't look at me. I'm too nervous to sit. I'll just pace backstage."

Lindy found her seat and sat down, feeling not nearly as glamorous as she had intended. Alone on opening night. How typical.

The houselights began to dim. Almost every seat was filled. She should have released Glen's ticket back to the box office to be sold.

"Is this seat free?"

She recognized the voice. She didn't even try to stop the tingling sensation that coursed through her. Bill sat down in the seat beside her.

"I thought you had had your fill of the theater."

Bill shrugged. "I decided to give it another chance."

"And?"

Bill gave her dress an appraising look. "It's growing on me."

The houselights faded to black.

Lindy didn't see him again. She had left him in the lobby after the performance. She walked down the stairs to the dressing-room door, feeling his gaze on the back of her neck. She wasn't ready to decide what kind of relationship they might have. She needed more distance—give her feelings time to segue him into the role of friend, or let him take a final exit. She was married. She was a mother. And anyway, she had a New York season to deal with. With one hand on the doorknob, she took one quick look back. She couldn't help herself. A fleeting smile from Bill and she shut the door behind her.

The rest of the week had raced by: rehearsing, dining with patrons, watching Biddy and Jeremy making plans for the company's future. And then it was over. On her first free day back in New Jersey, she was invited to see the videotape of the talent show she had abandoned.

She sat in the chairwoman's rec room drinking decaf coffee and munching gourmet cookies that tasted like cardboard. She was okay for the first half hour. She even made it through the Torville Family Puppeteers: mother, father, and two scrawny children mincing about behind their duck puppets and lip-synching to "Splish, Splash (I Was Taking a Bath)." But when Arthur Klein, his bald head topped with a red-and-white striped stovepipe hat, and his wife, Edith, her ample figure draped in the American flag, began to tap-dance to "God Bless America," Lindy suddenly remembered an appointment and fled, all the way to Rome.

For two glorious days she and Glen trekked through the Colosseum and Forum. For the next four days, he hobnobbed with executives from a multinational company, whose name had so many initials Lindy couldn't remember them all, while she wandered the streets alone. She made the rounds of museums and famous statues. She stared at the restored ceiling of the Sistine Chapel, which had been covered with scaffolding the last time she had visited. Finding herself at Trevi Fountain, she tossed in a coin.

In the afternoons, she haunted piazzas she had known.

Sitting at a table for one, she sipped Campari and soda and watched the heads of lovers at nearby tables, all young, beautiful, and thin. Sometimes she would join Glen and his clients for dinner, or else she would eat at the hotel with her latest mystery beside her and then go outside to watch the seven hills light up around her.

Glen had gone directly to the office from the airport. The limo let her off at the kitchen door; she dumped her suitcases in the middle of the floor. She looked at the pile of mail and *Times* bags stacked on the table, where they had been left for her perusal by the housekeeper. The phone rang.

"Seems like old times," she sang. She picked up the receiver and reached for the *Times*.

"Hi. It's Jeremy."

Lindy dropped the paper onto the table, unopened.

"Listen, I know you probably just got back. But I've got great news. We've lined up a West Coast tour for October. We'll have to start rehearsing right away; they want two different programs. I'll do another ballet and maybe a revival. Then there's a possible six weeks in Europe in February."

"Congratulations. That sounds wonderful."

"Thanks. I've convinced Peter to stay on. He's going to be okay. Andrea's making him see a therapist, though he doesn't like it much. And that new costume girl is a bitch on wheels, but funny. I think she'll work out. And then . . . " He paused.

Lindy waited.

"Well, actually, Biddy has consented to take over the business end. She's artistic, as well as financially savvy, and honest. So, the reason I'm calling is, would you at all be interested in coming along as rehearsal director?"

Lindy looked around her at the stacks of mail, the polished kitchen counters, her suitcases lying in the middle of the sparkling floor.

"Thanks, Jeremy, I'm already packed."